Sweetie Bogan's Sorrow

An Elder Darrow Mystery

Also by Richard J. Cass:

In Solo Time

Solo Act

Burton's Solo

Last Call at the Esposito

Sweetie Bogan's Sorrow

An Elder Darrow Mystery

Richard J. Cass

Encircle Publications, LLC
Farmington, Maine U.S.A.

Editor: Cynthia Brackett-Vincent
Book design: Eddie Vincent
Cover design by Deirdre Wait, High Pines Creative, Inc.
Cover images © Getty Images
Author photo by Philip McCarty

Published by: Encircle Publications, LLC
PO Box 187
Farmington, ME 04938

Visit: http://encirclepub.com

Printed in U.S.A.

"I have had only enough character to keep myself out of situations that require character."
—Kay Ryan

Dedication

For Anne, as always.
For my parents.
And for the newest generation—Gavin, Laken, Baby Spicer,
and all the ones to come—blessings on your heads.

Acknowledgments

Many thanks *encore un fois* to Encircle Publications, Ed Vincent and Cynthia Vincent-Brackett, for bringing this fifth adventure of Elder Darrow and Dan Burton to life. And, again, for Deirdre Wait at High Pines Creative for the beautiful and resonant cover for *Sweetie Bogan's Sorrow*. I don't know how she does it, but my sense of the book is inevitably broadened by the images she comes up with.

Thanks also to important early readers:

• My first reader, Anne Cass, who lets me get away with nothing.

• Zakariah Johnson, Brenda Buchanan, and Norman Olson, especially for the attention to various impossibilities in ages and timelines that apparently dog me. You all had a hand in making this book much better, and I thank you. A hat tip also to Zak for providing me the inciting musical idea that got me off the dime.

So: what a long strange trip it's been, yes. And will continue to be for the foreseeable future. Without trying to name names—because I would inevitably forget someone—massive love and gratitude to the crime writing community, not just here in Maine, but all over. We do our best to lift each other, to honor the work, to be grateful for what we have. Yes, kids, we will keep on truckin'.

And once again, a fervent thanks to our spouses, partners, families, and friends. We could not do it without you, and might not even try.

1

Rasmussen Carter slipped into Lily's life one Saturday afternoon at a country club in Westwood. She was singing with the trio from Berklee who called her whenever they had a wedding gig. The club was a long way from Jamaica Plain: the manicured green golf course, waitresses in uniform, an open bar.

"My," Rasmussen said, as she walked past his table to the ladies' room during a break. A row of tiny diamonds along the outer edge of his ear glinted when he moved his head. "That was something."

She might only be eighteen, but she could recognize a man who wanted something that didn't belong to him.

"Thank you." And she walked on.

He appeared at three more of her engagements in the next couple of months, persistent but polite. The first time, she thought about having the bouncer chase him off, but Rasmussen was a handsome man, if you ignored the colorless eyes that forced him to wear sunglasses indoors and out. She got used to him asking her, very formally, if he might buy her a ginger ale. She wondered how he knew she didn't drink.

One September afternoon, between sets at a golden anniversary party at the Congregational Church, he popped the question, not at all the one she had expected.

She had been daydreaming, thinking of the songs she wanted to sing in the next set, all tunes that filled her heart. She only sang for the way it lifted her, soft on the cloud of accompaniment, from what she could not otherwise escape: her weight, her menial job at the Stop & Shop, her father's way of looking at her as if she were

1

meat. Spoiled meat.

"You understand your voice is good enough for you to sing professionally?" Rasmussen said.

"Why would I ever want to do that?"

He wasn't talking about these random little shows, a few dollars for a Sunday afternoon.

He regarded her as if she were an exotic animal and his tone shifted.

"People adore what you're doing, darling. You have an honest voice, the way you phrase. Wouldn't you like more people to hear what you do? You could heal them."

Eighteen and wondering how her life would unfold, Lily liked the sound of that.

"I wouldn't have the slightest idea where to begin," she said.

"I can help you with that."

* * *

Her first solo date, in a ratty club Rasmussen found off Magazine Street near Dudley Square, was a disaster. The bar was a slumped box of plywood painted black, the shelves behind it bowed under the weight of the bottles. The piano player was so drunk, he kept fumbling the wrong keys into chords. And the sound system buzzed like the devil humming.

Halfway through "Misty," she stopped, losing the thread. Rasmussen, at a table in front, smiled and patted his fingertips together. She recovered and finished the song to a smattering of applause, none of it sober.

Tears in her eyes, she stepped down off the stage. He half-stood as she returned to the table.

"Lovely," he said. "A little hiccough in the middle there. But just lovely."

"I will get better." It was both a question and a statement.

"Of course."

A light-skinned man, older than both of them, stepped up to the table, gave Rasmussen a curt nod, and spoke to her.

2

"Miss." His deep bass voice warmed her. "Someone would like to meet you."

"I believe we were getting ready to leave," Rasmussen said.

"It's all right, Ras. I should always say hello to fans, don't you think?"

The man conducted her to a niche set in the far back corner, inside which sat a table for two. A black curtain was pulled to one side and the light from a candle played across the seamed face of an old woman, her hair a tangle of steel wool. Her eyes were as dark as the candle was white.

Lily started to sit down in the empty chair.

"No, no," the old woman said. "Don't make yourself comfortable. I don't want to marry you."

She cackled. The light-skinned man slipped away into the dimness. Lily's legs trembled, then she remembered her manners.

"Yes, ma'am."

The old woman turtled her neck, her lips working in and out. She picked up a tall glass and drank.

"You have the necessary magic, young lady."

Lily started to shake her head, automatically modest.

"Don't you dare deny it."

"Thank you."

"Be true to it, child. Don't ever fake a thing and you will go a long way. If that's what you want." The old woman's voice was suppler now, with hints of musicality. "Do you know who I am?"

Lily shook her head.

"Sweetie Bogan. They keep telling me I'm all done."

She trilled out the first few phrases of "Misty."

"Does that sound to you like I'm all done?"

The voice was rusty, but Lily could hear what it had been.

"The famous Sweetie." The old woman waved a claw, dismissing Lily. "You have the voice. If you want what it can bring you, go after it." She leaned forward over the table, nearly upsetting the candle. "Just don't sing 'Misty' any more—that song belongs to me."

She reached up and pulled the black curtain closed. Lily walked back between the tables to Rasmussen, who watched her approach as if she'd tried to escape him.

* * *

Eventually, Rasmussen found her better dates, consumed with his desire to make her a diva. His diva. She wasn't naive enough to think he wanted this only for her. But New York. He talked about New York.

She was slightly superstitious about what Sweetie Bogan had said, but not singing "Misty" didn't bother her. She avoided all kinds of tunes that didn't move her: love songs from the twenties and thirties, protest songs, that famous ballad of Billie's about lynching she couldn't bear to sing. And she saw Sweetie more and more often at her performances, as if the old woman had a stake in her.

Four o'clock, a rainy afternoon in October, no windows to look out of and not much to see in this neighborhood. Warm yellow light, Barry Manilow on in the background, which made her wince. This bar, today's showcase, was underground, a long steel staircase down from the street. Brown cork floors. Plants in brass pots. The Greenwood, Rasmussen called it, said it had just changed hands. Newer than some of the places she'd sung, but not top drawer.

"Tell me the man's name again. Edward Dare?"

"Lily, darling." Rasmussen tapped cigarette ash into the watery dregs of his Old Fashioned. "Try to remember. This is the man to impress if you want to get to New York. He books all the acts for the Blue Note."

She unwrapped a lozenge and set it on her tongue, aware of the tiniest scratch in her throat.

"And 'Misty' is his favorite song."

Rasmussen sounded proud of knowing that tidbit, as if he'd picked the man's pocket.

"Sweetie asked me not to sing that any more," Lily said. "And you know she's going to be here."

"She can't own a song, darling."

4

Lily shook her head. "She's not going to like it."

"Doesn't matter. Her day is gone and yours is dawning, believe me. Edward Dare."

* * *

Lily felt like she owed the old woman this much.

"Sweetie. I have to sing your song tonight. I'm sorry."

A cough, a weak laugh, the voice like shredded silk through the phone.

"You can't say I didn't warn you, then."

"I love it, Sweetie. You know that. It isn't like you're singing any more."

"That song belongs to me."

"You can't own a song, Sweetie. Not forever."

"You think you'll sing it better than I did?"

Lily's silence was the answer.

"On your head, child. On your head."

* * *

Lily was not surprised to see Sweetie totter down the long steel stairway of the Greenwood around eight o'clock, on the arm of the light-skinned man whose name, Lily had learned, was Alfonso. The owner of the bar, a twenty-ish black man in a pink linen shirt and bow tie under his long apron, wiped his hands and hurried to the bottom of the stairs.

Sweetie grasped both of his hands and kissed his cheek. He led Alfonso and Sweetie to a two-seater near the stage with a "Reserved" tent sign on it.

"Shoot," Rasmussen said. "I was hoping she'd stay away. Tonight of all nights."

His eyes were red when he took off the sunglasses to polish them. He smelled as if he'd been drinking all day.

"It will be fine," Lily said. "I'm flattered she's here. Don't worry so much."

5

Rasmussen made an inarticulate sound and walked up to the bar for another drink.

Lily wondered if she should go and say hello. But if Sweetie was angry at her, she might say something that would wound Lily's confidence. Lily pressed her shoulders back against the chair and sipped her ginger ale.

* * *

The piano player was a woman named Claudette Brown, and Lily knew from the first notes the woman played that she was as good a musician as had ever accompanied her. Halfway into a bouncy "Sunny Side of the Street," she knew Claudette would raise her singing beyond her best.

As they finished on the up-note, Claudette grinned from the piano stool, her gold front incisor flashing in the spotlight. The audience exploded in applause, but Lily was already feeling her way into "Misty."

At the break, she stepped down off the tiny triangular stage and picked her way through the buzzing crowd. The bar's owner, mixing drinks, threw her a broad smile and a nod. The man sitting with Rasmussen rose as she walked up to the table.

"Darling," Rasmussen said, as she sat. "Superb."

Flushed with joy, exceeding herself, singing past limits she hadn't known were there, she didn't need him to tell her.

The other man was sixty-ish, fit-looking, straight silver hair tucked back behind his ears. He wore a purple striped shirt under a cream linen jacket.

"Ms. Miller," he said.

Lily appreciated that he didn't assume he could call her by her first name. She accepted his hand, halfway between a squeeze and a shake. His palm was warm and dry.

"Mr. Dare?"

"I'm so pleased to meet you," he said. "Mr. Carter didn't exaggerate when he said you have a lovely voice."

Though she doubted Ras had said it that simply.

"Thank you."

She felt Rasmussen straining, wanting to push the conversation, force Dare to a decision. She wished she could reach over and calm him—she wanted this as much as he did, but they could not compel it.

"Mr. Carter must have told you 'Misty' is one of my favorites. I heard Carmen sing it one night at Ratso's, but you certainly owned it tonight."

A chair scraped at the little table down front. Sweetie's voice cut through the crowd noise like glass.

"I'm telling you, her breath control is for shit."

Lily looked over, appalled. Alfonso leaned his big head in next to the old woman, trying to calm her, or at least quiet her down. People at the nearby tables tried to look away and listen at the same time.

"She's going to have to fuck her way up," Sweetie cawed. "She has a lovely pair of titties, but a very ordinary voice."

Rasmussen stiffened.

"*No,*" Lily said.

"I will take care of this." Rasmussen rose and tucked his chair carefully in under the table. "Excuse me a minute."

"Ras."

A thin wedge of worry had slipped into her.

"It will be fine," he said.

He threaded his way through the tables toward the front.

Mr. Dare watched, unruffled, as if this wasn't the oddest thing he'd ever seen in a bar. His calm reassured her. He sipped from a rocks glass and patted his lips.

"You do have the voice," he said, as if continuing a conversation.

"What do you mean?"

"You have the singing voice to be a star."

She could not help the thrill.

"Like Sweetie?"

"Like Sweetie in her prime. But it takes much more than that." She held his gaze, waiting for the drop.

"Discipline. Support and guidance. Practice. The benefit of

someone in the business."

She glanced at Rasmussen, who had leaned over to speak to Sweetie.

"No," Dare said. "If you want your talent to reach its fullest potential, Mr. Carter is not the right choice."

Lily felt as if she stood on the end of a high diving board.

"And if I agree?"

"I can help you with all that."

Hard words from Sweetie made Rasmussen step back. His neck stiffened and he spit words at her, low and guttural. Like curses.

Alfonso stood, a blade suddenly catching the yellow spotlight from the stage. He buried it in Rasmussen's stomach. Someone screamed. Sweetie yelled. In triumph?

Dare was up and out of his chair in an instant, extending his hand.

"I think we'd better be somewhere else," he said. "You don't want to be associated with this."

Rasmussen folded and dropped to the floor. Sweetie leaned forward and spit on him.

As Lily scrambled up the stairs behind Dare, the old woman yelled at her.

"You free now, child! Go do it!"

Lily stood in the cold outside the bar on Mercy Street, wondering what Sweetie thought she was doing for her. She felt nothing for Rasmussen Carter, and wondered if that was her first lesson in being a star.

She threaded her arm through Dare's.

"I do want to see how far my voice will carry me," she said. "But let me be clear with you." She pointed a finger. "Sweetie Bogan taught me no one owns a song. And I don't want you thinking you can own a singer."

"Of course not," Dare said.

He shook his head as if she'd proposed something absurd, then lifted a long white hand to hail a cruising taxi.

2

Burton turned the unmarked car up E Street in South Boston and into the lot next to a one-story brick building, parking between a BMW 2002 tii from the early seventies and a bright yellow Hummer. He hoped the show hadn't started already. He'd never get Elder's attention if it had.

He had worried about his friend quite a bit after he sold the bar. The whole I can't be too much of a drunk if I'm in a bar all day theory hadn't seemed like the world's most intelligent sobriety plan, but it seemed to have worked for him. *Most* of the time. Without the anchor of the Esposito, though, Burton wondered what would keep Elder from drifting off into the ether somewhere.

The wide steel doors at the front of the building, where the trucks used to drive in, were pulled wide. A crowd milled inside. He walked around the side of the building to a faded red door that read OFFICE and tried the door handle. Locked.

Movement behind the grimy chicken wire window brought shadows toward the door. The knob turned and he pushed the door open, the hinges squealing.

"What you need to understand, Elder, is that Wynton Marsalis is on the path to ruin jazz."

Elder raised his eyebrows, inviting Burton to commiserate on the cocksure arrogance of the young. The young man with his legs draped over the arm of a steel and vinyl office chair alternately puffed on a vape pen and waved it in the air.

"Burton," Elder said. "You made it."

Three o'clock on a gorgeous October Sunday afternoon, Burton wondered why he was here. The temperature was in the high sixties, the sky high, dry, and blue as a summer ocean. No hint yet of winter to come. He wasn't here for the music—he needed a favor.

But they'd been out of touch for a couple of months, and their friendship—or at least its protocol—required him to show some interest in Elder's latest venture before getting down to business.

"So, this is the new venue?"

"Temporary," the kid put in. He wore skinny black jeans, and a white T-shirt that contrasted with his tawny skin. "If you dig what 'pop-up' means?"

His tone suggested he was sure Burton did not.

"Isaac," Elder said. "Burton, this is Isaac Belon."

"Bee-lawn, brother. Like the oyster."

The skin on Burton's neck tightened. "Somewhere we can talk?"

Elder read his face and nodded. If nothing else, they could still communicate.

"Isaac?" Elder said. "Check on the band, please? Make sure they have everything they need."

Isaac took a long regal toke, a pasha on his throne.

"I'm cool," he said. "Pretend I'm not here."

Elder hadn't lost the snap in his voice he had used to keep the Esposito under control. "Isaac. Screw."

Isaac unfolded himself from the chair as if his body was built of dry sticks and old rubber bands.

"Dig." He shook the legs of his too-short black pants down his shanks. "A dude can take a hint."

"Believe it or not," Elder said, after Isaac disappeared. "He's a very smart kid. Entrepreneurial. Valedictorian at Cambridge Rindge and Latin, and got a full boat to Stanford."

"Then why isn't he in California right now?"

"Deferred a year. Said he needed to make some money."

"Doing concerts?"

"Pop-ups, Burton. Get with the program. Nothing planned or formal. Spur of the moment, word of mouth."

Burton shook his head. Elder was just bored.

"Rasmussen Carter. You remember him?"

Rasmussen Carter had dated Elder's cook, Marina, during a period when she and Burton weren't talking to each other—back when Constantine Boutsaloudis was killed and they thought it had something to do with the Olympics coming to town, Carter had done some research for Elder.

"Sure." Elder tightened up, not wanting to talk about how Burton almost lost Marina to the man with ocular albinism, a condition that kept him out of the light. "What about him?"

"He's in Mass General. Stabbed in a bar fight."

He couldn't bring himself to tell Elder it had happened in the old Esposito.

"Interesting." Elder's attention drifted off to the warehouse, the blast of a trumpet. "Is he going to live?"

"Near as they can tell." Burton girded himself for the ask. "Wondered if you might take a look at it."

"It? What it? Why?"

"The situation. What happened."

"If he isn't dead, what do you care? Professionally, I mean."

"It's personal. For Marina."

"She's asking me to look into it? Not you?"

Burton stretched his neck.

"It's bothering her. I can tell."

Elder frowned.

"Bothering her or bothering you? It's not getting in the way of the wedding, I hope. I already bought a suit."

"Very funny. They've stayed friends. I think it would be good for her to know how it happened."

"Are you worried there still might be something there?"

"I just want her to know the details," Burton said. "And I can't look into it myself."

"So, what? I'm a private eye now?"

"Informally, I said. You've got the time."

Burton was also counting on a certain itchiness he'd detected in Elder since he sold the bar, an unwillingness to focus on any one thing for very long.

A semi-musical cacophony broke out in the warehouse.

"Come on out front and see what we're doing here," Elder said, "how I'm spending my time now."

Burton followed him out into the cavernous space, the concrete floor sticky and gritty underfoot. A small stage, maybe eight by eight, sat against one wall under a spaghetti of cables and a half-dozen spotlights.

Three musicians—a drummer behind an elaborate kit, a baritone sax player, and a woman with a trumpet—tuned up on the stage. Down on the floor in front of them milled a crowd of about fifty, swaying, expectant. A hand-lettered sign in neon green read TRICERATOPS.

The drummer wore a topknot of shiny black hair, his biceps bulging out of a sleeveless denim shirt. The sax player sported an electric blue beanie, red-framed glasses, and an orange jumpsuit. He swiveled his hips around as if warming up for a dance session. The trumpet player looked somewhat normal, the gelled pink hair shellacked into a helmet her only oddity.

Elder surveyed the band with the same kind of excitement he used to show for a good guitar player or singer getting ready to perform at the Esposito. But when they started to play, it was all Burton could do not to clap his hands over his ears.

The drums were heavily miked, and the beat from the bass seemed to move his ribs. The saxophone player commenced a honking like he was trying to decoy in a flock of geese, and hard metallic notes from the trumpet stabbed in and out of the whole mess. The sound was thick and hard, and he couldn't imagine anyone calling it music.

"Jesus Christ. What the hell?"

But Elder couldn't hear him, even if he had been listening. He and Isaac were both lost in the propulsive sound, the nasal repetition, the way the rhythm infected the crowd until it writhed and jumped and swirled like atoms smashing into one another.

He grabbed his friend's arm, raised a finger. One minute? And tipped his head back toward the office.

Elder resisted the pull. Burton saw his attention pinned to the trumpet player, a shine in his eyes Burton hadn't seen since Susan Voisine left town again. Uh-oh.

He tugged again. Elder yielded, gracelessly.

"Whoa!" Burton said as he closed the door. "The fuck you call that?"

"Brass house." Sweat gleamed on Elder's forehead. "New York thing, started down in the subways. Too Many Zooz? Moon Hooch? You like it, right?"

"Not much of a fan of anything out of New York. Except maybe Mariano Rivera. It does, uh, grab your attention."

"Love the drive," Elder said. "It bangs."

"Yeah. Look, I have to get going. You gonna help me out on this Rasmussen Carter thing, or not?"

"Why can't you do it yourself?"

"Well, for one thing, it's not a homicide."

"Not like you never did anything off the books."

"And it might be touchy if I get involved. Marina could think I was jealous."

Elder fixed him with the look that said not to bullshit him, shook his head.

"You're overthinking it. She might feel bad the guy got stabbed, but she's marrying you, right? Which means she's past her doubts. And she's enough of a grownup to tell you if she cared what happened to him. Give her some credit."

Burton shuffled his feet, not to the beat.

"I'm trying to avoid making it a problem for her."

"You need to talk to her, not me. I'm sorry, Dan, but I'm not getting in the middle. I never liked Carter that much. And the last thing I want is to get tangled up in your love life."

Burton's anger rose, but he didn't give in to it.

"OK. If you don't feel like you can help…"

"I don't." Elder spread his hands and nodded toward the warehouse. "I'm all about this right now. I'm done with the other stuff, the gangsters, the violence. That's your gig."

"Brass house." Burton tried to joke. "Sounds like a pack of monkeys shaking a garbage can full of silverware."

Elder's smile was more benevolent than the insult deserved.

"It's good to open up your mind a little, Daniel. Try something new. Change never hurt a soul."

Burton nodded, a little ashamed of himself for pressuring their friendship. Maybe none of it would bother Marina at all. Maybe whatever spark Rasmussen Carter had lit in her was well and truly doused.

The music—the noise—reached a crescendo and ended. Applause and shouting. A high fluty voice said, "Thank you."

"Moon Hooch?" he said. "Really?" And he walked out the door he'd come in.

3

Triceratops played for two solid hours. I envied their manic energy, the power that sparked that wall of sound. It had been a while since I'd paid much attention to anything but traditional jazz, and it was cool to feel as if I were learning something new. Even if the age of the band made me feel like an old fart. But I needed something to do if I didn't have the Esposito to occupy my time any more, and playing around in the music world felt right.

I counted out the sweaty crumpled bills from the take at the door into stacks, my fingers blackened by the money. I separated out two hundred dollars and passed it to Evangeline, the pink-haired trumpet player.

"Good show," I said. "Thanks."

All three of them had sweated through their clothes, but Evvie, as the drummer called her possessively, was the only one who smelled sweet.

"I thought we said three hundred. One apiece." Her voice was light and high, incongruous with her five-ten body. She must have weighed a hundred and fifty.

"We did not." I had dealt with enough musicians at the Esposito over the years to know how to stand up to them. There was always something wrong. The money was short, the lights too bright, the audience dumb. At least these guys couldn't complain people talked over their music. "Unless you never want to do this again."

Isaac looked on, puffing on his pen. I'd talked him out of buying black market THC cartridges by showing him newspaper articles about teenagers in the Midwest sick with lung infections, a couple

15

of them dying. He looked at the *Globe* like it was an artifact from the land of dinosaurs.

"Don't be an asshole, man." The drummer pitched in. "You can afford it."

That doubled my irritation.

"What's that supposed to mean?"

The sax player, his instrument laid in a case near the wall, shuffled around the floor like the music was still playing.

"We know your story."

"And what story is that?"

The drummer's topknot quivered, as if it were a barometer of his emotions. I disliked the way he was eyeing the pile of bills on the table, as if he was thinking about making a grab for them.

"Man. We know you're rich."

Evvie looked at me with new interest.

"Not true. But even if I were... what are you thinking? I should give you more and take it away from the guy who did all the work to set it up?"

Isaac had propped his skinny haunch against a corner of the desk, the vape pen out of sight. I waited for him to weigh in, assert himself. These pop-ups were his gig—I was only involved because he'd asked me for advice. I was supposed to be mentoring him, not acting as his shield.

"You want to weigh in here, Mr. Bee-lawn?"

I wasn't sure how he'd heard of me, but after the Esposito changed hands, I spent a lot of time hanging around Mr. Giaccobi's coffee shop. It was as if I couldn't get myself out of the neighborhood. I never did get sentimental enough to drop in and see what had become of my bar, though.

Isaac shook his head, as if he had been smoking the THC pods. I was about to ream him out when he stepped in.

"What?" he said. "There's a problem about the money?"

He confronted the drummer.

"Delmonico, my man. The money is what the money becomes."

He stepped over to the table and parceled the remaining bills into four stacks, none of them very thick.

"This one here." He pushed one stack to the side. "This is the rent. On the warehouse. Dig?"

He separated two more stacks.

"This one is the electrical work, to run all the fancy gear you brought in. And this other one: permits. And, well, bribes."

The last pile had maybe twenty ten and twenty dollar bills, some singles. He straightened their edges, tapped them into a neat pile, and handed them to me.

"That, my friend, is called the profit. For the risk I took in bringing you here."

I loved the way he made it look like I was getting the profit.

"You will notice," Isaac said. "That stack isn't any bigger than the one my man Elder handed you."

The drummer didn't flinch. Evvie crowded me a little, pushed her breast against my arm as if that might buy her something. I was intrigued.

"I'm not here to be some rich dude's hobby," Delmonico said. "We're people, too."

Isaac spread his hands in a peace gesture. A charge built in the room, the recognition that there were three of them and two of us. But you could not back down from this kind of confrontation. Isaac had to learn that.

"Look," I said. "I don't play an instrument. But I've loved music longer than you've been on earth. Ask around and see if I ever did anything good for anyone, music-wise or not. You don't like what you're hearing, don't come back. But don't try and hold us up."

Isaac nodded. "Righteous."

The sax player stopped his mincing dance steps, opened his eyes—which were a dull sea green—and focused on the bills Evvie was holding.

"Dudes." He made an unlikely surfer. "Time for chicken."

He plucked a couple of bills from Evvie's hand and started for the door. Evvie stepped away and sighed.

"C'mon, Del," she said. "Let's let these fuckers meditate on their greed a little while."

She grabbed the drummer's bicep and started him toward the

door. He tried to eye-fuck me on the way out, but Evvie was somewhere else already. Eating chicken, maybe.

After they were gone, Isaac pulled out his pen and fired it up, or whatever the correct terminology is.

"Well," he pontificated. "That went quite well, I believe."

I pushed the pile of bills he'd handed me back in his direction. I wasn't taking his money—he needed it more than I did.

"I don't know if you were lying to them about where the money went. 'Bribes?' But I'm advising you not to make a habit of lying to the people you need to put on shows. The word gets around."

"Those three?" Isaac shoved the bills into a padded envelope. "None of them's going nowhere. Except maybe Evangeline." He rolled the name across his tongue. "Woman has some chops. But Delmonico? The drummer? All hit and gristle. No music in him at all. And sax man? I call him Shemp. He's brassy enough, but his brain's too cooked to care. 'Chicken!'"

He grinned and I grimaced. I could help him learn the mechanics: hiring musicians, managing venues, putting together shows. What I wasn't going to teach him was how to treat people well.

"You're the driver here, Isaac. But I'm going to step on the brake if I think you're flying off a cliff. You need to understand relationships. Respect them. People are going to matter, if you want to succeed."

He made a face like I'd called him a name. He was an interesting kid, but his focus was entirely on what was good for him. Every decision he made was through the lens of personal benefit. What I was trying to pass on to him was the idea that you have to give to get. People can sense if all you are after is their money, and if they don't like what you offer, they'll drop you like a rock. They'll give you the benefit of the doubt if you build some trust, though. Because people didn't come to a bar or a concert for the music or the booze alone. They're reaching for community, something other than the solo life.

Isaac picked up a leather satchel from behind the desk.

"You good?" he said. "I'm in motion."

"You need a ride?"

He shook his head. I had no idea where in the city he lived. He always met me somewhere.

"I'm good. Next lesson?"

He was eager, but I wasn't sure I had much more to teach him. Most of what I could do for him now was plug him into my network, the music people I knew in the city. But I was holding off on that until I was sure his way of working wouldn't throw shade on my reputation.

"Let me think about it for a couple of days. You can call me." I pointed at the bag. "Don't go bribing everyone all at once."

"I hear you, Dad." He waved and left the building.

4

Marina found out about Rasmussen from a mutual friend, one of his "friends" that he thought she ought to know. She was unhappy with herself for worrying about him, especially since she and Daniel worked so hard to put that behind them, smooth the path forward. Carter had been a diversion for her and, let's face it, a screw-you to Burton, something to show him that an unbeautiful Italian girl could attract someone else. Their relationship—ha, their collision—hadn't lasted more than a month, but it was an intense time, and hearing Carter was lying in Mass General recovering from a stab wound cast her memory of him in a more tender light. She thought of going to visit him, but she couldn't see telling Burton she was going to do that, and she wouldn't lie to him, even by omission. They had learned the hard way not to hide anything from each other.

"Ma! How's it coming up there?"

And truly, she had plenty to worry about: her wedding in March to plan for, and of course, what was going on today.

Inarticulate grumbling spewed down the stairs from Carmen's bedroom. Marina had finally convinced her mother she wasn't safe on her own any more. The gerontologist said Carmen was suffering from neither dementia nor Alzheimer's, but her general forgetfulness caused Marina to worry every time she left her alone in the house. She came home wondering if a living room chair would be smoldering, or Carmen would be bleeding on the kitchen floor. And now with culinary school, she was out of the house more than she'd been when she was working at the Esposito.

"Do we need to do this today?" Her mother whined from the top of the stairs. "I think I have a doctor's appointment."

Normally, that would be a good guess, as Carmen was under care for a half-dozen other age-related conditions. But Marina cleared both of their calendars today, figuring once she got Carmen settled in the assisted living place, she'd spend the day with her, help her get adjusted. After that, the nurses could worry about her medical needs.

At least they didn't have to worry whether they could afford it. Carmen never wanted to touch the money Elder's father left her—there was a story there Marina didn't want to hear—but it made it possible for Carmen to move into a decent place in West Roxbury instead of a nursing home.

"Ma! Come on!"

They weren't exactly on a timetable, except the intake folks only worked a half a day on Monday. Marina needed to get this done today before her classes resumed on Tuesday morning.

"I'm taking your suitcase out to the car," she called. "And when I come back, we're leaving."

More grumbling.

She unlocked the door and carried the big lavender hard-sided case down the stairs. The outer door was bolted—Marina had learned to walk around the building every night to be sure Carmen hadn't left a window open or a door unlocked.

The October sun shone at a high enough angle to make her feel warm as she walked down the granite steps. Miracle of miracles, she'd found a parking space for the Mini right in front of the building last night, an unfamiliar token of good karma.

She slung the suitcase in the back and turned her face up to the sun. Maybe, after she settled Carmen in, she would go visit Rasmussen. Burton wouldn't care for it, but it felt like the right thing to do. He'd already learned she had a mind of her own.

She walked back up into the house. One thing at a time.

It was too quiet when she stepped into the living room.

"Ma! We're leaving."

"Coming, lovey."

Carmen had started to use endearments Marina had never heard from her before, still delivered in that rough maternal growl. It pleased her—maybe this transition would be easier than she thought.

A rustle came from behind the kitchen door. It opened and her mother walked out, clutching the black vinyl purse she carried everywhere.

Marina's heart skipped.

Her mother's upper half was tastefully clothed, a blue cardigan sprinkled with snowflakes over a white cotton blouse, but her bottom half was not. She wore tight purple sweat pants—Marina's from high school?—and over them a loose pair of nylon gym shorts.

"Mother!"

"What's that, darling?"

Marina felt the hopeless combination of laughter and despair that defined life with Carmen these days. Her mother smiled proudly, like a toddler who had tied her own shoes.

Marina took her mother's arm, thin as a broomstick, and reminded herself she wouldn't always have Carmen. Rasmussen Carter could worry about himself for now. She had more important things to do.

5

The administration kept trying to make Burton take a partner, but he'd avoided it for quite a while now. The brass loved his clearance rate, if not always the way he achieved it. His lieutenant wasn't trying to force a partner on him, but a deputy chief downtown was trying to get him off the street. The idea was Burton could train new Homicide detectives. How *not* to do it, Burton assumed.

He didn't hate the idea—he could see how passing on what he knew might help—but he was also slightly radioactive at the moment, on account of the lawsuit.

The long-lost heirs of Antoine Bousquet, the fashion designer Burton arrested for the deaths of two of his seamstresses, filed a civil suit against Burton and the city over Bousquet's death a year and a half ago. Burton was sure the heirs were really Belgian gangsters, but either way, no one coming into Homicide wanted to get close to him right now, in case his problems splashed over onto their shoes.

Which was a long-winded way of saying he was alone in his apartment on Monday morning, finishing up a plate of bacon and eggs, when he got the call for a dead body in the alley behind a bar off Portland Street in the West End.

He pulled up to the vehicles clotting the end of the alley: a patrol car, an unmarked, and the medical examiner's van.

"ME got here fast," he said to the uniform, as he signed the list of people present at the scene.

"Shitty day for golf, I guess," the patrolman said. "Watch out for

23

the grease. It's slippery down there."

Burton followed the narrow alley toward the knot of people. God help him, this work did get his blood up.

When he cleared his throat, the crowd parted to reveal a body sprawled face down on the pavement. Big enough to be male, wearing a black roll-neck sweater and gray corduroys, a short leather jacket. A dark pool spread under the man's head, the caramel skin of his neck taking on a yellowish tinge in death.

Tad Dankiewicz, the chief medical examiner, stood with his two assistants talking to Lieutenant Dennis Martines, Burton's boss. That was his first clue this wasn't an ordinary case. Dennis never came out to a scene.

No one shook hands. They were all gloved up.

"Slow day in the office?" Burton said to him.

Martines frowned at the levity, as he always did.

"This one's going to be a little touchy. You know who Sweetie Bogan is?"

"Vaguely. Musician? Artist of some kind?"

"Boston's answer to Lady Day. And a good friend of the Mayor's," the ME put in.

Dankiewicz, a tall weedy guy in his blue Tyvek overall, was a recent immigrant from the South, Atlanta or Nashville, and Burton already disliked him. The last scene they worked together, Tad moaned and groaned about not finding decent grits in the city, all while trying to scoop a week-old floater into a body bag. Must be why he brought the assistants now.

"Jazz singer." Elder would know who she was. "You guys going to let me at the body?"

Martines started to say something, shook his head, and stepped back.

"Go for it."

Burton half-knelt, careful not to drop his knee onto the greasy pavement, slick with whatever oozed from the broken bags at the foot of the dumpster.

"Well. I detect immediately this is not Boston's answer to Ms. Holiday, the body being male."

Tad glanced at one of the assistants, a thirty-ish redhead whose nervous twitching rustled her protective suit, and rolled his eyes. Burton marked him down for payback, down the line.

"Alfonso Deal-Jones," Martines pronounced. "He was Sweetie's companion for decades: manager, bodyguard, buffer from her adoring public. Supposedly her lover, too. The woman's eighty if she's a day."

Burton straightened and looked at Martines curiously. The man's entire professional being was devoted to climbing the police hierarchy. He was an unapologetic bureaucrat, and it was highly unusual for him to show interest in actual on-the-street police work. Which meant this was already more complicated than it appeared.

The lieutenant reached for his shirt pocket, a nervous tic. Sometimes there were cigarettes there, sometimes not. He wasn't smoking this week.

"OK," he said. "So I Googled her. And him."

"Clearly not a suicide."

Dankiewicz snorted, and Burton wondered why he kept trying to irritate the ME.

Alfonso might have been napping, if not for the cave-in on the back of his skull, a depression the size of a teacup. The blow had crushed bone inward and splashed blood and brain matter all over. The warmth of the day had slowed the congealing of the fluids. They were skinned over, but not completely dry.

"Lot of force," Burton said. "Fairly recent?"

"I don't like to speculate," Dankiewicz said. "But if Alfonso was standing up when he got hit, your killer was pretty tall. The impact was downward and this man is at least six one or two. Likely a male wielding the pipe."

He pointed to a length of iron pipe, stained at one end.

He didn't like to speculate, but he would anyway. Dankiewicz slotted himself firmly into the asshole category of Burton's taxonomy.

"To be determined," Burton said. "But thanks for waiting for me to get here. I know you didn't have to."

Martines's eyes widened in astonishment. Burton was rarely more than polite at a crime scene, too focused on getting after the killer. Dankiewicz looked troubled, as if he'd expected worse.

"You're not mellowing out on me?" Martines said quietly as they walked back up the alley, leaving the ME's people to do their work.

Burton was already planning what to do and didn't register Martines's remark completely. He didn't like it, but he was going to have to drag Elder into this, whether he wanted to or not. Burton knew squat about the local jazz scene or this Sweetie Bogan. Of course, he'd have to drag Elder's attention away from the pink-haired trumpet player he was drooling over.

"Why don't you come have a coffee with me, Lou? Bring me up to speed on all the politics here."

Martines scrunched his forehead, as if he sensed trouble.

"Ah, sure, Dan. Let's do that."

6

I'd disliked hospitals from the time my father died, and the hatred only intensified as I got older and various parts of my own physical self started deteriorating: knees and back from fourteen-hour days on the hard floors behind the bar, for starters. And who knew what shape my internal organs were in after three decades of hard drinking? But I was operating under my personal rule that said anything I didn't want to do was usually the right thing, so when I pushed back so hard on Burton's request, I felt guilty.

But, I told myself in the elevator Monday morning, I was visiting an acquaintance in the hospital, not committing myself to some half-assed investigation into what might have happened.

Carter's room was at the end of a hallway. I slipped inside. It was very quiet, a private room with no TV blaring, and far enough from the nurses' station you couldn't hear them. The shades were drawn and the lights very low, I suspected in deference to Carter's eye problems.

The man himself was sitting up in bed, dark glasses reflecting what little light was available. I couldn't see if his eyes were open. I paused in the doorway, suddenly unsure why I'd come. The change in the shadows must have registered.

"Someone there?" Carter said, a hitch in his voice.

"Elder Darrow, Rasmussen. Sorry if I startled you."

Carter's laugh was rough, his voice not the smooth confident manner I remembered.

"Pretty much everything startles you when you been stabbed in the guts. What are you doing here?"

27

He sounded aggrieved and frightened, which I supposed I understood. An attack like that had to shatter your normal assumptions, that you were going to live forever.

"No agenda," I said. "Heard you were in here and thought I would look in. You need anything?"

Carter's hands pulled at the light blanket covering his legs.

"You here on Burton's account? I know he hates me."

"On my own, Ras. Visiting someone in the hospital. Nothing more."

He ignored what I was saying.

"Because what happened with Marina, that was just a little fling. You can tell him that. He never had a thing to worry about."

It was unlikely Carter cared anything about the relationship between Burton and Marina, or whether Burton was jealous. Unless maybe Burton had threatened him? Maybe he was afraid Burton had sent me on a revenge mission. Getting stabbed had to make you at least a little paranoid.

"You're healing up?" I said. "Everything going to be OK?"

His cockiness surfaced. He must have decided I wasn't here for anything but what I'd said.

"Missed all the important parts." He was almost bragging, as if that was anything but luck. "I wouldn't have stayed this long, but the cut got infected."

At least I could tell Marina that Rasmussen Carter was going to survive. It might be tougher on her if he died. I wasn't sure why I thought that. And I wasn't curious enough to push any deeper. I was only curious about one thing. Rasmussen wasn't brave enough to start a bar fight.

"This came out of the blue at you? Like a random thing?"

He made a sour face.

"You know, Elder Darrow? I'm not really feeling like I need to talk to you about this." He lifted his pale moony face and tipped his head back and forth, as if mocking a Ray Charles move. "I'm not really believing in the benevolence of your being here."

I'd been known to bang my head against a wall, but I'd also learned which ones were important enough to expend the energy on. Rasmussen Carter didn't qualify.

"All set, then? Glad you're healing up. You'll be back on the streets in no time."

"Doubtful," Carter said. "I'm done with all that."

I thought what that meant was he didn't intend hanging out in bars any more. Turns out I was wrong.

* * *

I'd done what I could for Marina. If she asked, I could ease her mind. Burton's plan was a lot murkier, but that was his problem. Carter was healing, and the fact that he didn't want to talk to me meant I had no reason to get involved. Knives in play? No, thank you.

I walked out through the parking lot to my new Volvo station wagon. The Cougar had given up the ghost over the summer, and I'd researched cars seriously, looking for something reliable that was good in the snow. Burton made a bunch of cracks about returning to my roots, which actually would have meant driving one of the Mercedes-Benzes my father was so religious about. I liked the Volvo—it was comfortable, anonymous, and I didn't feel the least bit guilty about spending the money.

My phone dinged, a text from Isaac.

Evvie wants a meet. Proposition!

He ended it with emojis of a woman dancing and googly eyes. I shook my head.

Manana, I texted back. I couldn't figure out how to type the tilde.

And as I drove back down into the city, I thought about the woman, the improbability of her paying me any serious attention.

29

7

The Western Addition was a new-looking brick building, three stories high, cupped around a curved driveway in front. The plantings around the foundations were seasonally appropriate: maroon and yellow chrysanthemums and bunches of corn stalks. Marina didn't see any pumpkins yet.

A young woman in a lavender scrub top, stretch jeans, and thick-soled white nurses' shoes met them under the portico. Marina was impressed someone had come out to meet them.

"Mrs. Antonelli?" she said. "Welcome to the Western Addition. I'm Kim."

Carmen looked at Marina, confused. Her eyes narrowed and Marina almost convinced herself on the spot to cancel it all, shut the car door, drive Carmen back home, and deal with her by herself.

"What are we doing here?" Carmen said. "Is this the jail?"

Marina lost her words. Kim slipped her smile a bit, but rallied.

"A little vacation for you. From your daughter." She reached into the back of the Mini to pull out Carmen's suitcase. "Oof. What are you carrying in here? Your rock collection?"

Marina fought with an unreasonable anger at how light Kim was.

"Go with her, Ma. I'll park the car and meet you inside."

Kim nodded and winked, which Marina thought was supposed to make her feel better. It didn't.

She sat in the driver's seat watching Kim help Carmen navigate the concrete ramp toward the double doors. She had another selfish impulse, to turn the car around and drive like hell, head back to

30

Boston, and pretend she was alone in the world. She could not imagine Carmen, once she realized Marina intended to leave her at the Western Addition, would not pitch a blockbusting maternal fit, unleashing all the gods of guilt on her only daughter. For the first time in forever, Marina resented the fact she had no siblings to share the load.

She backed the Mini into a visitor's slot and locked it, then dawdled up the path to the entrance. Inside, a chest-high reception desk with a tall vase of summer flowers at either end greeted her, as did a handsome twenty-something Arab man wearing one of those Broadway-actor headsets.

"Ms. Antonelli?" he said pleasantly. "One-oh-nine." He pointed a manicured fingernail. "Left after the first bend in the corridor."

She told herself to toughen up, but this was harder than she had anticipated. She and Carmen had lived together all of Marina's life—even after she went to work, Marina stayed at home, saving money. There was plenty of room and she liked Carmen's company.

And the support was mutual. Marina's first cooking job at the Esposito was Carmen's doing, a connection back to the Darrow family for whom she'd kept house for so long.

But marrying Burton was going to change all that. She couldn't ask him to move in with her and her mother, and Carmen was not safe on her own any more. Her mother had given her a lot, and now it was Marina's turn to take responsibility. Mostly, she feared not doing the right thing.

She paused outside the door to 109, listening to the voices inside, straining to hear if Carmen sounded angry or sad. The door was too thick to pass nuance. Privacy was something the marketing department stressed about the Western, that residents—patients? inmates?—could interact as much or as little as they chose.

Marina knocked lightly, dread welling in her chest. She could sit with her mother a while, help her get accustomed to the new situation, but at some point, she would have to leave and go back to the house. And Carmen would stay here, alone.

She wiped her eyes and opened the door.

One of the suggestions the Western made to ease the change

was to set up Carmen's new apartment, a two-room suite, with familiar furniture and personal items. The people here did a nice job of making the smaller space homey. Paintings of country scenes from Italy that used to hang in Carmen's bedroom were already up. The headboard of the old bed, dark walnut carved with grapes and vines, sat against the wall, with the matching bedside table and a brass lamp Marina knew only lit the first setting of a three-way bulb. A small Ikea bookcase held a dozen of Carmen's paperback romance novels.

Marina raised her eyebrows at the sight of Kim sitting on the bed, her legs straight out in front of her. Carmen sat in the familiar green recliner that used to grace the TV room at home.

Kim chattered away familiarly about activities Carmen might like to take part in: yoga, drawing for seniors, water aerobics. Marina could not see her mother in a swimming pool. Carmen used the remote to cycle through the channels on the flat screen.

"Look at this." She failed to notice Kim's light frown at being ignored. "They have the Red Sox."

Their house in Boston sat in a strange zone contested by two cable TV companies, so they never received the TV station that broadcast local games for more than a month at a time. She did her best to radiate approval, but she hoped Carmen wasn't planning to sit and watch TV the rest of her days. It was her choice, however.

"That's great, Ma. You'll be able to watch the World Series."

Carmen shot her a hard sharp look, and in its pure lucidity, Marina understood that her mother knew exactly what was going on and why. And she was fine with it.

A knot in her chest eased, and she was overcome with love for a mother who, even now, was mothering her. She nodded.

"Maybe some nights," Carmen said, "you can come over and we'll watch a game together."

8

Burton had not been back to the Esposito since Elder turned it over to the new owners back in June. His friend had gone back and forth over the decision, but the chance to stick it to one of the real estate developers speculating on the Boston Olympics must have been irresistible. Elder had crowed about being overpaid.

He still wasn't sure it was Elder's smartest idea, selling off the brick wall that kept him from falling back over into his alcoholism. The bar was more than a business to Elder, had been as long as Burton had known him. He'd asked Burton and Marina both for advice about selling, but Burton knew Elder had a hard enough head that he might have been looking for an opinion he could contradict. Both of them had begged off the chance to weigh in.

It was late Monday afternoon, so the lights inside weren't as low as they might be later. He didn't know if the place even hosted live music any more. As he descended the familiar steel stairs, he saw the complete transformation.

All the old black and white jazz photos were gone. The walls and ceiling were a soft off-white, giving the room a glow. Vintage incandescent bulbs swung from a web of wire crisscrossing the ceiling, and teacup-sized potted plants hung in lighted niches on the walls.

He thought fern bars died out in the Eighties, but the new Esposito was a frightening resurrection of that old idea. Elder would hate it.

He walked across the spongy floor—cork tiles—and up to the

bar, where a young black man, maybe six foot six and thin as a garden rake, regarded Burton with suspicion. He must have made him as a cop.

Up close, the man looked thirty-five or so. His pink bow tie bobbed when he spoke.

"Detective."

He knew the correct way to address Burton, which made him wonder. Had the man collided with law enforcement before today?

"Love what you've done with the place," Burton said.

He didn't, but no sense starting off wrong-footed. The barman caught his tone, though.

"Ah. Another of the original habitués." He wiped his hands on a bar rag. "Back in the olden days of the Esposito?"

"What are you calling it now?"

"The Greenwood." He pointed to a large oil portrait on the wall near the door to the kitchen, a fierce old man with no chin and muttonchop whiskers. "Chester Greenwood. Invented the ear muff."

Burton couldn't wait to tell Elder that.

"And you are?"

"Baron Loftus." He reached across the bar to shake hands, his fingers long like a pianist's. "What can I do for the Boston Police today? I gather the department was familiar with this address, back in the day."

Burton hated that expression. He defended Elder *in absentia*.

"Long time ago. The previous owner cleaned it up quite a bit."

Loftus sighed showily.

"Not all the way, I'm afraid. I've had to ask a few of the old clientele to find another place to squat on a bar stool all day."

Burton refocused on why he was here.

"Understand you had an incident here Saturday. More Esposito than Greenwood."

Loftus made an exaggerated show of thinking, frowning, finger to his lips.

"Oh. That woman. I was trying something out, a nice quiet jazz evening on a Saturday night, if you can imagine that. Low lights, a special cocktail, some cabaret music. Then that lunatic gets into a knife fight over something the old witch said."

He popped his lips in exasperation.

"Sweetie Bogan?"

"One and the same." Loftus ran some cola from the soda gun into a glass, but didn't offer Burton anything.

"And which lunatic are we talking about? Alfonso Deal-Jones?"

"Oh, god no. The man with the sunglasses. I don't know his name. He's one of the people I'm going to ban."

"Rasmussen Carter."

Burton doubted he was planning to return.

"If that's the man they carried out on a stretcher, yes. It's the last time I'll have live music in here, I'll tell you that."

"No music? Place used to attract a decent crowd, you know." Burton skidded off-topic again.

Loftus pointed up at the speakers in the corners of the room.

"Spotify, my friend. No more junkies or drunk guitar players for me. No fuss."

Burton knew Elder hated all the online music services, for the predictable playlists and the fact the musicians barely got royalties.

"So. Sweetie Bogan."

Burton had found no address for her anywhere in the city databases, rentals or property owned. Alfonso Deal-Jones, likewise. They must have split before the responding officers collected IDs.

Loftus's heavy sigh made the starch on his white shirt crackle.

"Yes," he said. "Another of the many mistakes I've made in buying this bar."

Burton had assumed he was the manager, not the owner.

"Meaning?"

"The divine Ms. Bogan, Detective, is my dear departed mother's sister. Darling of dive bars and low-rent concert venues everywhere."

Interesting—Burton's sense was Sweetie Bogan was better-known and a bigger talent than Loftus was saying.

"And where does she live? I'd like to speak with her."

"Wouldn't everyone?"

Loftus wrote out an address in a part of the city Burton knew too well, a condo building in what used to be the Charlestown Navy Yard. The Nautica.

"That is her current home," Loftus said. "I think you'll find out she doesn't go out much any more. Living in the glow of past glories. She's not welcome in here again."

Strains in family dynamics were always interesting. Motives were made of less.

"You must have known Alfonso, then?"

Loftus shook his head.

"I wanted nothing to do with all that, in any way, shape, *or* form. That was the first time Sweetie and her paramour came into the Greenwood, and it was a fucking disaster."

The curse must have tasted bad, the way he spit it out.

"'Paramour.' Her lover? I understood Ms. Bogan is in her sixties."

Loftus smiled archly.

"Little ageism there, Detective? I would not advise taking that tone with my aunt. Who prefers Mrs. Bogan, by the way."

"Alfonso?" Burton felt like he was following a twisty path through a cartoon wood.

Loftus poured himself a shot of Bacardi and tossed it back, again not offering Burton anything.

"Consort to the queen," he said. "Bodyguard, manager, all-around factotum. They were together for eons."

"You didn't like him?"

"Only in that he took a lot from Sweetie and gave her very little. The way he handled her finances, for example. Kept her on a small allowance."

Money motives always perked up Burton's ears.

"Really. You saw a problem there?"

"A man in his fifties, more or less at his peak, squiring around a woman in her sixties? Living off her royalties—which are still substantial, by the way."

Burton filed the fact Baron Loftus was conversant with the state of his rich aunt's finances. And his obvious feeling a family member ought to treat him a little better.

"You know anyone who might have wanted Alfonso dead?"

Loftus couldn't control a spark of pleasure.

"Is that what this is all about? His murder?"

Burton leaned over the bar.

"You know he's dead? How's that?"

They'd found the body eight hours ago, and Boston was still the kind of town where the death of a black man who wasn't a politician, a businessman, or a sports figure would not be breaking news.

"Would you find it offensive if I used the term 'jungle telegraph?'" Loftus picked at the corner of his mouth. "The story was out in the world quickly, if not officially."

"I'd be interested to know where it came from."

Probably someone from the investigative team—there was almost always someone with a connection to the paper or TV—but to what end?

Loftus rolled his shoulders.

"Around. People assume all bartenders are deaf, you know."

Something Elder had said to him more than once. People said outrageous, even criminal things, on the other side of the bar, assuming he was a drink-dispensing automaton.

"You didn't answer my question," Loftus said. "But let me infer. You want to talk to Sweetie because of what happened to Alfonso. But I think you will find the two of them weren't talking to each other lately."

"And why was that?"

Loftus showed that sly avidity gossipers use to pretend they aren't tattling.

"Alfonso recently developed an affection for what used to be called the marching powder." He tapped the side of his nose, as if Burton might not know what he was talking about. "More like a major love affair, in fact. I believe she cut him from the payroll two or three weeks ago."

"And yet he was in the bar with her on Saturday night."

Burton never forgot how serendipity played into his work. You followed the facts where they led, but you didn't let them dictate what you thought. You kept your eyes and ears open for what was happening out on the fringes, those whiffs of fancy, possibility, ideas that filled in the spaces around the cold hard facts.

Loftus shrugged.

"No accounting for the desires of an old woman."

"Is it possible Alfonso ran up a debt to someone? Over his choices?"

"Possibly. I emphasize that he did not buy his drugs here, nor anywhere close by. The old reputation of this place was bad enough. I'm trying to upgrade, if that wasn't clear."

Burton smirked. That was exactly how Elder had talked about the place, back when it was a true bucket of blood. The notion was in the eye of the beholder. But for a young man with pretensions to elegance, Loftus seemed to know a lot about lowlifes.

"Then where did he go?"

Loftus stretched out his skinny arms, the wrists' bony protuberances well past the stiff cuffs on which diamond cuff links sparkled. He paused dramatically, but Burton had put up with more crap for lesser reasons.

"Well. In a city so tightly controlled by a particular gangster, you would have to ask yourself who that might be. Ultimately, that is."

Burton's head started to hurt. He wondered if they'd been edging in this direction. He'd hoped not.

"You're talking about Mickey Barksdale."

Loftus lifted a shoulder and dropped it, like a shy chorus girl.

"More likely some minion of his, yes. But ultimately? Yes. Mickey B."

9

The Red Sox were on a West Coast swing before the playoffs started, but I was damned if I was going to start watching a game at ten o'clock at night. Tuesday morning, the Cask and Flagon was almost deserted, not completely cleaned up from the night before.

The transformation of Evangeline blew me away. In fact, when I walked into the Kenmore Square bar, I almost didn't recognize the put-together young woman sitting with Isaac. She wore a long-sleeved button down blue Oxford that concealed her ink and a black pencil skirt. Her hair was black today, skinned back and braided into a bun resting at the base of her neck. I would have pegged her as a young executive from the financial district, slumming for lunch.

Before either of them saw me, as I walked under the hanging TVs and through the scattered tables and chairs, I watched them. Evvie rested her hand on Isaac's arm and leaned into him a little more than I would have been comfortable with, but Isaac didn't seem to mind terribly. It reminded me how she'd leaned into me at the warehouse, and I wondered if it were a conscious ploy.

"The man." Isaac caught me walking up to the table and stood up to shake hands. "Thanks for coming."

As if he were already the business mogul he intended to become and I was coming to his office. Evvie looked up at me with cool gray eyes.

"Evangeline," I said.

She held my gaze a beat longer than necessary, then nodded her head toward the chair between them. I laughed to myself. Isaac was reading business strategy books again.

"OK. I'm here. What is it?"

"Can we get you something?" Evvie raised her hand for a waiter. "I'm having a Long Island Iced Tea."

For breakfast? Isaac shook his head fractionally, but she didn't see. He obviously hadn't clued her in to the fact I was a drunk and that it would take one sip of a Long Island Iced Tea to set me walking down a long lonesome road. No, not walking—running.

"Nothing for me, thanks." I raised my eyebrows at Isaac. "Your call—what are we here for? I hope no one's trying to renegotiate Sunday's take again."

This was only the second time I'd been around Evangeline, but I could already tell she was a manipulator. She probably didn't care what anyone thought of her, as long as she was moving in the direction she wanted. The question was how relentless she would be in pursuit of her goals.

"Isaac," she said. "You explain it better than I can."

Isaac saw through her, too, but he was young enough to think he could impress her, give her something on the theory that she might be grateful enough to give him something back. I could have told him otherwise, but some lessons you have to learn yourself. She already knew I trusted him more than her, which had to be why she drafted him.

"Evvie, she wants to..." He hesitated, as if looking for the most flattering way to say it.

"Evvie, she wants out of Triceratops." She was impatient. "Evvie's tired of making music in the subway. She's got some better chops than honking like a parking lot full of drunk kazoo players."

"Who's your favorite trumpeter?" I said.

Isaac frowned. But she saw where I was going. And that I might be taking her seriously.

"Chet Baker."

"Before or after?" When he fell in love with heroin, his playing changed radically. And not for the better.

"Before. The dope just ruined him." She sounded sad, but I couldn't judge how good a faker she might be.

Though, I approved of her answer. There were still, in the twenty-first century, young jazz musicians enamored of the dark romance between drugs and creativity. That was how Bill Evans got himself a heroin habit, thinking it would make his playing more authentic. I still didn't trust her completely, but I had a better sense of how she thought.

"Tell me what you think I can do for you."

She worked her hands around the tall glass of amber liquid the bartender delivered, as if mining herself for words. She caught my glance at the iced tea.

"The bartender knows to make them nonalcoholic," she said. "I don't really drink."

I gestured for her to continue.

"I like those two guys. Well, Spud, the sax player? No one really gets to know him too well. They're basically good guys. I'm just not into what they're doing any more. Isaac says you used to run a bar. Hire bands and all that?"

I nodded.

"I was thinking maybe you could help me connect with some folks. Get into clubs where I could play music that people listen to."

"You don't want me to manage your career."

"No. You must have contacts in the city, though, right? The bars? You could introduce me to the people who own clubs. People who hire bands."

"There's not much demand for a solo trumpet player," I said.

"I can pull a trio or quartet together if I have to. But I really want to sing."

I looked at Isaac for his reaction. He probably thought he was doing me a favor, bringing me another opportunity, like my mentoring. I wasn't sure I wanted any deeper connection with Evvie, though—didn't know if I trusted her. But Isaac's pop-ups weren't going to feed my need for something to do. And if I let myself get bored, I might lapse back into drinking.

"I can't guarantee I can help you. I was one guy with a small club and a very small budget. But I can do my best to connect you with the people I know."

"Excellent," she said.

Her thanks didn't gush. She patted her hands together as if applauding. Me? Or herself, for getting what she wanted.

Isaac acted relieved, an odd reaction. I had an uneasy feeling I'd just agreed to something I might regret.

"Drinks for the house." Evvie laid a hand, cool from the glass, on my forearm. "How about a nice Virgin Mary?"

10

Burton left the Greenwood, formerly the Esposito, with the sense Loftus was holding back something about what happened the night Rasmussen Carter got stabbed, or something about Alfonso Deal-Jones. Or both. The fact that all three of them were black would make it harder for Burton to investigate. Not because of race, but because they came from the same part of the city. The perpetual problem of working in Boston was how the individual neighborhoods were so Balkanized. It was a situation the city's power brokers encouraged. It kept people divided and fighting for the crumbs among themselves, not challenging larger issues. The rich got richer, and gained more control.

The Nautica condos at the Navy Yard were a perfect example of how the city was eating itself. Older low-income neighborhoods were razed to provide the city with more tall shiny-glass-and-steel towers full of apartments for the high-income, high-maintenance young lawyers and professionals who swarmed the city, driving the price of everything to the moon.

He loved his city, but he did not love what it was becoming, a kind of upper-class theme park, a homogenized shrine to youth and money, craft beer, kombucha, farm-to-table restaurants, and massage therapists who didn't offer hand jobs as an extra service.

The next morning, he parked, walked into a high bright atrium, and badged the uniformed man at the desk.

"Sweetie Bogan?"

"Mrs. Bogan is on the penthouse floor." The guard picked up his handset. "I'll ask if she can see you."

"She'll see me," Burton said. "And let's not bother her ahead of time."

"Building rules. It's worth my job."

Burton considered whether to teach him a lesson about cooperating with law enforcement now or later, then focused. He headed for the elevator.

"Hold on," the guard said. "She said she'll see you."

He jogged around the front of his desk, key ring jingling.

"This is a secure building." He inserted a key into the hole on the elevator panel. "Lots of weirdos in the neighborhood."

Burton hoped so. As the door closed on him, he wondered how much of a pain in the ass it would be to lose a key, or forget it at home?

The car whooshed upward a little faster than he was used to, what the developers probably called "an amenity." He'd done a quick search on his phone and priced out a penthouse apartment at about ten grand a month. So Sweetie wasn't hurting. His stomach floated as the elevator stopped, somewhere above the tenth floor.

The door slid open onto a foyer, a single entrance in front of it. The penthouse door was wide open, a diminutive black woman in a bright yellow head scarf and a cream-colored double-breasted linen suit stood silhouetted by the strong sunlight behind her. She was barefoot, her toes knobbed and curled under.

"You would be Detective Burton." Her voice was a pleasant whiskey-rasp he could imagine caressing ballads in a dark and smoky dive. He hadn't given the guard downstairs his name, which meant Baron Loftus must have called to warn her he was coming. Good to know the family tie was tighter than Loftus pretended.

"I am. And you would be Ms. Bogan."

She stood aside and swept him inside with a hand.

"I am Mrs. Sweetie Bogan," she said with an icy bite. "I was married to that bastard long enough. I don't want to forget him."

She slashed a smile at him as they started down a hallway lined with black and white photos.

"Son of a bitch up and died on me. For which I will never forgive him."

Burton caught images of familiar jazz players—under other circumstances, he would have been tempted to stop and look. As it was, he saw Sweetie with a young Eubie Blake, Ellis Marsalis, and Johnny Hartman.

She clocked his interest and sighed.

"Oh, god. Not another fan."

Her acerbic tone brought him back to why he was here. He reminded himself to tell Elder about this.

Sweetie sat down with her back to a wide glass wall looking out on the harbor, as if the view were old hat to her. The sunlight made him squint.

"Alfonso Deal-Jones," he said. "Employee of yours?"

Her laugh trilled promises.

"Oh, darling. So much more than that. Rest his rambunctious little soul."

"You know he was murdered, then?"

It made sense, if she'd talked to Loftus. The speed of gossip could still surprise him. Especially in less favored circles, where not knowing what was coming at you could be dangerous, he understood. Didn't help him do his job, though, losing the element of surprise.

"Of course."

"Maybe you could tell me a little bit about your relationship."

"Sit, please. I can't bear to have someone hover over me." She pointed to a red velvet chair next to a round mahogany table that looked like an antique. "Can I offer you something? It's nearly afternoon."

She spoke to fill the space between them. It didn't feel like she was nervous.

"Nothing. Thank you. Alfonso?"

"Yes." She looked past him, focused on the middle distance, the wall behind him. "Alfonso and I—how do I say this delicately? We had a mutually enriching life together. Nearly twenty years."

Her voice snagged. He couldn't forget she was a performer.

"And? Something happened?"

"When I started out in this business, I was a naive young girl from Roxbury. My father was a house painter and my mother was what you call nowadays a stay-at-home mom. She worked harder than he did, most days. They knew nothing about music, that world. How the thieves and the vipers would treat a young girl."

Burton folded his hands and listened. When someone started rolling, it was enlightening to see where the ramble took them.

"Alfonso was my first lover after Mr. Bogan. I was forty and he was shockingly young." She smiled at the memory. "My protector. He took care of all my business, let me concentrate on singing."

"Your manager, then?"

A tear appeared in the corner of one eye. She dabbed it with a tissue.

"He was my wall, Detective. Standing strong between me and a world that always tried to get over on me."

"Did he make some enemies along the way? In your business? Maybe someone who didn't like how he treated them? Or how he protected you?"

She nodded.

"I wasn't really fair to him. The singing was so important to me that I didn't pay attention to anything else. Certainly not budgets or paying my bills on time. I let him smooth every path for me."

The regret felt more professional than personal, Alfonso's passing an annoyance more than an emotional loss. She would likely mourn Alfonso for as short a time as was polite, absorb the loss, and move on. He felt a certain sympathy for the memory of the man.

"Would you know anyone in particular who might have wanted to harm him? Recently?"

Her thin torso stiffened, but the outrage felt fake, something to disguise a lie that might be coming.

"Well, Detective. He did have to stab that fellow who tried to attack me last weekend, didn't he? In Baron's bar?"

Shit. Alfonso was the man who stabbed Rasmussen Carter? Why hadn't he known that? Because he was staying away from it, because he'd asked Elder to investigate. Because he'd been avoiding the details in his haste to step away.

Sweetie eyed him with malicious pleasure.

"You didn't know that."

He gave her a quick nod.

"Then he's the first man you should talk to," she said.

"Mr. Carter is still in the hospital. And I think it's probably unlikely he checked himself out long enough to kill Alfonso, then checked himself back in. He's been in a lot of pain."

"Good," she said.

Burton was angry at himself. Normally he was on top of the details, but this time he'd ignored learning more because he didn't want to deal with Marina's past.

"He must have friends." Sweetie bore in, as relentless toward the weakness in his argument as if they were knife-fighting.

"I'm sure he does." He struggled back from the defensive. "You were recently estranged from Mr. Deal-Jones, I understand?"

Her face tightened up, the probe a little too personal.

"You could only have heard that from my nephew."

"I can't comment on where the information came from. But it was true?"

She closed her eyes, as if in pain. Her years on the stage, behind the microphone, had taught her acting as well as singing, shifting to please an audience. She coughed lightly, a ringed hand over her mouth.

"Alfonso owned what I would call an addictive personality. There was very little he was willing to do halfway."

She grinned salaciously.

"As you can imagine, many aspects of our life together benefited from that single-mindedness. He was a man who paid exquisite attention."

That sounded like a decent epitaph, but her wriggling and posing were starting to irritate him. And interviewing people in a murder investigation rarely irritated him.

"I understand he was a cocaine addict," Burton said. "Do you have some sense of how deeply he was involved?" He apologized mentally to Baron Loftus, who was going to get an earful from his aunt about discretion. "If you cut off his funds, for example, would he have tried to deal on credit? Maybe gone into debt with a dealer? Or maybe he stole money from you?"

She sniffed and delivered another surprise.

"I didn't cut him off because he was tooting. If I abandoned everyone I knew who did something illegal or had a weakness, I would have no friends left at all. Or family."

She peered at him.

"Do you trust anyone? Is there someone in your life you would believe in unconditionally?"

She was hijacking the interview again, forcing answers from him rather than questions.

"Of course." Marina. Maybe Elder.

"Alfonso had a dream," she said. "A late life one, I guess you'd call it. He was tired of being my consort. Male ego, I'm afraid. He borrowed a large sum of my capital without asking and invested it in a scheme having to do with drugs. Illegal ones. I didn't know more than that, and I didn't want to."

"How much?"

She waved a hand.

"It doesn't matter. I recovered it all before he could do what he planned."

There was a motive, if Alfonso had brokered a major drug deal with someone who didn't like having it canceled.

"Do you know who he might have been dealing with?"

He didn't expect an answer, but he had to ask the question.

"I do," she said. "But I don't believe you'll find him in Boston. His name is Edward Dare."

11

"This used to be your place?" Evvie said as I parked the Volvo at the curb on Mercy Street on Tuesday afternoon. "Shitty neighborhood."

I was getting tired of her world-weary attitude. She was by turns snippy and sarcastic, and she didn't seem to appreciate the fact I was going to introduce her to bar owners I knew and try to help her make connections. This was absolutely the last help I was providing for her. The main reason I'd started here was to see what the new owners had done with the Esposito.

The blank steel door at the street level had been replaced with a carved wooden one with a small octagonal stained glass window in the center of the panel. I rapped it with the back of my hand and it reverberated like real glass. The neighborhood hadn't gentrified that much and I wondered how often the new owner—the list in my hand read Baron Loftus—replaced it.

I shouldered the hefty door open and stepped onto the landing. My first sense was that it did not smell like the Esposito. A tinge of ozone in the air said Loftus had invested in state-of-the-art air scrubbing apparatus. The atmosphere was dry and characterless, like an airplane cabin at thirty thousand feet.

I let Evvie precede me down the stairs so I could take in the changes.

The walls and ceiling were so light now, they almost glowed, and even in late afternoon, the lights were still high, as if the bar was now proud of its darkest corners. Plants hung on the wall under mini grow lamps, the shiny black lacquer furniture all matched, and the bar top was covered with sheets of hammered copper. Kenny G was playing on a better sound system than I'd ever been able to afford. My head started to hurt.

"Seriously?" Evvie sniffed. "This is like a place old yuppies go to die."

I snorted, trying not to care. The bar wasn't mine any more and that was fine.

"Not the way I ran it," I said.

A couple dozen patrons eyed us as we walked down the stairs, or rather they eyed Evvie, who wore a tight strappy top that highlighted her narrow waist, big shoulders, and sleeve tattoos. A pair of flowing blue silk pants clung to her hips and billowed out below.

"Mr. Loftus?"

I walked across the floor, which rebounded slightly underfoot, and stuck out my hand to the very tall young man behind the bar in a starched white shirt and onyx cuff links. He must be a neater bartender than I'd been. By the end of a good night, my apron would be smeared with maraschino juice, beer stains, and who knew what else.

"I'm Elder Darrow. We spoke on the phone."

He was a stranger to me. He had not attended the closing at Attorney Markham's office, nor had any of the other principals in the sale been African-American. I wondered if Murray Carton, who ended up with the bar after the Olympic bid collapsed, either hired a black manager to make the place seem hipper (though the Neil Diamond decor worked against that), or flipped it to this guy.

"You used to own the place."

Loftus's voice was high and reedy, as if strained out of him by his height and thinness.

"I did." I expected some comradely platitudes about running a bar, maybe an invitation to compliment him on what he'd done.

"You know how the dishwasher works? It keeps getting jammed." Evvie snorted beside me.

"There's a catch in the feed tray that gets stuck sometimes. Let me show you."

I followed him into the kitchen where nothing had changed except the grill and the fryer were cold.

"You're not serving food?"

Loftus lifted one side of his mouth.

"Only on the days the inspectors come around."

I questioned the decision. Having Marina in my kitchen had added a slim but necessary layer of profit, and food gave people a reason to linger over drinks. Not my bar, I reminded myself.

"Here."

I reached under the hood of the Hobart and freed the jam.

"See it? The belt gets gummed with food scraps sometimes. Easy enough to fix."

Loftus looked horrified at the idea of putting his clean white-shirted arm into the old monster.

"You called me yesterday? About a quartet you're trying to book?" he said.

I wiped my hands on a rag hanging on the side of the dishwasher.

"Yeah. You are hosting live music?" I thought about the new decor, the background music. "Might not be the kind of thing your clientele wants."

Loftus stared at me, maybe insulted.

"You know we had a little trouble with a girl singer here?"

I tipped my head. "How so?"

"You must be the only person in Boston who doesn't know. Some wannabe impresario got mad when someone heckled his girl. Got himself stabbed." He pointed out the kitchen door. "Right out there."

Rasmussen Carter was stabbed here? In the Esposito? It made me sad to think that the bar's original roots had resurfaced after such a long time. And all the work I'd put in trying to clean it up. And then I got pissed at Burton, who should have told me about it. Warned me.

"Then you're probably not looking for live artists, at the moment."

"*Au contraire, frère.* The notoriety brought business. The place has been jammed. I guess people like a little dive in their bars. Can she sing?"

"You'd have to ask her," I said. "But I imagine so."

"Well, let's go do that, then."

He clapped me on the shoulder and led me out of the kitchen, as I pondered his sudden friendliness.

12

Everyone agreed the lawsuit was bullshit, but there was apparently no way to dodge it.

"They actually said they'd drop the personal suit, if the city settled." Bridge Willos, his PBA lawyer, held up his hands. "But the city won't go the settlement route any more, not unless they're sure they're going to lose in court. And they aren't."

Elder had offered to pay for a private attorney for Burton—hell, so had Marina—but if he understood correctly, even if the verdict went against him, he wouldn't be personally liable for damages.

"It could hurt the city more if they lose, though, right? I mean, I've been in courtrooms where the jury was happy to stick it to the cops on general principle."

Willos sipped at the coffee Burton had brought to his office and looked impressed.

"Not the usual precinct swill—you pay for it yourself?"

Burton shook his head impatiently.

"And the people on the jury don't stop to think that if the city's paying damages, it's coming out of their pockets. The taxpayers. We have the names of the people bringing the suit?"

"Unnamed heirs of Antoine Bousquet. Some LLC with the identities held by their sleaze bag lawyer."

Burton almost cracked about tautology, but Willos was a lawyer, too, and probably wouldn't appreciate the joke.

"They can do that? File a lawsuit anonymously?"

"Eventually, they'll have to come out. But for now, it's a corporate entity."

"And of course corporations are people nowadays."

"I don't mind meeting with you, Dan. But you really have nothing to worry about here. And the PBA can't get involved in court. City's got white-shoe lawyers up the ass."

"Yeah. And none of them's looking at it from my point of view." Willos shrugged.

"You've been in court. You know what it will be like. Their lawyers will challenge everything you did or didn't do, every decision you made, and try and make you look like some troglodyte baton-wielding throwback. They'll claim excessive force made him more vulnerable to what happened afterward. The stress of being arrested."

"Jesus, that's a long pull."

Willos drained his coffee.

"They don't really give a shit about Bousquet, whoever it is. They're trying to play the city off against the Feds. Feds want to seize Bousquet's assets under RICO. I guess the lawyers think a local suit will confuse the issue."

"Good luck with that. The Feds love their RICO."

RICO cases allow the Feds to seize the assets of criminals convicted of crimes that are associated, however loosely, with organized crime, the assumption being those assets are fruit of the criminal enterprise. More than one Federal law enforcement office in the country is flush with money, guns, and vehicles forfeited in RICO cases.

"A little *ex post facto* at this point," Burton said. "But I suppose the lawyers know what they're doing. Oh, wait. We're talking about political appointees."

Willos frowned. A little too close to home?

"It's not going to be a problem for you unless you make it one, Dan. Unless they find a very sympathetic judge, it's going nowhere. They're counting on the city blinking on a settlement."

"Which the city's done before."

"They're pretty adamant this time around. But for three buildings in the heart of Chinatown and whatever else Bousquet owned, they must think it's worth a try. One of the foremen took over and the business is doing well. Apparently he had a better business head than his boss—straightened out the criminal crap, started paying the seamstresses. Helps that he's Chinese."

"What's his name?" Burton said. "Could he be the one behind the suit?"

"Shit, I don't know. Chin Ho? I doubt he has the shekels to hire Baker and Barney."

Another thing you could count on the old-time Irish guys for was a racial crack. Baker and Barney was the Boston criminal defense law firm that filed the suit. Their price almost guaranteed organized crime was involved. B&B didn't do *pro bono*.

"So what you're telling me is to wait, and if it does go to trial, be prepared to get shit all over. But don't take it personally. I'll get my day in court."

Willos snorted.

"Week, more likely. No, the whole thing is very close to a nuisance suit. A hard-ass judge could kick the whole thing out."

"Film at eleven, then," Burton said. "Thanks for the update. Not that I love what I'm hearing. I do have real work to do."

"Don't worry about it. The lawyers will run up some billable hours and crap on you, but you're used to that. You have nothing material to worry about."

Burton wished he was as confident as his lawyer. People liked to think the law was a rational and objective system, but experience told him the opposite. Where people were involved—egos, power, politics—anything could happen.

He stood up and collected the coffee cups.

"I hope you're right, Bridge. 'Cause the city always looks out for itself."

13

She wished she didn't feel so guilty, as she parked the Mini Cooper in the lot on Parkman Street and walked into the lobby of Mass General on Tuesday. She and Burton had dinner together last night, and she should have told him what she was planning. The argument with herself ended when she decided that the difficult thing—what she didn't want to do—must be the right thing. Visiting Rasmussen Carter in the hospital wasn't sending him a message she still cared about him. It was the kind of thing a friend would do.

Then why was her stomach knotted?

A young woman in cartoon character scrubs at the kiosk gave her the room number. Marina took the elevator to the sixth floor. Her throat tightened as she paused outside the door to his room.

She took a deep breath and entered. Rasmussen lay on his back, bare to the waist. A nurse smoothed a gauze bandage over his flat abdomen and taped down the edges. Marina was shocked by a physical memory, the feel of Carter's body on hers, and she flushed.

"Looking much better, Mr. Carter." The nurse patted the bandage and pulled up the blanket to cover him. "No sign of infection. I'd say you're not long for this bed. Day or two more."

But his eyes were on Marina in the doorway, his expression a mix of longing and anger. She was the one who dropped him, after all, and it looked as if it still pricked his ego.

"Marina. Baby."

"Rasmussen. How are you feeling?"

He pushed the sunglasses up on his nose. The nurse bustled out.

"What do you think?"

The silence grew like a balloon filling. She fiddled with her bag.

"Nurse said you're getting out soon. That's good, isn't it?"

Those sunglasses made it so hard to read him. He pulled the blanket to his neck and raised the bed so he sat up straight.

"It's nice to see you again, Marina. Wasn't sure I ever would."

She sat down in a hard plastic chair, wondering if they were designed to be so uncomfortable so people wouldn't linger.

"I'm sorry about the way things ended," she said. "I just couldn't find another way."

She'd ignored the calls and texts, even sending Carmen to the door one time to say she wasn't there. His possessiveness had started to frighten her.

"I hear you're getting married," he said.

Marina shook her head. She was not discussing her personal life with him.

"What happened to you?" she said. "Did I hear correctly you were attacked in a bar? Over a woman?"

"Not true. A misunderstanding. You're the only woman I'd ever fight over."

"Pretty serious misunderstanding for you to wind up in here."

"How's your Moms? You know I always liked her."

"She's been better. I moved her into an assisted living place in West Roxbury. Much better for her."

"And better for you, too. I imagined the three of us..." He dropped the thought when he saw her face. "Better for your fiancé, too."

"None of your business," she said. "We all make the best decisions we can."

Reminding him of the decision she'd made about him.

He shifted, winced, pointed to the rolling table with the water pitcher.

"You mind? The antibiotics make my mouth dry."

She stood and rolled the apparatus over, poured him a cup of water. He wrapped his hand around her wrist.

"What are you getting married for? You have to?"

"None of your business."

"To a cop."

"To a decorated Homicide detective on the Boston Police Department."

"Are you going to have babies?"

The conversation ranged too far afield for the relationship they had: a dozen "dates," three sleepovers. A lot of light talk about not much. For her, a fling—had she misread his intentions? Had he wanted more?

"Again. None of your business."

"Because you and I would have made some beautiful babies."

Blood heated her cheeks.

"Not a chance."

She gathered herself to go, the visit having met her minimum requirement for politeness.

"I will be out of here in a couple of days, as you heard," he said. "I would like for us to take up again."

The shock silenced her for a good ten seconds.

"You wormy little man. What on God's green earth makes you think I am not happy with what I'm doing? Did you think I've been pining away for your sorry self all this time?"

He regarded her calmly, his expression blank.

"No, Marina. But I know Burton, from working for Elder. He's not a steady man. And he's always going to be working for a salary. I've got better prospects than that."

When they were together, she'd read him as a quick-hit artist, looking for the big chance. He was not someone who believed in building anything, in sustained and focused work, in sticking with something—or someone—for long. She could not imagine tying her future to someone with a boom-or-bust mentality, then or now.

"Looks to me like your prospects almost got you killed," she said. "Maybe you need to rethink your priorities."

His face twisted and he ripped off the sunglasses. Both the irises and the retinae of his eyes were eerie-pale, setting off the bright blue pupil in relief. He pointed the earpiece of the glasses at her.

"The man who stabbed me? He took something away from me that I earned. Earned with hard work and patience. Don't think I'm letting him get away with it."

She stepped back, stunned by his fury.

"I know what's mine," he said, with a low laugh. "And I don't give it up so easily." He slipped the sunglasses back on. "You can expect to hear from me."

His laugh echoed behind her as she stalked from the room, nearly colliding with a nurse. It horrified her that he'd gotten the wrong impression, that he thought she still cared for him. As the elevator dropped, she worried that she might have set something in motion that she hadn't intended. Probably would have been better if she didn't come at all. Trying to do the right thing with Carter had backfired. Horribly.

14

Rasmussen shook his head. He hated losing control, and most especially with Marina. He should never have intimated that he had plans for her, but for some reason, the woman wound him up beyond his capacity to control himself. It would have been better not to warn her he was coming to punish her for leaving him, but it was done. He'd work around it.

All of his revenge would be sweet, once he was out of here. He knew Lily must have gone with Edward Dare, and he'd cut himself in on that deal Alfonso was working up. He understood now that the man hadn't been protecting Sweetie Bogan so much as covering for his own scheme. Opportunity, as one of his heroes was fond of saying.

He lay back against the pillow, his sunglasses filtering the low light in the room down to the dimness of late dusk. Yes, he was going to have his revenge on Marina Antonelli and her cop boyfriend, too. And then cut himself a large piece of pie.

The ambient light darkened. He thought a nurse had come into the room. He had tried to talk the one last night into a hand job, but no soap.

"Trudy? That you, darling?"

The nurses preferred quiet patients, sleeping ones. Maybe she was bringing him some pills.

Strong hands pushed a pillow down over his face, pinning his head and shoulders to the bed. The sunglasses cut into the bridge of his nose and he bucked against the pressure. Sparks danced in front of his eyes. He gasped for breath, the little bit of air he took in full of the smell of starched cotton. His chest heaved, trying for more. He arched his back and bucked hard, but the weight pushing down on him increased until it felt as if a whole body lay on top of him. He was a slight man, and it was not very long before things went darker than normal, and then the final curtain fell over him at last. Gratitude was his feeling at the end of it. He was thankful there was no more pain.

15

Burton ignored the new voice mail from Bridge Willos. This soon after they'd met, it couldn't be good news, and he didn't need the distraction of thinking about the suit while he was working. This wasn't the first time someone he'd arrested or their family had complained about him. Hell, it wasn't even the first time he'd been sued. He couldn't control what Bousquet's heirs did. His job was to catch killers.

Sweetie had been unemotional about losing Alfonso, her companion of many years. If the guy had been stealing from her, that could chill a relationship. But now that he had the connection, he could use it as a pry bar with Carter. You never knew what you'd run into—some days he felt like one of those dogs rooting around in the forest for truffles.

It was after the morning rush hour but the Parkman Street entrance to the Mass General complex, in front of the surgical building, was choked with traffic, vehicular and human. He waited in a slow-motion line of taxis and private cars picking up and discharging people with walkers, people on crutches, people in sweat suits and pajamas. No johnnies, thank goodness.

Past the bottleneck, he parked the slickback nose-out in an "Official Business Only" slot beside a huge generator and slipped the BPD placard onto the dash. It was a toss-up whether the notice would get him ticketed or towed. He dodged the halt and the lame and their slow-moving families as he walked in the main door.

He wondered when Marina had come to visit Carter. She was too kind not to. Whenever she talked about him, she sounded flip and dismissive, as if the time she'd spent with had Carter meant little. But he sensed something deeper. His head still spun with how the two of them got back together so fast. Some days, the notion that they were getting married felt like fantasy. In a good way.

Rasmussen's private room was occupied by a pale obese woman with peach highlights in her hair, sitting up in bed crocheting something with red yarn. She stared at him wide-eyed when he walked through the door.

"Sorry. Wrong room."

He backed out and followed the corridor to the nurse's station.

A thin black-haired nurse, senior in status and age, looked up at him skeptically when he stopped in front of the U-shaped desk. He saw her recognize him as a cop and lock her jaw. Nurse O'Toole wasn't the type who saw cops and nurses as partners in helping people. He was an interloper she needed to guard against. Her lips pulled back against nicotine-yellow teeth.

"Rasmussen Carter?" he said.

Her face shifted. Something had happened.

"And you are?"

He sighed, flashed the badge. If anything, it made her stiffer.

"Not family, then."

He breathed.

"The man is a person of interest in a homicide case. I would appreciate it if you would tell me where to find him."

She considered her options, and while he could respect the professionalism, she was slowing him down. But more pushing would only get him more push-back.

He watched her parse her options, then guessed what she was going to say.

"He passed," she said.

He hated that weak word for dying, as if the deceased had floated off in a cloud of gas.

"I thought he was healing fine from the stab wound. What happened?"

O'Toole bucked her shoulders again.

"You know I can't discuss patient information with you." She slapped her pencil down on the desk. "HIPAA."

An all-purpose excuse and another word to hate. The government owned your DNA, your Internet browsing history, and a list of everything you took out of the library, but people still pretended something like privacy existed.

"Maybe you'd like to have a subpoena added to your permanent record card."

In a case last year, he discovered by accident that hospital administrators purely hated dealing with law enforcement. It was the people below them in the hierarchy who clogged things up who were often punished.

She puffed her chest up under the baby blue scrubs.

"I've been working in this hospital for thirty-seven years," she said. "You come for me, they better have some damn good lawyers on tap." She pointed the pencil at him. "And you better, too."

He knew when resistance was futile, and he'd learned to control his rage when he was thwarted. O'Toole wasn't an intern or a first-year nurse he could browbeat. The more he shoved, the harder she'd stand.

A short blocky Hispanic man standing behind O'Toole raised his eyebrows at Burton and tilted his head toward the elevators.

"Marie," he said. "I'm going on break now."

Still staring at Burton, she waved a hand at him.

"Well," Burton said. "Thanks so much for your cooperation. I'll be sure to mention it to your supervisor."

Her doughy face crinkled in a smile.

"Sonny-boy. I am the supervisor."

Out at the elevators, the male nurse—Randy, by name tag— looked around as if to preserve the fiction they were meeting by chance.

"That fucking witch," he said. "She ought to work for ICE. You want to know about Rasmussen Carter?"

"He died?"

"He was the one with the stab wound, right? Healing up?"

Burton nodded.

"We were all ready to discharge him tomorrow. Then he supposedly got MRSA—a really bad strain that came on fast."

"An infection killed him? Overnight?"

Randy nodded as the elevator bell dinged.

"That's why Nursey there's so tight-assed. Hospital's worried about a suit. But there was something else."

"What?"

"Not sure. They whipped him down to the morgue too fast. But he looked blue and he had those tiny blood bursts in his eyes."

"Petechiae," Burton said. "He might have been suffocated?"

Randy shrugged. "That's your job, right? All I know is what I saw."

Burton didn't trust gift horses.

"Why are you telling me all this?"

"My brother's trying to get me on the department. Better pension. Can you help me out?"

Burton leveled a look of disgust.

"Probably not."

He walked out the revolving door to the sidewalk, spotting the ticket on his windshield before he got there.

"Shit." He stuffed it in the glove compartment.

The voicemail chime on his phone sounded and he keyed it open. Willos's voice echoed in the cheap phone speaker.

"Burton. We need to craft a response here. The brass is talking about suspending you until the suit is resolved. Call me. ASAP."

"And double shit." He slapped the shifter into Drive and headed out. His Wednesday wasn't getting any better.

16

Marina was enrolled in a two-year culinary arts program at
Bunker Hill Community College. Along with taking care
of Carmen, she was so busy, I hadn't heard from her in a couple of
months. One of the things I missed about the Esposito was seeing
and talking to her every day. We weren't friends, really, but she had
a practical bent, and I used to talk some of my decisions through
with her. We also had the shared history of the bar itself, some of
the crazy things that happened there.

Which is to say I was glad when she called me on Wednesday
morning and asked me to meet her for breakfast.

Tara's Kitchen was a long narrow storefront on Columbus Ave.,
just this side of Mass. Ave. It looked like an old storage warehouse,
dirty brick walls, exposed pipes, and what looked to me like a
retro version of a Woolworth's lunch counter: round steel and red
leatherette stools along a Formica counter extending the length
of the room. The kitchen, if that wasn't too grand a term, was
crammed behind the counter: Bunn-o-Matic coffee maker, small
refrigerator, pie case, glasses, plates, flat top, and a fryer. There was
barely enough room for two people, as long as one of them never
left the grill.

"Elder." Marina unwound a chenille scarf and tucked it in the
pocket of her short wool jacket, hung it on a row of hooks on the
back wall. "Are you drinking?"

Was she looking at my bloodshot eyes? I'd only been sitting
at the counter long enough to get my mug filled with coffee—
weak and bitter, the way most of the automatics did it—and it was

early in the day for me. When you spend years working until three
in the morning, your body doesn't adjust to a different schedule
that quickly. Eight-thirty in the morning was like midnight for
someone who had my rhythms.

"Not so's you'd notice."

I removed the newspaper I'd used to save her stool and she sat
down beside me.

She frowned at the ambiguous answer—I should have reassured
her I was staying sober, but I didn't want to lie, especially to her. It
wasn't as if I was drinking the way I used to.

The counter person, a whippet of a man with pale lavender
highlights in his curly hair and black onyx earlobe gauges, stood in
front of us, vibrating with the need to take our order and get on to
the next thing. I looked at his hands to see if they were clean and
wondered if Tara hired speed freaks. Short order cooking was not
a deliberative practice.

"Scrambled eggs and lox, English muffin, toasted not grilled," I
said. "Small V8. More coffee."

"Wheat toast and a poached egg," Marina said. "Please."

The man favored her with a fawning smile, slapped down
napkin-wrapped cutlery, and zipped back up the counter.

"Lovely to see you," I said. "We should do this more often.
How's your mother?"

During the year before I had shed the Esposito, Marina and
I had both come into money from the same source, but for far
different reasons. Hers was enough to take care of her and Carmen
for quite some time, but it took a while to get Carmen to accept it
from my father's estate.

"I put her into assisted living." Marina stirred a second spoonful
of sugar into her coffee. "So far, so good. I didn't think it would go
as easy as it did."

I thought about my own mother, who'd died in a car accident,
and my father, a victim of cancer. I wasn't sure how gracefully I
would have presided over a slow wasting away of either one.

"Good, then. That it was easier, I mean."

Our food arrived, steaming. I was pleasantly surprised to find the eggs scrambled soft, the way a French chef would have cooked them. We ate in silence for a minute or two, until she looked over, spreading strawberry jam on her toast.

"I went to visit him in the hospital," she said.

I knew then she hadn't called me just to catch up.

"Rasmussen Carter."

She nodded. "I thought it was the right thing to do. Regardless of what happened."

I finished my juice. I didn't know what happened. Didn't *want* to.

"Then it probably was."

I had been startled, last year, watching the attentions of Rasmussen Carter turn her head. I knew, from as far back as her weird symbiotic relationship with the drug dealer Carlos Tinto, that she'd never thought of herself as attractive.

Her frown etched the sides of her mouth.

"You didn't hear?"

I shook my head.

"He died. Last night."

"I thought he was supposed to be mending," I said. "When I saw him…"

"You went to visit him, too?"

"He seemed all right. In pain, but healing up. They didn't think he was in danger. What happened?"

"They're saying it was MRSA. Some fast-acting bug that got into the wound?"

I couldn't guess why news of his death relieved me, but it did.

"Good reason to stay out of hospitals, then. That's too bad."

She shook her head.

"I was there yesterday. A couple hours before it happened. He was fine."

I felt myself tense. The dalliance must have been a little more serious than I thought.

"This stuff happens a lot. Hospitals, doctors: they're all human, right? That woman in Medford?"

A couple months before, a young woman suffering an allergic

reaction collapsed in the street outside her local hospital, unable to rouse the medical people behind the locked doors of an ER in that shady part of town. Marina shook her head.

"That kind of infection takes days to develop. Weeks, even. My aunt got infected when they took out her gall bladder. It's not an overnight thing."

"Tell Burton, then. That's his part of the world."

She shook her head. Maybe I was being stupid. Or maybe I sensed what she was pushing me toward.

"Sure thing. I ask him to investigate the mysterious death of my old boyfriend. How do you think that would go over?"

"Marina."

"I'm not asking you to go all private eye, Elder. But you know people. You could make some calls, find out if there's anything not right about it."

Her assuming I had connections in the city was a mistake a lot of people who knew me made. My father had run the family bank for decades, leveraging all kinds of access to the city's power brokers, but that wasn't something he passed down to me. The money was enough. I had no desire to be a wheel in the city's machinery.

We finished our food. The breakfast crowd had thinned, so I nodded yes to more coffee.

"I don't know what it is you think I can do," I said. "He could have had the infection going into the hospital. It doesn't have to be their fault."

She shook her head.

"Something feels wrong. That's why I'm asking you for help. Didn't your father used to be on some advisory board for the hospital?"

I shook my head. Thomas had been very clear with me about his role, especially when he was suffering from the cancer.

"He was a trustee. Purely ceremonial. For fundraising and so on."

I wished I could help her, but I had no pull with the movers and shakers in the city, nor did I want any. My father's name could get me in to talk to someone, but that was about all.

"I wouldn't have an idea where to start. You know I don't have Thomas's kind of pull."

Her eyes darkened.

"If you won't do it for me, maybe you'd do it for Burton?"

"That's not fair. I couldn't do it for either one of you. I don't have the access."

Her pressuring me was so unusual I had to wonder what else was going on. I'd help her if I could, but I was irked at being maneuvered into something I didn't want to do, only because I couldn't say no to her.

"You'll try, then?"

"Let me think about it. But tell me what you think is wrong. Something about the way he died?"

"A hint I got. I heard about the MRSA from a nurse friend. But they wouldn't tell me anything officially because I'm not his family. But infections don't work like that. They're don't kill you instantaneously. Maybe they missed it and they're trying to cover it up."

Someone at the hospital now knew she was interested in Rasmussen Carter's death. It was unlikely there'd been foul play, but that was what she was implying. I'd have to step carefully, but there might be a couple things I could do. Any reasonably intelligent doctor could explain the probabilities. I wouldn't have to bumble around with the leadership of the hospital. And Marina had never asked me for a favor this large before.

"I will ask around. But no guarantees. And if you don't like the answers, that's it. We're not speculating."

"Fair enough." She laid a twenty on the check. "For that, I'll buy you breakfast. But Elder…"

"I know. Not a word to Burton."

She nodded. "Call me when you know something."

17

One of the more difficult parts of not having the bar to run any more was my lack of a daily schedule. Instead, my days had a loose progression, starting with coffee and three newspapers in the morning and, if I didn't meet with Isaac, puttering away after that with whatever small chores I could find to do. One of the main reasons I'd agreed to mentor him with his brass house pop-ups was the sense I had that I needed to find something useful to do, to get my ass out of the apartment.

The bar had also given me a physical location to be, public enough that I had to shower, shave, dress, and put on shoes to go there. Taking on what Marina wanted me to do would at least give me a reason to get out of the house.

I finished my lunch, a variation of the keto diet that favored bacon and steak. I hated the fact I couldn't have pasta, though, and I refused to put butter in my coffee.

The buzzer on the apartment door, followed quickly by a knock, came as I was pouring my third cup of Sulawesi out of the big French press. I hadn't gotten as persnickety as Burton, with his Japanese pour-over pot and exotic roasts, but my morning cups were as important as blood to me.

Whoever it was, it couldn't be Mrs. Rinaldi. She couldn't climb that many stairs any more. She had gotten very frail in the last few months, unable to keep working with the opera set designers who bought her miniature set renderings to recreate on stage. I feared she was going to go the slow way Henri Voisin, my other old tenant, had gone—first to a nursing home, then on to assisted living, and then dementia care.

The knock repeated, less forcefully. I swore softly and levered myself out of the kitchen chair. Not being on my feet behind the bar every day meant I'd gained a few pounds, as well as a certain morning stiffness in the muscles.

I undid the locks, opened the door, and surprise crashed over me like a rogue wave.

"Susan." My voice almost shook, but I didn't mind. As soon as I saw her, I wanted her to know I had missed her.

"Elder Darrow, as I live and breathe."

Which is what I wanted to do, put my arms around her and breathe her in, her hair, her skin, her scent. I settled for opening my arms, letting her decide.

She stepped into the hug, her head only up to my breastbone. I felt a frightening exhilaration at the sense she was back, whatever it might mean.

She let out a low sound in her throat that I heard as contentment, although she could as easily have been trying to warn herself. She'd run away so many times by now, she must know that fear.

"Maybe we should close the door?" she said.

I gave up the embrace unwillingly. It might be all I took from her this trip. She'd knocked on my door, but she didn't seem overjoyed to see me.

"You're here," I managed to get out.

She regarded me with that amused look so many women in my life had given me.

"That's pretty well established. What I don't understand is the Greenwood."

"You went to the bar first?"

She laughed, but an edge came with it.

"That's no bar. It's an airport lounge. What happened?"

I ran down the events of the last half-year for her, glad for something to talk about other than where she'd been and what she'd been doing. I was irked all over again that she hadn't been here to experience it with me—I could have used her support.

She walked into the kitchen while I spoke and turned on the gas under the tea kettle, rummaged in the cupboards for a mug.

"Make yourself at home." But I muttered it to myself so she wouldn't hear.

"So I guess you don't need to get to work this morning. Are you still drinking?"

Straight and bald, there was the question, and the reason why we never really completed the connection—the reason, she claimed, why she didn't stay in Boston. Had something changed to bring her back? Could I let my hope go free?

"One a day," I said. "Like the vitamins. No more and no less. Two ounces of the most expensive single malt there is."

Her entire body stiffened.

"Dicey choice," she said.

And my pleasure gave way to a deep irritation. She had told herself so many times that my drinking was the problem that she couldn't hear any solution that allowed me to wet my lips.

The water boiled and she poured it into her mug, dunked the tea bag up and down without looking at me.

"So what brings you back to Boston?" Sensing it was not the chance to reignite things with me.

She turned away to squeeze the tea bag against a spoon.

"Nothing earth-shaking." She dropped the bag in the trash can. "I wanted you to know I was here. Thought it was time I cleaned out Dad's apartment so you can re-rent it."

Before, she had always called him Henri around me. Maybe nostalgia was taking hold. I knew the further I got from my own father's death, the dimmer the memories of the ways he'd irked me became, the brighter the bright spots.

I could have told her how much I'd missed her, how much I wished she would stay here in Boston, but I was also frightened by how her sudden appearance could shift my balance. My life after selling the Esposito was still precarious, personally, I mean. I wasn't sure the fragile structure I was building could hold up under another unsuccessful try with her.

"Good, good," I said. "You do know the rent's paid through the end of the year?"

Of course she did. She'd written the check.

She scrunched her eyebrows down.

"I won't be a bother. I came by to say hello. And warn you there'd be someone in the apartment for a while."

Which I could take as a warning. Or an invitation.

"Of course. Maybe we can have dinner some night."

I saw her smile at the quasi-formal tone we'd taken on. All I could say to myself in the moment was I didn't know whether I wanted to make love to her or fight.

"Maybe." She sat at the kitchen table. "So, catch me up on everybody. How's Marina? And Burton. Did they kick him off the force yet?"

I leaned against the counter, not wanting to be too easy. She was already acting a little too comfortable here for my taste.

* * *

Susan rinsed out her mug and turned it upside down on the drainboard.

"I better get going," she said. "I have an appraiser coming to look at Henri's books."

Her father had been a bookbinder and restorer, as well as a collector of old books. I was still twisted up with things I wanted to say but couldn't find the words for.

"So," I said, as I held the door for her. "Dinner sometime soon?"

"Maybe lunch." She smiled. "Less commitment that way."

Cleaning up the kitchen after she left, I was glad I had this small charge from Marina to occupy myself. It would keep me from thinking too much about what Susan's reappearance meant.

Marina had suggested I contact people in the network of the rich and powerful, people she thought I had access to. What she didn't realize—what most people don't—is how transactional people in prominent positions, people with power, are. If you want something from them, they want to know what you are offering in return. It would be much easier to make contact if I had something valuable to offer, and while money—for which the appetite is insatiable everywhere—was the obvious answer, information would be more useful. I needed a better idea of how Rasmussen Carter ended up in the hospital in the first place.

* * *

The Greenwood—it would take a while for me to get my head around that name—was half full on a late Wednesday afternoon, which started me off with a shot of envy. I liked that Loftus hadn't tried to muffle the steel stairs leading down from the street. It was about the only thing he hadn't changed. I couldn't control my wince at the treacly instrumentals oozing through the speakers.

I crossed to the bar where Baron Loftus stood reading a magazine. I lifted the cover to see what it was—the *Atlantic*.

"Good article?"

He looked put-upon, as if irked by my interruption. Great customer service vibe he gave off.

"Mr. Darrow, isn't it? I can change the music if it offends you that much."

So, he had been paying attention as I walked into the place.

"You never told me how you like what I've done with it?"

It was such an obvious trap, I didn't step into it.

"Wondered if you had a chance to audition Evangeline." That was my pretense for being here, for asking other questions. "Did she work out for you?"

He nodded.

"Evvie's going to be fine. Will you have a drink?"

My one-a-day plan rested on ceremony. Only in my apartment, only at the end of the day, a precise two-ounce pour of Dalmore Single Malt Alexander III in one of the Waterford crystal shot glasses I'd rescued before my parents' house on Beacon Hill was sold. A slow meditative sipping, making it last, until I finished and cooked my dinner.

"Club soda, please."

Loftus gave me the look I remembered dropping on tourists who wandered in off the street on a hot summer day and asked for a glass of water. Hard to make any money that way.

He set the glass on a coaster.

"Dollar and a half."

I craned my neck to look up at him, past the green polka dot tie, to see if he was serious. He didn't break a smile and I fished a dollar bill and three quarters out of my pants pocket, slapped them on the bar.

"Keep the change."

"Evvie is singing here Friday night," he said. "But that's not why you're here."

"No?"

"Your reputation precedes, Mr. Darrow. At least the part that says you're friends with the police and a person who likes to insert himself into situations."

The club soda was almost flat, something wrong with the CO_2 charger.

"Rasmussen Carter," I said.

"You see what happens when you try and do something nice for someone? Trouble and more trouble."

"You were doing Carter a favor?"

He burned me with a sneer.

"That little hoodlum? No, I was helping out my auntie and her friend from New York."

I nodded, inviting him to ramble, with no idea where he was going.

"The young lady singing that night? My aunt was giving her a break. A venue and a chance to shine. Unfortunately, that riffraff came in the door with her."

"Sweetie Bogan is your aunt?"

Loftus's Adams apple bobbed when he nodded.

"I told her I didn't want any of that old school dive bar crap in here. And she said it was all cool. She knew the girl, she told me. What she didn't tell me was the baggage the girl came with."

"Tell me the story," I said. "Top to bottom."

I was prepared for him to tell me to fuck off, but his outrage won out. He rested his hands on the bar top, lowered his voice.

"Sweetie helped arrange the gig for this girl, Lily, a singer. I got the idea Sweetie wanted to help launch her career. The girl sings like a dream, but then Sweetie takes off on her, yelling about how bad she is, how her breath control sucks. This Rasmussen goes over to shut her up—something I wouldn't even have the balls to try—and when he doesn't back off, Alfonso stabs him."

Outside of that one odd detail—that Sweetie had heckled the singer she was supposed to be promoting—it made a little more sense. Maybe Alfonso had gone over to the hospital to finish off what had started in the bar that night.

"You know Rasmussen is dead," I said.

Loftus tipped his head. Of course he did.

"Couldn't have been Alfonso, though. If that's what you're thinking."

"And why's that?"

"You and your police chum ought to talk a little more. Mr. Alfonso, he's dead, too. And I believe it happened before Carter went down."

My first idea faded, but I wasn't disappointed. The easy answer was almost never the right one. But I was starting to believe that, if Rasmussen Carter hadn't died of a virulent infection, something very dark indeed was behind his demise.

18

Isaac and I spent the next day or two planning out a series of popups for late winter. I didn't hear anything from Burton, so I assumed he was still working the Alfonso Deal-Jones murder.

Thankfully, by Saturday night Loftus had lost his usual playlist of Neil Diamond and Kenny G. My foot bounced to the big band version of "Take the A Train" coming out of the speakers, while Evvie sat in the chair beside me, waiting for her introduction.

I wouldn't have bothered coming out to watch—I didn't like what Loftus had done to my bar—but in return for introducing Evvie to him, she promised to take me to dinner after the show. I was still thinking vaguely lustful thoughts about her, and dinner together would tell me what might be possible and what was just an old man's fancy. Susan's return to Boston wasn't offering me hope, and I had a life to live.

"Thank you again." Evvie laid a warm hand on my arm. "I can't tell you how much this means. Singing for actual grownups."

She was the magazine image of a jazz chanteuse, in a slinky smoky-red gown, floor-length, backless, and held up in front by who knew what magic. She looked so different than she had the afternoon I'd seen her play the trumpet with the brass house boys, I had to look twice to be sure it was her.

The small crowd worried me a little. I did recognize four or five people from when I owned the place. A guy named Frank Merwin who worked in the financial district, a rabid fan of saxophone music, came over as Evvie stepped up to the edge of the stage. Baron Loftus stood at the mic, his shadow as tall as a tree, and his silver bow tie sparkled in the footlights.

"I heard you let the place go." Frank put a hand on my shoulder. "I get you taking the profit, man, but Jesus! Neil Diamond? I hope this…" he nodded at the stage, where Evvie was talking to the band, "bodes well, shall we say? Not enough places to hear decent music these days."

He walked off, heading for the bar before I could answer, but his words made me feel like I had done some good when I ran the Esposito.

Up on the stage, the drummer shushed his cymbals into the intro to "Our Love is Here to Stay," and I sat back in my chair to hear what Evvie had to offer.

"It's very clear…"

And I was off into a reverie of long-ago times and the voice of Alison Somers, the first female singer who ever played the Esposito, back when I'd just started out. Her death was what pushed me into my friendship with Burton and kicked off my amateur crime-solving. Alison had the charisma of a more sophisticated singer. I heard the promise in Evvie's voice, but she had a ways to go.

I looked around, saw an old black woman, frail and thin with steel wool hair, sitting off at a two-top, Baron Loftus in the chair beside her, talking low. Was that the infamous Sweetie Bogan? It seemed unusual, given what Burton had said about her long relationship with Alfonso, that she'd be out on the town only a week after losing him. But I'd learned not to bet money on any of my assumptions when it came to other people.

Evvie rounded off the end of the song where she should have had an up-note. Light applause came, and I had the sense very few people in the Greenwood were there because of the music. I couldn't tell why else they'd be here—when the band took its first break, no one hurried to the bar to refuel. Loftus handled a slow stream of customers, mostly light beer and white wine.

Evvie slipped into the seat beside me, flushed with her performance. I had another flashback to Alison, how singing in front of people overcame her natural shyness, allowed her to communicate. Not that Evvie was in any way that subdued.

"Fuck," she said. "I'd forgotten how good that feels. It's almost better than sex."

I'd heard that line from people before about different activities. I only agreed it might be possible there was something better than sex because I knew what it would be for me: the big glass of Scotch. I gave her an eyebrow.

"Really."

She mock-vamped me, pooched out her lips.

"Theoretically, I'm sure. We're still on for dinner afterward? And whatever?"

The hint something might come after dinner was an idea I liked. It was a while since I'd been out on the town in any way, and even the chance to flirt with her felt like a win.

"Whatever and beyond," I said.

"Good."

Loftus gave her the high sign the break was over. She slid out of her chair and started for the stage. I watched her rear end move under the sleek red dress and thought some lustful thoughts I'd quashed in the last couple months. Her heels shone like red silk in the lights from the stage.

Loftus said something to her as she climbed the three stairs and she flashed him a smile. The piano player keyed in the first few notes of a song it took me a second to recognize, a note-for-note rendition of a video I'd seen of Ella Fitzgerald singing "Misty." Evvie stood tall, resplendent in the spotlight, and as she took a breath, something odd happened.

Baron Loftus drew his finger across his throat several times, the sign for the band to cut the music. Evvie looked confused, then gestured back at the piano player, whose notes dribbled away. Once he picked up on the fact they weren't playing that tune, he swung into the syncopated start of "Girl from Ipanema." Loftus relaxed back into the chair beside Sweetie, and the old woman patted his hand, as if thanking him.

Another man had joined them while I wasn't looking: sixty-ish, gray-white hair slicked back, black suit, and an open-collared purple shirt. I pulled a double-take at his shoes. I hadn't seen a pair of white-over-tan spectator shoes since that Charlie Parker biopic.

I was watching Evvie and fighting my memories of Alison and the clubs we'd been to, so I didn't realize the man was standing next to my table until the applause started again. He leaned over to speak to me.

"Is this seat taken?"

His voice contained what I thought was a Scottish burr, until I found out later where he came from. There were three open chairs around the table, so I couldn't say no. He sat down next to the one where Evvie's clutch purse rested.

Was this a come-on? I'd been approached that way more than once when I tended bar, as if a sympathetic ear and a friendly demeanor meant I was also amenable to all kinds of love.

"Do I know you?" I said.

The man turned the chair's back to me so he could see the stage, directing all his attention to Evvie's performance. She sang two more songs, "Ain't Nobody's Business" and a torchy version of "Send in the Clowns" that shouldn't have worked that way, but did. She had a little better musical sense than I thought.

As she stepped down off the stage for the second break, I saw Sweetie beckon her over to her table with a long bony finger. Loftus got back behind the bar to sling drinks. Evvie took the open chair next to Sweetie, who had something to say. I only hoped the old woman wasn't trashing her voice the way she'd apparently done to the last girl.

The interloper at my table watched Evvie closely, giving me a better idea why he'd foisted himself on me. He stood up, turned his chair around, and stuck out a hand for me to shake. His hands were large for his body, scarred and big-knuckled.

"Edward Dare," he said. "Extraordinary, isn't she? May I buy you a drink?"

I held up my glass, half-full of club soda and lime.

"I'm fine, thanks. Should I know your name?"

Dare chuckled modestly and picked up a rocks glass full of amber. My nose twitched: bourbon.

"I should doubt that," he said. "Unless you're a diehard New

81

York jazz fan. I book talent for the Blue Note."

Any jazz fan knew the name of that club. But I was skeptical that he'd come to see Evvie specifically. On her very first singing gig?

"You came all the way for this performance?"

His gray eyes were colder than winter, as if I'd been impertinent.

"Happenstance, actually." I didn't believe him. "Why, do you represent the young lady?"

The small favor I'd done for her with Baron Loftus didn't count that high. I shook my head.

"A friend."

The mystery of why he'd colonized my table was clear, as Evvie left Sweetie's table and walked back to ours. Dare half-stood and bowed.

"Evangeline. I wanted to say hello. I'm Edward Dare."

She was still exhilarated by her performance, the tops of her breasts blushing above the gown's bodice. She took his hand and did a little bunny-dip in the tight dress before she sat down.

"That's Sweetie Bogan," she said to me. "She said she liked what I was doing."

"Of course she did," Dare said.

"Elder?" Evvie begged prettily. "Would you see if Baron has any champagne behind there? Kir Royale?"

Sweetie must have also told her who Dare was. The sudden appearance of someone who could further her career had transformed her into a diva with a speed that spun my head. I frowned to let her know I didn't like being treated like baggage, but I did get up.

"How about you, Edward? Get you something?"

I must have put a little challenge into the question. He shook his head, not taking his attention from her. Phony as hell, but Evvie was eating it up.

"Thanks." He held up his half-full glass, mocking the way I'd done it before. "I'm good."

This time, the bar was busier. As I waited for Loftus to get to me, I watched them from the corner of my eye. Whatever lines

Dare was laying down, she was picking up. Her eyes glinted and her teeth flashed as she laughed at his no-doubt polished words. Somehow, I wasn't surprised when she picked up her clutch, took his arm, and started for the stairs with Dare.

"Where's she going?" Loftus demanded, as if I were responsible.

"Damned if I know."

"Then order a drink, or sit down."

"Nothing right now." I turned away. "I'm good."

But I was sure I was not. And I worried about her.

19

"Who told you that?" Martines yelled. "I can't have you suspended right now!"

Burton paused in cleaning the items out of his desk that he didn't want to leave around if this went longer than a few days. For some reason, this suspension didn't piss him off as much as the one he'd gotten for cold-cocking Antoine Bousquet in front of God and the assembled Boston media. Probably because he knew this one was purely political. He hadn't done anything wrong, in his own eyes.

He was getting tired of the push-pull of politics in this city, anyway. Everything that happened had some kind of subtext. And being technically off-duty wouldn't keep him from investigating Alfonso Deal-Jones's murder. This wasn't a job you took on because it was a nine-to-fiver or you wanted to please your bosses.

"Better check with the brass pants up the line, Loo. I heard it from my PBA lawyer, and he doesn't tell lies."

Martines took the Marlboro pack out of his pocket and passed it from hand to hand like he was running a rosary.

"Bullshit. They know you're my best detective…"

He must have remembered how little that counted for when the bosses got involved.

"I suppose I see it," he said. "If they put you out of sight for a while, maybe the whole Bousquet suit thing goes away. But you can't leave now."

"It's fine." Burton hoisted the small cardboard box. "It's the same old shit. It'll blow over in a week or two. I can use the time off."

"No. I mean you literally cannot leave right now. There's someone here I need you to talk to."

Ready as he was to wave a middle finger at the bosses, he couldn't leave Martines high and dry. The man did his best to support him through the Bousquet thing and keep the assholes off his back. He stopped. The least he could do was start his suspension on a positive note.

"Does it have anything to do with one of my cases?"

"It might. Interrogation one." Martines flipped open the top of the cigarette box. "You're still working the Deal-Jones killing."

Burton pointed at the whiteboard where all the detectives' names and their cases were listed. The lieutenant nodded.

"This might connect. Or it might not. Go talk to this woman." He held up a hand when Burton started to ask a question. "I don't want to prejudice you in advance. Just go talk to her."

* * *

Kaylen Miller was the ruin of a beautiful black woman. Her eyes were so swollen he could barely see they were hazel, and the loose skin underneath them was the grayish brown of a winter garden. Her angular face blotched light and dark, a motley of grief. She was slim and sat very erect.

"Ms. Miller. Daniel Burton. How can I help?"

He sat down at the table carefully, as if she might shatter if he jostled it. Martines had given him no clue why she was here, and her deep emotion made him uncomfortable.

"Doctor Miller," she said.

He waited out her pain as she gathered what she wanted to say, hindered by what? Fear of a white cop? Not an unheard-of reaction in this city. She raised her chin, cleared her throat.

"The Lieutenant said you might have some information about a case I'm working on. Did you know an Alfonso Deal-Jones?"

"I did not," she said. "But I believe a man named Rasmussen Carter kidnapped my daughter."

Burton rocked back in his chair, caught the edge of the table.

"That's a strong accusation," he said. "I assume you have some evidence to support it?"

She reached into a purple net bag piled on the table in front of her, took out a pill bottle, and unscrewed the cap.

"May I have some water, please?"

He was accustomed to people he was interviewing trying to interrupt the rhythm of his questioning, but her intent wasn't malicious. Anyone else, he would have bulled straight on, but he'd learned when to flex, and when not to.

He returned with a squat bottle of water and waited while she shook out two pinkish pills with crosses on them.

"Acetaminophen," she said. He hadn't asked.

She was avoiding telling him why she'd come here, and he wondered again if he were intimidating to her. But she seemed to realize her presence was not something she could revoke.

"Your daughter. And Mr. Carter."

The water or the pills refreshed her. She sat up straighter, and he sensed the attention she could muster when she had to.

"My daughter Lily is a singer. She has a very fine voice. She started out singing in our church, and in the last year or so, she's taken lessons and performed in public." Her voice snagged. "She had—has—the desire to be a professional singer. Jazz."

Burton sat with his hands in his lap.

"This Mr. Carter." She spoke Rasmussen's name with a bite Burton wouldn't want to hear applied to anyone he cared about. "Fed her and her fantasy, false hopes."

"You're saying he convinced her she was better than she was? To his advantage somehow?"

He could believe that easily, Carter being the slick lounge lizard with the perpetual eye on his own desires.

"No," Mrs. Miller said. "She has, as I said, a very fine voice. She can sing as well as anyone. No, her talent is not at issue."

Burton waited.

"I am a physician, Detective. Burton, is it?"

He nodded.

"A pediatric surgeon, actually, and my specialty is separating conjoined children."

"Siamese twins?"

She pursed her mouth. He judged he'd stepped over a line.

"Go on."

"I'm also a black woman. I won't bore you with specifics, but suffice to say, I've been faced with challenges. I tried to teach my daughter that people might try and take advantage of her talent."

Burton's patience slipped.

"Are you reporting unlawful sexual conduct from Mr. Carter? Assault? How old is your daughter?"

"Lily has disappeared, Detective. The last time I saw her was in the company of Rasmussen Carter, a week ago Saturday night. On her way to sing in a nightclub."

Her voice cracked.

"She was very happy, almost giddy. I believe she thought she was taking the first step toward a professional career."

"And she didn't come home." He could think of a thousand reasons why not, not least, the pressure of living up to the example of her mother's accomplishment. "Did you speak to Carter afterward?"

"I heard he was in the hospital and I went to visit. He insisted she'd left the bar without him and that he hadn't heard from her since. What is more important is that I haven't heard from her. We've had a touchy relationship since she turned eighteen. If you have children, you'll understand. But we agreed to stay in touch always. Phone call or text. I've heard nothing for ten days."

"I'm not sure how we can help you, ma'am. If your daughter is eighteen, she can do what she wants."

Mrs. Miller dipped her head.

"Understood. But I had concerns when I heard the man who stabbed Mr. Carter was killed. Is my daughter involved somehow?"

"I don't know. But I'm not aware she has any connection to Mr. Deal-Jones's death. There's really nothing I can do, unless you want to file a missing person's report. That would be a different division."

He wondered, if her sources were good, why she didn't know Rasmussen Carter was dead.

She frowned, let slip a little anger.

"But if she got killed, it would be your department?" She waved her hand. "Can't you, I don't know, interrogate this Rasmussen Carter?"

Except for a tenuous connection to the Alfonso Deal-Jones case, Burton couldn't tell why Martines had sent him in here.

"I'm sorry to tell you Mr. Carter died in the hospital last Tuesday night. There wouldn't be any way we could interrogate him now."

Kaylen Miller reared back as though he'd tried to slap her, but a lifetime of self-control took over.

"Then I believe my daughter to be lost, Detective. I don't know what he could have done with her. But she must be lost."

Her self-control shattered and she dropped her face into her hands. He sat there while she sobbed, trying not to dismiss her belief in a connection between her daughter and the two deaths.

20

Marina's class was making timbales out of rice, avocado, and crabmeat, when her phone vibrated in her pants pocket. She was grateful she'd remembered to turn the ringer off. Last week, one of the teaching chefs plucked an iPhone away from a texting student and tossed it in a vat of boiling bone broth.

"Excuse me," she said. "My mother."

Chef frowned, jerked his head toward the hallway.

She recognized the caller ID, but didn't get out of the kitchen fast enough to answer. As the door closed behind her, the buzzing stopped.

She took a quick breath before pressing Redial, guilty about the fact she'd only been out to visit her mother three times in the week since she went into assisted living.

"Western. How may I direct your call?"

"This is Maria Antonelli. I had a call from this number."

The receptionist gave a gasp. Marina had the impression of noise and urgent conversation at the other end of the call.

"Ms. Antonelli." The receptionist's voice was replaced with the crisp assured tone of one of the nurses. Marina recognized the faint Irish uptick at the end of her sentences. "Could we ask you to come in to the facility, please. We've had a bit of a kerfuffle with your mother."

Marina froze.

"As soon as I can. Is she all right?"

"Carmen is fine. Nothing to worry about. But better we don't discuss it over the phone."

"This time of day," Marina said, "I'll be about forty minutes."

"We'll be here," the nurse said. "Please. Not an emergency."

Marina ended the call, wondering what was an emergency, if it wasn't a mysterious summons to come right away.

* * *

The young woman at the front desk was in a giggling conversation with a tall black man who had a pale birthmark high on his cheek. Marina thought he was an orderly, but since no one at the Western wore medical garb—part of an effort to make the patients feel at home—he could have been a doctor. They separated quickly when she walked in through the sliding glass doors, as if they'd been flirting, or talking about something they shouldn't have.

The receptionist flushed and sat up very straight as Marina crossed the lobby.

"I'm Marina Antonelli. I had a call about my mother?"

A smirk crossed the orderly's face, almost too quickly for Marina to see.

"I'll get the nurse, Rosemary." He walked off down the carpeted corridor.

Rosemary flicked her hair back off her forehead, and Marina assumed the two of them had been gossiping about the patients. Not uncommon. She and Elder used to make up stories about the customers when business at the Esposito was slow. The memory tweaked at her.

She recognized Nurse Donahue, steaming down the corridor, from Carmen's pre-entry physical. The nurse, barely five feet tall, had bright red hair and the carriage of a dancer. She held out both hands to Marina.

"Marina. Thank you for coming so quickly. Let's go to a conference room."

Walking away with her, Marina heard a stifled giggle behind them. Nurse Donahue stiffened, paused, then continued on, opening the door to a small square room with a card table, three folding chairs, and a Keurig machine. Marina's throat was dry.

* * *

"You found her doing what?" She struggled to keep her voice calm.

Donahue was careful and clinical, not betraying a jot of amusement. Marina understood what Rosemary and the orderly had been laughing about. It might have been amusing, if it wasn't her mother they were talking about.

"She was in Mr. Barksdale's room, sitting on the bed, with her hand inside his pajama bottoms."

Marina was appalled and curious why her mother would suddenly display any interest in sex. As far as she knew, Carmen hadn't had contact with a man since Marina's father died, three decades ago. And like any child, she found it difficult to think of her parents as sexual beings, despite the evidence of her own existence. Especially now.

"I don't know what to say. Is it dementia?"

"This isn't behavior you've observed in your mother before? When she lived at home?"

Donahue made herself coffee from the machine, offered Marina a cup. She shook her head.

"Not that I know of." She supposed, with all the time she spent out of the house, first working at the Esposito, then going to school, her mother could have been entertaining a whole male entourage. Or a female one, for that matter. "Is this common at this age?"

Donahue sipped the coffee, made a face.

"I wouldn't say it's typical. But it isn't unusual. As people age, they sometimes regress. Their sense of boundaries slips. I'm sure you've known elders who were very frank about what they said and thought. I think being closer to the end of life than the beginning loosens the strictures."

That was a lovely way to describe an old woman groping a bedridden man.

"Well, obviously, we can't have that happening," Marina said.

Donahue relaxed, and Marina realized the nurse had been worried about how she'd react. Had she thought Marina would argue with her? Call her a liar?

"Of course not. We're not really set up to confine her to her room, however. She doesn't need Memory Care. And she isn't a danger to herself or anyone else."

Except maybe their virtue.

"There are pharmaceutical approaches," the nurse said. "And I think that's our likely course of action, if the behavior continues."

Marina's anxiety roared back with visions of Carmen zombified, staring into space.

"You'd drug someone to control an impulse like that?" The idea horrified her.

Donahue set the plastic coffee cup to one side, leaned across the table.

"We don't have the personnel to monitor your mother 24/7," she said. "Did you know that, nationwide, the incidence of sexually transmitted disease is higher in nursing homes than on college campuses?"

That was too absurd to contemplate. Marina found herself up on her feet.

"You will not medicate my mother without consulting me first. Now. I would like to see her."

21

Monday night, I was sitting in my old leather armchair in the bay window with a view of Commonwealth Avenue, my single nightly tipple almost drunk. If Alfonso had been dead before Rasmussen, he couldn't be the killer—if there was one. Marina must be wrong. I needed to catch up with Burton, find out if Carter actually died of an infection. It wasn't unheard of for someone in the hospital to succumb to a complaint they hadn't gone in for. Maybe it was as simple as that.

A knock on my apartment door made me jump. Susan was out somewhere, and I was faithful about latching the downstairs door. Since Mrs. Rinaldi was hardly going out these days, she wasn't leaving the door ajar the way she used to.

"One minute."

With regret, because that was not part of my ritual, I tossed off the last sip of whiskey and rinsed out my mouth out with water. If it was Susan or Marina, I didn't want either of them to worry. I set the glass in the sink and unlocked the door.

"Evangeline."

I was surprised to see her, and a little concerned she knew where I lived. She tipped her head, a half-smile in place.

"I squeezed your address out of Isaac," she said. "He did say you were protective about where you lived."

She was carrying a paper shopping bag from Savenor's, the gourmet grocery.

"You going to let me in?"

"Of course." I stepped back, breathing in her scent as she passed, warm with a touch of cinnamon. "What's in the bag?"

She headed for the kitchen as if she knew where it was and set the bag on the table, unpacked containers of chopped celery, onions, green pepper, and white paper-wrapped packages from the butcher shop. Or fish market—I caught a whiff of shrimp.

She turned around, took my face in both hands, and kissed me. Seriously.

"That's just the appetizer," she said. "For everything you've done for me. You have no idea how much."

I enjoyed the feel of her lips, the closer encounter with her perfume.

"You must have flour and butter." She rumbled through my cupboards and pulled out the six-quart All-Clad pot, set it on the stove.

I resolved to roll with whatever she had in mind. Except for the promise of the kiss, it seemed harmless enough.

"Canola oil OK?" I reached over her into the cupboard. She slipped a hand under my sweater and rubbed my bare stomach.

She turned on the heat under the pan and poured in a cup. The oil started to sizzle.

"Flour. And a long wooden spoon, if you have one."

I watched as she stirred flour into the sputtering oil.

"Always a pleasure to see you," I said. "But what's the occasion?"

My reactions were off, but I set it down to the fact she'd caught me after my daily drink and before I had anything to eat. By this time of day, I'd shut myself down, given up on the notion of human interaction.

The flour mixture darkened. She stirred faster, then moved her head to kiss me again.

"Mmm. I thought I tasted Scotch. You sharing?"

I reached down the Dalmore from its high cabinet and poured her a good shot. "Water?"

"Are you serious?"

"Why are you here, Evvie? Other than cooking me dinner and making cryptic promises?"

The roux was a caramel brown. She stirred in the chopped

vegetables. The pan hissed and the kitchen smelled wonderful.

"Nothing vague about them," she said.

I switched on the exhaust fan under the stove hood.

"Look," she said. "Isaac told me you knew your way around the city, that knowing you could help my career. I didn't expect anything good to happen this fast, though."

"Meaning?"

She stirred the pot, added canned tomatoes, turned the heat to low.

"I'm sorry I left you hanging the other night. At the Greenwood. It was a very unclassy thing to do."

Not a lie, and I couldn't tell her I was used to that these days, not connecting sufficiently enough with people to keep them interested.

She lifted her glass. "You're not drinking."

I poured myself another, not as large as hers.

"Tell me why we're celebrating," I said.

She poured vegetable stock from waxed cardboard containers into the pot and turned the heat back up.

"I'm sorry. I didn't mean to be mysterious. I thought Isaac would have told you."

"How about you tell me now?"

She danced a two-step and waved the spoon.

"N'Awlins, baby. The Big Easy." She pirouetted on the linoleum. "Two week gig at the House of Blues. Starting Thursday."

"That was the guy at the Greenwood? I thought he said he booked for the Blue Note."

"Edward Dare," she said. "He books all over."

Fucking New Yorkers, I thought. Always trying to puff themselves up, especially in Boston.

"He's not someone I know." I remembered how uncomfortable he made me feel. Something about the flat demeanor had seemed calculated, as if he didn't really care about the music. "I'm not recommending him."

She stirred the pot, fragrant steam rising into the air.

"Baron knows him—he said he's good people. That's enough for me." She set the spoon on a ceramic rest and turned to hug me. "But you were the one who got me in the place first. I am pumped."

This had happened fast, which made me nervous for her. I was more inclined to situations that developed at a measured pace, so I could anticipate what could go wrong.

She shut off the gas under the pot and pulled me out of the kitchen by hand.

"That gumbo's got to meld a little while," she said. "We've got some time to kill."

22

Burton sat in his Jeep in the parking lot overlooking the back side of the airport. Being suspended meant he didn't have use of an unmarked car. Technically, he was still working, but he came out here sometimes to watch the planes take off and land, and to think.

Now he needed to start pulling on the connection between Rasmussen Carter and Alfonso Deal-Jones. He doubted Carter had checked himself out of the hospital and shot Alfonso, but he could have contracted a hit. Rasmussen had those kinds of connections in Boston.

He sipped from the to-go cup of Dunkin's, knowing it was going to give him an acid stomach, but he needed the caffeine. His cell buzzed: the ME's office.

"Burton."

"Tad Dankiewicz, Dan. How are you?"

"Working. What do you have?"

"You deal with a body named Rasmussen Carter?"

Burton frowned. "I know him. Natural causes? Some kind of infection? How did you get ahold of him?"

"He shows up, we do the cut," Tad said. "But, cause of death."

"What?"

"Not any infection. The hospital trying to cover its ass, I bet. He was smothered."

"Shit."

"No. A pillow, it looks like. Cotton fibers down deep in his throat. And all the other colors and tissue characteristics of hypoxia."

"Huh. You tell Martines?"

"I thought you could do the honors. Since I'm only the doctor."

"Sure, sure. Thanks for the heads-up."

He cut the call. Two murders now. Even if Rasmussen had killed Alfonso, who had killed Rasmussen? Sweetie Bogan involved here somehow? She's a nasty woman, and he'd known too many female killers to discount her.

He checked his watch. Marina asked him to meet after her classes to talk a little bit about the wedding. He thought things were pretty well firmed up. He'd been married once before, and it hadn't been a bed of roses, but he and Marina fit well together. More importantly, Marina was independent. She had her own work, her own interests, and she liked it that way. She'd organized Carmen's move into assisted living like a general manager. He hadn't had to do a thing.

A 737 with the Southwest logo on it lifted off from the near runway. Fall was coming on, the air was getting cooler, and he'd promised to take some time off so they could go someplace warm this winter. During her school vacation, of course. Hell, he might not even have a job by then, and today he wasn't sure he hated the idea. Police work was starting to feel more and more like a corporate gig than the calling he felt it to be when he started.

He opened the car door and dumped out the remainder of the shitty coffee. He'd take Marina out for dinner and they could talk through whatever she wanted to discuss in peace. Then, he might take tomorrow off. He wasn't going to quit on Alfonso's murder, but now he had to factor in the death of Rasmussen Carter. Maybe it was time to catch up with Elder.

* * *

"I just don't know if I can go through with this right now," she said.

Marina toyed with her spoon. The crème brûlée sat between them untouched. Burton picked up his water glass, concentrated on not gripping it too hard.

"You want to call it off?" he said. "Because there's no way in hell

I want to do this, if you aren't sure of what we're doing."

"No, no." She rubbed her hands over her face, leaving her cheeks pink. She'd been quiet all through dinner and only now had she finally spit out what was bothering her. "It's just Carmen's having a hard time adjusting to the assisted living place. I had to run out there this morning, in the middle of my class."

"She was sick? Why didn't you call me? I could have backstopped you." She knew he was on suspension.

She shook her head, broke the brittle crust of the dessert with her spoon, but did not eat any.

"No. It was something else. But I need to be sure she's stable there."

"We can postpone it," he said.

Though they'd already prepaid the hall and the band, scheduled the church. Changing dates and times now would cost them. A year ago, he'd been so relieved to get rid of Sharon, he hadn't been thinking about marriage again. Maybe he wasn't cut out for this yet. Maybe he was giving Marina a vibe that said he'd be a lousy husband.

"I don't know."

"You're the boss," he said.

"I am not. We need to make this decision together."

"Postpone? Or cancel?"

"I love you," she said. "Nothing's changed there. But I need to feel like Carmen's stable. That I can leave her and she'll be all right."

"You weren't planning on her coming to the wedding?"

"I guess I was hoping. But probably not. I don't want to have to medicate her so she can make it."

At least she still wanted to get married. At least, he thought so. He spooned up a little custard.

"I'm with you, whatever we decide. But if we're going to postpone, there are logistics."

She emerged from her thoughtful funk long enough to pin a look on him.

"I get that, Daniel. Really. I'm not an idiot."

There was no good response to that, except to signal for the check. He pulled out his credit card, took her hand.

"I do want this, Marina. And I know you do, too. We'll make it work."

She patted him absently, as though still worrying about her mother.

"I know," she said. "It will work."

23

"I'm not sure this is going to work out," Burton said.

I'd been on my way to meet Isaac, who was running another brass house pop-up, but when Burton called, I diverted to a bar in Chelsea to meet him. He had three empties lined up before him and I knew that meant he wasn't working today.

"Marina's tough," I said. "You've know that from the get-go. She'll figure it out."

He shook his head. If I were going to worry about his drinking, it would be that he was downing straight rye, not his usual whiskey sours.

"I'm getting the feeling this doesn't have anything to do with Carmen at all," he said. "How much do you know about her thing with Rasmussen Carter?"

I took a long swallow of the Virgin Mary the bartender reluctantly made me—no profit in tomato juice. Guilt poked me. I hadn't told him Marina asked me to look into Rasmussen's death, but maybe it was time.

"I think his death shook her up, regardless of whether they were close," I said. "Out here in the civilian world, we don't see that many dead and dying people every day."

"How close do you think they really were? She always acted like it was a fling, mostly something that would piss me off. You think it was more than that?"

"Be reasonable. What else is she going to tell you? He was the love of her life until you came back?"

He knocked back the rest of his fourth rye.

"He was killed, you know. It wasn't an accident. *Or* infection."

"Whoa. You don't think she killed him?"

Burton shook his head impatiently.

"No, but I think she's still irked I didn't take her seriously. Investigate it. I'll have to now."

I held my face straight.

"In fact," he said. "If I thought there was something else about Rasmussen Carter's death someone wasn't telling me, I would be mightily pissed."

24

To hear Sweetie Bogan tell it, Alfonso Deal-Jones was collaborating with this Edward Dare character on a large-scale cocaine deal. Using her money. If Rasmussen Carter hadn't killed Alfonso for stabbing him in the Greenwood that night—which Burton had eliminated as a possibility—then another likely suspect for Alfonso's death would have to be Sweetie Bogan.

She was actually a better suspect, in ways. As Deal-Jones's long-term friend, lover, and business partner, she would have been shocked to find out he was stealing her money. And having met Sweetie, he didn't think she would forgive very easily. She might not have shot Alfonso herself, but in a long life in the bars and back alleys of the jazz world, she'd no doubt rubbed elbows with unsavory types, people who would take on that kind of job.

Before he braced her again, though, he needed to understand exactly what Alfonso and Dare had been planning, how much money Alfonso misappropriated, and what became of the deal when Sweetie reclaimed her money.

Which meant he was due to have a chat with Mickey Barksdale, still the axle around which any organized version of crime in the city rotated. Burton had known Mickey since third grade in Charlestown. Mickey had been trying to move his operations to the right side of the law—ever since that abortive attempt to bring the Olympics to Boston—trying to legitimize himself. More of his criminal activities were falling in line with what the politicians, developers, and business types did to earn their money.

Even so, he was too much of a control freak to abandon any

interest in major criminal activity going on in the city. The numbers, pot, the street-level prostitution—let the rest of the clowns fight over low-value scraps. But a high-dollar cocaine deal would have attracted his attention.

Once he'd made contact with his old schoolmate through the required number of intermediaries, Burton was directed to an office building in a respectable part of town, on the edge of what used to be called the Combat Zone. Pi Alley was where most of the old printing businesses had been, back in the days of hot lead type, and then the neighborhood transformed into what the city fathers and mothers like to call "the adult entertainment area." Bars like the Pilgrim were vestiges of the Combat Zone, but with naked women and pornographic videos available to anyone with a computer, he had to believe their days were numbered.

Burton entered through a door at 47 Lagrange Street, noting the glass had the dull sheen of bulletproof material, or at least shatterproof. The foyer was narrow, leading to a stairway of old marble steps scooped in the middle from hundreds of feet. He wondered what the building had housed before Mickey took it over.

"Nice," he said, stepping to the left into the open door of a self-service elevator straight out of a Gilded Age hotel, the brass shining, the paint fresh. Mickey wouldn't try and compete with the glass and steel decor of the high-rolling firms farther downtown— he was too cheap, for one thing—but Burton knew that people who'd grown up the way he and Mickey had put a lot of weight on a prosperous public appearance.

At the top of the ride, the elevator doors squeaked open, and a monster stood before him, blocking out the light. His body was like a refrigerator topped with a concrete block for a head. He fluttered his fingers at Burton.

"Weapons."

Burton shook his head. This was all theater—Mickey knew he handed over his service weapon to no one. He also understood that if and when Burton came for Mickey, it would be with the tools of the law, not a pistol.

"Try again."

"He's fine, Tiny. Let him through."

Mickey's throaty voice floated down from the open door to the left of Man Mountain Dean, who was giving Burton a look that was supposed to convey how lucky he was to still be alive. Burton set his forefinger on the front of the thug's shirt, right where the knot of his tie would have been if he was wearing one. When Tiny looked down, Burton raised his finger and hooked the end of Tiny's nose. A Three Stooges original. Nyuk, Nyuk, Nyuk.

He stepped past his latest enemy and walked into Mickey's office, which was decorated with the care and high design of a big-time lawyer's digs: mahogany partner's desk, pale figured Oriental carpet, even a frigging hunting scene on the wall: horses, hounds, and men in red jackets.

"Tiny?" he said, taking a leather club chair. "Seriously?"

Mickey waved a burning cigarillo at him. The smoke smelled as if garlic was embedded with the tobacco.

"And you're still smoking those Parodis. The Italians on your mind that much, huh?"

"Nice to see you too, asshole. Always glad to help out someone from the old neighborhood."

Reminding Burton that he'd come looking for Mickey's help, not the other way around. To be fair, he never pushed Burton for a *quid pro quo*, what had become America's favorite concept this year.

"Alfonso Deal-Jones."

Mickey stubbed out the little cigar. It continued to smolder in the ashtray. For effect. Mickey was always calculating his words and actions for maximum impact. He was as unlike the sloppy legendary crime figures of Boston history as Burton could imagine: focused on profit and discipline, a proponent of violence only as an extreme last resort. The abrupt shift away from the traditional model may have been why he got away with so much.

"Who d'at?"

But his merry face told Burton that Mickey was fucking with him. And Burton had to play along.

"Come on, Mick. You know why I'm here. You wouldn't have

given up your new business address if you didn't have something to tell me."

Mickey stubbed the smelly butt the rest of the way dead, waved smoke away with a pudgy hand.

"I know. It's just, I never see you unless you want something from me, Dan'l. A little pleasantry makes for a smoother relationship."

"There's no relationship here. Don't make that mistake."

Mickey acted unimpressed, which didn't mean he hadn't heard.

"Pretty big talk for a guy whose ass I…"

"Not one more word, Mick. Alfonso."

Unlike most of the hoods Burton dealt with, Mickey knew when he'd reached the limit.

"That asshole."

Burton held a beat.

"OK. He was an asshole. Elaborate."

Mickey sat back and folded his hands across his vest like a banker.

"Let's say, for the sake of argument, someone with business interests on the darker side of the law was doing his best to legitimize things."

He peered at Burton, who didn't respond.

"You know what I mean. And an acquaintance from his past, the side of life he was trying to extricate himself from…"

Burton chuckled.

"What? You think I don't know any big words? I have an Associate's from Bunker Hill."

"Your friend," Burton said. "Not a local?"

He was reading ahead. This acquaintance came asking Mickey for a favor. If he'd been from Boston, it wouldn't have been remarkable. There was a well-defined way to ask Mickey for favors that didn't require a personal audience. And Mickey wouldn't call him an acquaintance unless he considered whoever it was a peer.

"An old friend from the Big Easy."

Another one of the too many things that pissed Burton off was people who used half-assed nicknames for places: Frisco, The Cape. It was a convenient way to tell who'd been there and who hadn't.

Mickey slipped another gnarled cigar out of the red and green box. Burton shook his head.

"Please, god, no. Give me the short version and I'll be out of here in five minutes."

Mickey's eyes flashed, Burton recognizing the rage that was never far from the surface, no matter how polished Mickey tried to be. He met the stare—it was never a good idea to show Mickey you were intimidated.

"You want it straight."

He lit the cigar, blew the smoke off to the side, away from Burton.

"This gentleman I know contacts me, knowing that even as I'm trying to transition my organization, I still have certain interests in the city and how things are run."

Mickey may have been pushing his criminal enterprises underground, but he wasn't going to eliminate them. He was only insulating himself, without losing any profit. Because the one thing Burton knew from their shared boyhood was the bottomless greed of Mickey Barksdale. Burton remembered fifth-grade Mickey sandbagging, literally, a hapless kid who wandered down the wrong block in Charlestown and refused to pay Mickey's nickel street tax.

"So, this friend of yours from New Orleans wants to do a deal in Boston and comes to you for permission. Cocaine, I'm told. In quantity."

Mickey moved his mouth, as if the cigar tasted bad. He never liked talking details.

"And he was dealing, pardon the pun, with Alfonso Deal-Jones."

Mickey held up his hands.

"He only wanted my blessing. You know I don't work with criminals of the colored persuasion."

"Unless there's something in it for you. How much was your taste of the deal?"

Mickey nodded.

"I was in for a small percentage. An access fee, you might call it, like one of those lines on your cable bill. But I have no idea who my, uh, acquaintance was working with. No detail."

And yet he'd known Deal-Jones was black.

"I'll bet you were underwhelmed when the deal went south. Loss of income?"

Mickey smirked.

"My fee is my fee. I don't do contingency, like some ambulance-chaser. The fellow who backed out of the deal was on the hook for it, or so I heard. I got paid."

"Not your acquaintance."

"The story I heard? My acquaintance was ready, willing, and able to continue the transaction. It sounds to me like an amateur getting in over his head, losing his financing without a backup plan."

"And maybe getting himself killed because he screwed the pooch?"

Mickey shook his head.

"I had no part of that. I'm on the periphery. But I doubt my friend from New Orleans would resort to that. Blood from a stone, if you get my meaning."

Burton agreed with him. No one killed someone who owed them money, even if any gangster could be as greedy and self-righteous about what they thought they were owed as any politician. But he wasn't taking Mickey's word for it, that the New Orleans thug was the nonviolent type.

He stood up to go.

"Thanks." Mickey was an invaluable source once more. Neither of them was completely comfortable with Burton using him, though.

"Wait." Mickey heaved himself out of the chair and walked over to the small refrigerator with the potted jade plant on top, pulled out a bottle of champagne with an orange label. "I hear you're getting ready to tie the knot."

Burton shook his head. The last thing he wanted was his personal life common knowledge among the criminal classes. He did not reply.

"I wouldn't expect to be invited to the wedding. And I won't ask you to drink with me." Mickey picked up a felt-tipped pen and wrote something along the side of the label. His voice held a vein of sadness, maybe that the two of them would never be friends. "But you can accept a little gift, can't you?"

He pushed the bottle into Burton's hands.

"*Mazel tov*, as our Hebrew brethren say."

Burton was both touched and appalled.

"Thanks, Mick. And for our little chat." He found a jot of charity. "Appreciate the help."

Mickey winked.

"Boston boys, Burton. Beantown all the way."

Burton exited onto Lagrange and headed for the Boylston Street T station. No one but a tourist brought a motor vehicle down here. Outside the MBTA kiosk, a raddled woman in a faded Boston Patriots jacket—seriously vintage—was panhandling. She turned away as he approached, reading him like a cop.

He thrust the bottle of champagne, an expensive one, into her hands.

"Here," he said. "Go wild."

He was on the third step down into the subway when she called to him.

"You need this note?"

He sighed and re-climbed the stairs. She held out the bottle. Along the edge of the orange label, in Mickey's parochial school cursive, was a name. Edward Dare.

"No, darling," he said. "But thanks for asking."

25

I was playing amateur detective again, as much out of boredom as to help out Marina. Without a job or a business, I didn't have much to do. I also couldn't pass up a chance to talk to a jazz legend like Sweetie Bogan. It took a couple tries to get her on the phone, but when I told her I wanted to talk about Alfonso Deal-Jones, she brightened at the chance to dish about her old lover, and maybe her own history.

The apartment she had down in the old Navy Yard implied that her career had done well, or at least, she'd held onto the money she made. The music industry was rife with tales of financial malfeasance, and I wondered how much Alfonso had to do with managing her money and what that might mean, now that he was gone. These condos rented in the ten- to twelve-thousand-a-month range, and Sweetie had one of the best, a penthouse unit with views of the harbor and very little else man-made in the way.

She was standing in the doorway when I got off the elevator, a tiny woman with the carriage and fine bones of a princess. Her gray-white hair was slicked back against her delicate skull. She looked ancient and fragile, an impression she blew away as soon as she opened her mouth. The instrument, her voice, was strong.

"You're white." She sounded surprised, as if she'd assumed something else from my jazz knowledge.

I didn't have an answer for that, spread out my hands. No argument there.

"Well, come in anyway."

I assumed she was joking, at least partially. I knew enough about how race worked in this country, and in the music, that I figured I owed her a dig or two on principle.

We walked down a long hall lined with black and white photos, mainly of singers and songwriters whose faces were as familiar to me as family: the Duke, of course; Earl 'Fatha' Hines; Ella and Billie; Tad Dameron.

She felt me trying to pause, gawking. We stopped in front of a picture of her and Sarah Vaughn, holding up champagne bottles to the camera.

"My rogues' gallery," she said, in a whiskey-and-pebbles voice. "Most of them gone to memory by now."

She ushered me into the living room—aggressively modern furniture, steel and white leather, with a few antiques sprinkled in—and sat me down with my back to the view. She perched on the edge of a Boston rocker, spindly as her legs, and eyed me.

"Well, I won't offer you a drink, since I understand you have what we used to call the 'Irish disease.' I could make you a cup of tea."

It shouldn't have creeped me out that she could find out things about me, but I didn't love technology so much that I didn't mourn the days when you could be anonymous.

"Well," I said. "If you looked me up, you must know I'm a fan. Of the music and you. I used to own a bar in the South End."

"It's called the Greenwood now, if I'm not mistaken."

Her attention on me and my answers was complete, bright as a spotlight. Was she trying to convince me she wasn't senile? I nodded, acknowledging she'd done her homework.

"Formerly the Esposito," I said.

"Much better name for a Boston bar, I have to admit. And you miss it, don't you? The nights? The people? The music?"

Especially the music. I felt warmed by her empathy, the way she seemed to understand.

"Night life," I said.

"That mean ol' sporting life." She half-sang the words. "You'll go back to it one day. There are people who are born to work in the daylight, and people who come alive at night. I can tell which kind you are."

I shook off a feeling of being bewitched, though I felt how audiences would have reacted to her charisma. I imagined her in a shimmering blue dress under a single spot, singing a ballad like "Fly Me to the Moon," every man in the place, and some of the women, certain she was singing only to them.

I shook myself.

"You may be right. But I really came by to talk about your friend Alfonso."

"'Friend.'" She chortled. "What a polite way to say it."

She reached a hand, gnarled with arthritis, and laid it on my knee. It was cold.

"Lover, business partner, and my cross to bear. Nothing much we didn't share. Even an old woman has needs, you know."

I blushed.

"Not what you're thinking." She retrieved her hand. "Intimacy. Someone to talk to. A friend in need."

I felt pulled in and warmed by her words, their rhythm, the comforting fabric of her tone of voice.

"He stabbed a man I know."

She nodded.

"Our world, Elder. Yours and mine. The night world? You know as well as I do it's a violent and dirty place. Alfonso cast himself as my protector."

She projected vulnerability now, which could be its own kind of protection. I doubted she needed much help.

"I didn't come to rehash what happened. As you say, things happen late at night that might not, out in the sunshine. What I wanted to ask was if you thought Alfonso might have carried a grudge, gone after Rasmussen Carter again because he thought you were at risk. Or out of his own anger?"

She shook her head.

"Alfonso was a man who lived in the right here, right now." Her stare looked deep into me. "You have no idea what it's like to have to hide what you think all the time, do you? To bow and scrape and nod, when what you want to do is scream? Alfonso lost his filters years ago—'how' isn't important, but its effect was profound. He made a point of being and acting as closely to his vision of himself as he could. And despite some of the tricks he pulled, he was loyal to me. He was unhappy that he had lost his temper and stabbed another black man, but he believed I was under attack. He would not hold a grudge. Mr. Carter died?"

I didn't know whether to tell her he'd been murdered.

"He developed a severe infection in the hospital."

"How terrible." She put her hands to her mouth, but it was a stagy move, the first false note I'd seen. "I assume you know how Alfonso was killed? Beaten, the detective said. Perhaps something to do with whatever else was going on in the bar that night?"

I considered that.

"Was there something else?"

Her sigh sounded exhausted.

"You wouldn't have any idea who else might have a grudge against Rasmussen Carter?"

She widened her eyes, innocent as a summer cloud.

"I'd barely heard his name. Why don't you ask my nephew, Baron. He runs the bar."

"Baron Loftus is your nephew?" Did Burton know this? "Was he involved in Alfonso's business at all? Maybe that was why it all happened in the Esposito."

"The Greenwood," she corrected me, her eyes amused. "I don't believe that young man has the wherewithal for anything that complicated. Or criminal."

A rustling behind us startled me. I'd assumed we were alone. I turned to see who'd come into the room and strained my neck.

"I think Mrs. Bogan is ready for her dinner. Aren't you, Sweetie?"

The man was blocky, built like a middleweight boxer, and had the palest skin I'd seen on a man, almost translucent.

"Enzo. Thank you." Sweetie looked vacant, as if she'd forgotten why I was here. "Enzo likes me to sing for my supper. You can stay for that much, at least."

She cleared her throat, spit into a tissue, and in a voice only slightly cracked by time, began to sing.

"Look at me. I'm as helpless as a kitten up a tree."

26

Burton walked away from the conversation with Mickey feeling grubby, but in possession of facts he hadn't had before: a connection to New Orleans organized crime, and a name—Edward Dare. Time for some actual police work, even if he wasn't supposed to be doing any.

The homicide bullpen was eerily empty for a Tuesday afternoon, which he hoped didn't mean there was a load of new cases all of a sudden. It had been a relatively quiet autumn.

Lieutenant Martines's office door was closed and locked, but Burton looked at his watch and wasn't surprised. It was after four. Martines was hoping to rotate out soon for an administrative position in headquarters. He must have been trying out his new schedule.

Burton slipped the spare key to Martines's office out of his pocket. He was certain enough that the bean counters monitored phone calls and Internet usage that he never called long distance from his own cubicle. And he never touched his computer except to file reports or search databases. Assuming he couldn't find someone else to do it for him.

He locked the office door behind him and turned on a small desk lamp Martines used to read files. The office windows were opaque and anyone outside would see only a low glow, which could easily be taken for a computer monitor left on.

The air smelled of stale cigarettes and cold coffee. Burton smirked at the cliché. He could have used a cup of coffee himself, but he wasn't going to be here that long.

He leafed through his little black address book of phone numbers for a direct line to the detective in New Orleans he'd talked to last year, when he was researching Kathleen Crawford on Elder's behalf.

"Bordaine," a rusty-sounding voice answered after eight or nine rings.

Burton used that strategy himself, letting the phone ring long enough for someone to give up.

"Antoinette the man-eater." He didn't know where the nickname came from, but he liked it. "Dan Burton. From Boston?"

"Home of the beans and the cod." She cleared her throat. "I know you're not calling for my boudin recipe."

People who only heard her name mistook her occasionally for a semi-famous TV chef and travel guide. The two also shared a lanky build and wiry salt and pepper curls. Of course, Antoinette was clearly female. He knew she'd used the name confusion to her advantage at least once to jump the reservation line at Galatoire's, after the TV chef had killed himself weeks before.

"Your fair city is in my sights again," he said. "You up on your local version of organized crime?"

Bordaine worked burglary, of which New Orleans had a shitload, and that was how Burton found out Kathleen Crawford was a professional thief. But cops tend to focus on their professional silos—the most he could hope for was a name.

"More or less," she said. "There's a certain amount of overlap at the lower levels. And this city's not that big, once you're in it. I can only get you so far, though."

Burton understood the subtext, that she had to be cautious about helping people, even another cop, from outside the local chain of command. The police force in New Orleans was still rebounding from the terrible stories, mostly apocryphal, about their behavior during Katrina. And no cop, honest or otherwise, cared to attract attention from above.

"I hear you," Burton said. "Edward Dare."

Bordaine whistled, low.

"Mr. Man. You always want to start at the top, don't you?"

The tickle of anticipation made him shift in Martines's chair.

"You've heard of him, then."

"Never met the man. But he is one of the chief lieutenants of the Asshole Army down here. A front for one of our Tier One gangsters, Frank Vinson. They call him Clean-Head, for obvious reasons."

Not obvious to Burton, but that was all right.

"What's his specialty? Or is he more of a generalist?"

"Frank? He's into about everything you'd expect."

"Cocaine deals, young ladies crossing state lines?" Burton was remembering Kaylen Miller and her worry for her daughter.

"Except drugs, actually. He got popped on marijuana possession as a boy, back when it wasn't the lollipop it is now. Did ninety days in county and did not, I guess, enjoy himself. No drugs for anyone in his organization. On penalty of separation."

"Would Dare go off and do a drug deal on his own?"

He heard a lighter click and the rush of breath as Bordaine exhaled.

"Not too likely, if he wanted to keep Frank sweet. On the other hand, he doesn't earn a ton being Frank's procurer. Girls and boys. Clean-Head likes to have someone on his arm when he goes out. It's like a signature, always a musician or a singer."

Burton felt a pang of recognition.

"And Dare finds them for him?"

"Frank tends to use people up. But as you might remember, there's a fair amount of tolerance for sexual variety down here."

Burton preferred not to remember his one-night trip down Bourbon Street with Antoinette.

"Would this Dare go out of state for anything?"

"Have to, if he was doing a drug deal." Bordaine was thoughtful. "I can't see Frank allowing it here. Someone said his latest squeeze might have come from up North."

"Can I ask a favor? Check that rumor out? It might link up to something I've got going on here."

"Sure," she said. "Between all the nights I spend on the town and the lack of crime in the city? You ought to come back, Burton.

We had ourselves a time, as I recall."

Better to let that night fade into the mists of time.

"I tell you I'm getting married?"

"No. So?"

"But who knows? I might be back again. Not around Mardi Gras, though. I'd be sucking down blue drinks with the rest of them."

"Ha-ha." She huffed smoke again. "I gotta boogie. Call you at this number?"

"Uh, no." He gave her his cell. "Work phone—don't leave any cute messages."

"Well, Burton." She deepened the drawl. "Didn't know y'all worried about things like that. *Ciao*, baby."

He replaced Martines's phone, wiped it down with a tissue. You couldn't be too paranoid about the bean counters.

The door to the office latched shut behind him and he headed out, wanting to get out of the precinct before anyone found him there.

27

I'd known Marina longer than I'd known Burton. When she couldn't get child care, Carmen used to bring Marina to my parents' house, when they were still together and lived on Beacon Hill. I had memories of us playing together once or twice, although Carmen had had an overdeveloped sense of propriety about our relative social classes. And my own mother's class consciousness didn't help.

But Marina was one of the reasons the Esposito had worked out. She was a solid presence in the kitchen for as long as I owned the place. I'd always owe her for that. And the fact that she'd been so steady made it harder for me to hear her so unsure of herself.

"I don't know why I should be so confused," she said.

I met her for coffee at Mr. Giaccobi's espresso bar, up the street from the old Esposito and not far from the culinary school. I don't know that I would have sold pastries this close to where professional students could critique them, but the place was serving a steady stream of people in chef's whites, knife rolls under their arms, buying juice and coffee and muffins.

"Burton and I have been through a lot together. I know it'll work its way out eventually. But I have this weird feeling something's not finished. That Rasmussen dying interrupted something."

"You know I never married," I said. "So I don't speak from experience. But isn't it normal to feel uncertain about it? You're putting the rest of your life in someone else's hands, risking what you know and how you've lived. It's got to be unnerving."

She picked at the remains of an orange pecan muffin, a

combination that didn't sound like it should work. Rolling the crumbs into a tight little ball, she flicked them into her empty coffee cup.

"I get that," she said. "It's Burton I'm worried about."

I was already tense enough for both of us. I refused to play referee between two people who were the closet to friends I had. I'd come to meet her this morning to tell her I didn't see any sense in continuing to look into Carter's death. Now that it was a murder, it was Burton's call. And while it had been interesting to meet Sweetie Bogan, she hadn't given me any ideas where to look once I learned Alfonso couldn't have killed Carter.

"Rasmussen Carter is gone from the planet now," I said.

She frowned at me.

"What I mean is… I don't know. He isn't a presence for Burton any more, is my guess. It doesn't eat at him because he can't do anything about it. He knows he was being a jerk."

My espresso was cold. I drank water.

"Oh, it still bothers him," she said. "He's still holding onto a lot of that you-belong-to-me stuff, deep down. Part of his charm."

She grinned stiffly.

"You know as well as anyone no relationship is going to be perfect."

"I think I might have loved him," she said.

I didn't like the past tense.

"Burton? What? You don't any more?"

She shook her head.

"Rasmussen. Something in me cannot let go of him. I'm not going to be specific about what he did for me…"

For which I was grateful.

"But he had heart. He treated me well. Raised me up." She shook her head, baffled by her own emotions.

"Well, even if you want to, you can't go back and change any of it."

"I know, I know. I just can't get it out of my brain. And I need to, if I'm going down this road with Burton."

I looked at the travel posters of Firenze and Venice on the walls behind Mr. Giaccobi, the drawings from his granddaughter's school class. The espresso machine hissed a comment on my competence as a friend. I wanted to convince her it didn't matter any more.

"I don't know what to tell you. Look, Burton told you he was killed, right?"

She looked shocked.

"No! How?"

I hoped I hadn't given away something Burton needed to keep to himself.

"Suffocated."

"Did he do it?" she said.

"Burton? Are you serious?" My voice skyed.

She shook the thought away.

"Then it was the old lady?"

"Sweetie? I doubt it." I wondered why Marina's mind had gone there. "Look. You have doubts? Talk to Burton. He's not the dinosaur he likes to pretend he is."

"Yes." She crumpled the muffin papers and stood up to clear the table. "But if he and I are really supposed to be together? Why is it that the most comforting thing I can think to tell myself is: if it doesn't work out, we can always get divorced?"

28

Despite the fact that she had an excellent motive, the fact that he'd tried to steal her money to finance a drug deal, Burton doubted Sweetie was responsible for Alfonso's death. The conversation with Antoinette gave him another idea what might have happened. He could see a scenario where Edward Dare took revenge on Alfonso for screwing up the deal, especially if it left Dare vulnerable to Frankie Vinson.

Doubling back to Sweetie wouldn't gain him anything. Except for the missing cash, she wouldn't have known details of Alfonso's deal, the principals or the terms. All she'd have cared about was her money.

But Dare had been at the old Esposito the night Rasmussen got stabbed, and one other person might have some insight into all the characters. Elder was fond of saying bartenders were ignored. Maybe Baron Loftus saw or heard something that would help Burton move forward.

He didn't like his second look at the Greenwood any more than the first. He missed the black and white photo of Dizzy Gillespie blowing his horn, cheeks distended like apples. He missed the smells of Marina cooking, the good jazz in the background instead of this smoothed-out sugary crap. The stairs rang under his feet as he descended, the only familiar thing left in the place.

Loftus sat at a table near the bar with two thuggish-looking characters. The conversation seemed civil enough. Burton didn't recognize either one, and he realized, with Mickey moving toward respectability, the time would come when he didn't know any of the low-level hoods. The petty crimes would be staffed by strangers.

He walked to the end of the bar and sat, watched Loftus write a check, tear it out of the book, and wave it in the air to dry.

One of the thugs snatched it and grinned at Loftus, exposing gray teeth the shape of corn kernels. Burton tensed, but the two stood up and left the bar, boots hammering the stairs.

Loftus stowed the checkbook under the bar, adjusted his bow tie, and pulled down a bottle of Knob Creek Bourbon. He poured himself a tot and tilted the neck toward Burton.

What the hell, Burton thought, and nodded.

"Trouble?"

Loftus looked tempted to dump his woes, but only shook his head.

"Delivery guys for one of my suppliers."

Who had him on a cash-only basis? Elder had worked his ass off getting the Esposito to the point where his food and booze deliveries didn't depend on how much he had taken in the night before.

"Business not going well?"

Loftus tossed off his shot, looked at the bottle, shelved it again.

"It's all good," he said. "People don't go out as much any more. Netflix and chill, some shit."

Burton sipped the bourbon, not his usual drink, but he never turned down a meal, a drink, or a chance to pee.

"Edward Dare." He watched for a reaction. Nothing.

Loftus rinsed out the glass and set it in a dishwasher tray.

"What about him?"

"Friend? Customer? Supplier? Vendor?"

Loftus relaxed. Burton had the sense he'd asked the wrong question.

"Friend of my aunt's. Someone introduced him to me."

Burton sat up straight.

"Your aunt? Not Alfonso?"

"They're pretty much the same. It was Alfonso who brought him in that night."

"The night Rasmussen Carter was stabbed?"

"Was that his name? He started it, you know. Alfonso was defending Sweetie."

"But Edward Dare was here? Sitting with Alfonso?"

"No." Loftus rubbed down the spotless counter. "He sat with the chick. The singer."

"What singer?"

"You guys really don't talk to each other, do you? Carter was, like, this girl's agent. He talked me into trying her out." Loftus's face shifted with the memory. "Said the bar used to do real well with live music."

"So Carter was here with the singer and, what? Where did Dare come in?"

Burton thought they might be talking about Lily Miller, the missing daughter.

"He kind of pushed his way in, to be honest. Carter was sitting by himself listening, and Dare just sat down at Carter's table. But mostly he talked to the girl, on her breaks."

"He wasn't a regular?"

"First time I'd seen him. He took off right around the time of the fight."

"And not by himself," Burton said.

"With the girl. But he wasn't forcing her. She looked happy to go."

"Any idea where they were headed?"

"Once they're out the door? They're not mine. Not my circus, not my monkeys."

Burton shot back the rest of the bourbon and laid a card on the bar.

"You see this Dare again, I'd like to know."

Loftus raised his eyebrows.

"You think your friend might want his bar back? I've about had it with this shit."

"Nah. He came into some money. I don't think he's doing anything but hanging out these days."

29

I'd asked Susan out to dinner twice since she'd come back. The first time, she said she still felt jet-lagged, which I took to mean she thought it was too soon. The second, she'd been apologetic but had an appointment with a second appraiser to evaluate Henri's books. I was dubious about an appraiser who only came out at ten o'clock at night, which was when I heard her let someone in the street door.

Without turning it into an axiom, the third time I asked, she agreed, but she wanted to stay in the building. She'd renewed her acquaintance with Mrs. Rinaldi, who was getting frailer by the week, and said she'd promised to have tea with the old woman later that Wednesday night.

I believed that was her escape hatch if she didn't like how the evening turned out.

But here she was in my kitchen, sitting up on a stool at the island while I stirred the marinara. It made me hopeful, if not downright happy.

"The appraiser from Gross Street." She gestured with her wine glass. "Total crook. I think he forgot I used to do business in this kind of field."

When I first met her, she was selling celebrity memorabilia and making a decent living out of the bibs and bobs that people collected. "Reflected celebrity," she'd called it.

People always underestimated her. She was well short of five feet tall and proportioned to her height, which made people, men in particular, assume her brains were also in proportion to her size.

She'd started cutting her hair short in Oregon, and it only added to the waif look.

"Is that the little short guy, with the frog face?"

"Nope. What are you cooking?"

I caught a whiff of her perfume mixed in with the notes of garlic and tomatoes and thought the combination could make me happy for a good long time.

"Nothing heavy. Fettuccine, red sauce. Salad."

"I can smell the garlic," she said. "I hope it's not too strong."

She looked innocent, but I caught the subtext, bad breath and kisses. Not really a tease, because I knew if she was implying, she planned to follow through.

She poured herself another glass of the Montepulciano. For such a small woman, she had a remarkable tolerance.

"You're still not drinking? Other than that nightly tipple?"

I'd even forsworn that tonight, because even that might be a point of tension. She never told me so, but I believed there was alcohol addiction in her family somewhere. She'd always been tough on me about drinking, and I wasn't about to test the subject, unless it looked like we might get together again.

"Still not drinking."

Today, I said to myself. Tomorrow? Well, it depends.

"So I know you don't have the bar any more. What have you been doing with yourself?"

She watched me pour steaming pasta into the strainer in the sink. I'd set the table on the kitchen island, her stool the only seat high enough for her.

"Odds and ends, mostly. Helping out this kid Isaac who wants to be a music impresario. I got a good price for the Esposito, so I don't have to work anymore."

Not to mention the chunk of money my father left me, which I had resolved never to touch.

She grabbed the basket of bread and the butter dish from the counter, climbed back up on the stool.

"You still haven't learned, have you?" She picked up her wineglass again.

My back went up.

"What? That bar was a hell of a lot of work. I don't think it's a terrible idea to take a little time off."

"But how long?"

"What?"

"How long since you sold the place?"

"Five or six months."

She cocked a thin eyebrow at me.

"I have a feeling you know down to the day," she said. "But whatever you need to tell yourself."

I tonged the fettuccine onto the plates and ladled sauce, pushed a small bowl of grated Parmesan in her direction, and sat down.

"And that's important why?"

She twirled noodles around her fork and put them in her mouth.

"Delicious," she said. "A man who cooks won't have trouble finding friends."

I was irritated in a way only she could manage. I'd forgotten the feeling, but here it was again.

"So why is it important how long I've been out of work?"

"You still don't get why you were there, do you? It wasn't the bar that kept you from drinking, Elder. It was the work. You need something to do, the structure. Going to work every day was your anchor."

Though I'd managed a couple of spectacular falls off the wagon during that time, she was mostly correct. Running the business, dealing with customers and vendors, it had given my days and weeks a skeleton. I couldn't have drunk the way I had been before I owned the place and still run it at all.

"Even if that's true, it doesn't mean I can't find another way."

She started eating again. I was disappointed we kept coming back to this.

"I would bet myself," she said. "That this occasional drink—you're not binging, so you're telling yourself that it's under control. That just one won't kill you?"

I wasn't going to lie to her.

"I'm proving to myself..."

"Proving what?" She ripped a piece of bread apart. "You can slide down that slope on one drink as easily as twenty. When do you stop kidding yourself?"

I set down my fork. I'd never wanted a glass of Scotch as much as I did at that moment.

"I'm trying to find my way through." I didn't like the faint whine I heard in my voice. "Not throwing the baby out with the bath water."

She stared at me.

"What does that even mean, Elder?"

The doorbell rang, the street door. I wasn't sure if I was relieved or angry that we had to interrupt our conversation.

"What?" I bellowed into the intercom. "Who is it?"

"Evvie, man!" Isaac's voice was strident with panic, squeaky. "She's gone!"

30

Burton wasn't sure of the value of what he had learned from Antoinette. Suspended as he was, no one was going to pay him to fly to New Orleans and look up Edward Dare. Without any more evidence, in fact, he wouldn't have been going even if he had been on duty. Words of a bartender and a gangster wouldn't count for much with Martines. He'd have to hope Antoinette Bordaine came up with something he could take to his boss.

In the meantime, he needed to talk to Elder, who'd been doing for Marina what Burton had asked him to do in the first place, looking into Rasmussen Carter's death. The whole mess got more tangled every time he turned around. Maybe they could bounce some ideas off each other.

When he got to the apartment building on Comm. Ave., though, he ran into more confusion. The street door was wide open. He climbed the stairs and knocked on Elder's door.

"Hey," he said, when Susan Voisine let him in. "I didn't know you were back in town."

He'd never really cottoned to her. She was the first in a string of women Elder didn't know how to deal with. She'd clouded up the situation around Alison Somers severely, and Burton knew she hated the fact that Elder took a drink. Apparently, she didn't like him much, either.

"Burton," she said.

Elder was sitting in the living room with that black kid who'd run the brassy music thing a couple weeks ago. On his way past the kitchen, he glimpsed an aborted dinner for two, wine and candles, and wondered what happened.

"Burton." Elder looked up. "How did you hear so fast?"

"Hear what? Something happen to Marina?"

The kid—Isaac, he remembered now—snorted and turned away, as if he'd never expected help from a cop. Burton took a step in his direction before Elder got between them.

"No," Elder said. "Nothing to do with her."

Burton heard the clink of a fork on a plate. Susan was eating her dinner before it got cold, which seemed sensible.

"A friend of ours has gone missing." Elder nodded at Isaac. "You remember the trumpet player at our brass house gig?"

Burton remembered sleeve tattoos and gelled pink hair.

"Evangeline."

"She was supposed to sing at a gig in Roxbury last night, before she left for New Orleans. She never showed."

"She's been gone a whole day?" Burton said.

"She would never miss a gig. Believe me. She just got a leg up in the business, and she knows better than to build a reputation as someone you can't count on."

"Cop doesn't believe in millennials." Isaac picked at the skin of his cuticles. "We ain't all the fuckups you think we are."

Burton only held his temper because Elder was so worried.

"Less than a day, really," Elder said.

Isaac, sullen. "She is missing."

Burton shook his head.

"You know that's not long enough to open an investigation. Officially."

"This woman had giant ambitions," Elder said. "She's not a doper. Or a drunk." His eyes went to the kitchen, as if he wanted Susan to hear something. "She's a professional. She's not going to blow off a gig."

Burton thought his friend was probably kidding himself, especially since he'd seen Elder eying her. Many of the new jazz scene youth bought into the older mystiques: hard partying, lots of booze, thinking of drugs like heroin as a gateway to creativity.

Chances were very good that the young woman was shacked up somewhere with a bottle or an envelope of white powder. Or a guy.

He gentled his tone.

"Do you believe she's injured? In danger? You've checked her living space? The places she hangs out?"

"Dude thinks we're maroons," Isaac said. "I told you the copsters weren't going to help."

"Shut up," Elder said.

Burton's eyes widened. Elder was never straight-out rude. He was more likely to withdraw, go all passive-aggressive and sarcastic.

The apartment door opened and closed. That was Susan out of here, then. Probably for the best. Elder thought her problem with him was the drinking, but Burton knew enough cop groupies to recognize their opposite, someone who was afraid of crime and violence, who wanted no contact with it at all. And Elder kept finding himself in these situations. His drinking was the convenient excuse for her.

"I know you can't do anything right now," Elder said. "But, yeah. We can do all the usual things. What else?"

"Well, where do trumpet players practice? Does she have a rehearsal space? At Berklee, maybe? Contacts there?"

Isaac rolled his eyes and walked out to the kitchen. The refrigerator opened.

"She doesn't play trumpet any more. This gig she didn't show up for? She was performing as a singer."

The ping shocked Burton.

"Singer. OK. When's the last time you saw her?"

"She was here, Monday night," Elder said.

"Before that?"

Elder caught his excitement.

"Saturday night. At Baron Loftus's place. The Greenwood."

He didn't call it the old Esposito. Burton couldn't decide if that made him sad.

"She was singing there? Not playing that brass mouse shit?"

"Jazz. She left with some guy who claimed to book acts in New York."

"Shit." Burton breathed out. "You have any whiskey? I think I know where she might be."

Elder nipped to the kitchen while Burton thought. He heard Elder trying to soothe Isaac, whose voice was teary.

Burton raised his eyebrows when Elder returned with a bottle of Scotch and two glasses, filled them both. But it wasn't his job to comment on Elder's drinking. Never had been.

"Talk to me," Elder said.

"The guy she left with," Burton said. "Was his name Edward Dare?"

31

I was appalled by the story Burton was telling, and afraid for Evvie. I'd seen too many examples of bad faith in my little corner of the world to feel good about where she might have gone and what was happening.

"You're sure about this?" I said.

Isaac had shed the tough-kid act and looked scared.

"I can't be certain," Burton said. "But coincidences don't usually grow that big."

"We gotta get her out of there, man."

I let Burton calm Isaac down. We were in the cop's universe now.

"We don't know there's anything actually wrong," Burton said. "This other girl who went missing—Lily?—she was running with that same dream, of being a star. As far as I know, she's down there headlining in New Orleans, career on the rise. She's just too busy to call her mother."

I knew from the calculated way he was trying to talk Isaac down that he thought, as I did, there was a better chance Lily—and maybe Evangeline—was being used and abused.

"What are we doing about it?" Isaac tried to sound calm, but he knew he was in over his head.

"What's this 'we'?" Burton said. "I'm already hanging by my thumbs with the department. I can't go running off to New Orleans on a whim. I'd have no status. And I'd probably lose the rest of my job."

"Hold on." I tried to bring a little rationality. "Nobody's charging off anywhere, just to find out no one needs rescuing. Am I right?"

Burton shook his head.

"We can't assume. These are not nice people. Gangsters. If what I think is going on, their attitude is that Boston's so far from New Orleans, no one's going to make the connection. Dare's coming up here, seducing female musicians with the promise of a career."

"You don't know they're walking into a bad situation," I said. "You said it yourself. I don't want to be the reason someone's dream gets derailed. Maybe they really are taking a chance on a career."

Burton didn't like it. I knew I was arguing the other side, but these women were adults, too.

"Dare is also the guy who was putting together the cocaine deal with Alfonso Deal-Jones," Burton said. "A drug deal his boss wouldn't want him to do."

"So we know Dare's a gangster." My experience with music and bars told me you didn't always get to deal with the most savory characters.

I turned to Isaac.

"She leave a note or anything? Voice mail, email? That she wasn't going to make the gig for some reason?"

"No, for fuck's sake! I told you already."

"Easy," Burton said. "It won't help anyone if you go off all half-cocked."

He turned to me.

"I have a contact on the police force down there. I already asked her to look into Dare for me, whether he might have something to do with Alfonso's murder. Let's give this a day or two and let her get back to me. I can ask her specifically to look for Evangeline. And Lily."

Isaac still boiled with a need for action. Burton crooked a finger. "You have a picture of her?"

Isaac extracted a snapshot from his wallet, of him and Evvie standing in front of the Swan Boats in the summer.

"I want that back," he said.

His voice quavered. Burton gave him a respectful nod. I was embarrassed by the night she'd spent with me. I hoped she hadn't flaunted it with Isaac.

"Seriously, Isaac." Burton turned a stern look on the young man. "I am not fucking around here. These appear to be very serious people, so let's not run around stirring things up. Word?"

Isaac's look was equal parts pain and hatred.

"I have your word?" Burton said.

Isaac nodded, looking like a child told he couldn't have candy before dinner. Burton pointed at me.

"You, too, hotshot."

I raised my hands.

"I don't play with the bad kids any more. I'm not going anywhere near this."

Though I couldn't deny a rising excitement. I'd been bored silly by life after the Esposito, but I didn't plan on getting in any gun battles with gangsters. On the other hand, the prospect of helping someone escape a bad spot was appealing.

"Seriously," Burton said. "No one does a thing until I hear from Antoinette."

"Seriously," I said. "Until then."

Burton searched me with a look and nodded to himself. He knew I was already preparing for what came next.

32

I pushed Isaac out the door, telling him to stay close to home in case Evvie returned. I didn't want him haring off on his own, especially if Evvie didn't need rescuing.

Burton didn't mind the cold pasta, but as we sat at the kitchen island, I couldn't help regretting the nice domestic scene Isaac had interrupted.

"Susan's back in Boston?" he said, wiping out his bowl with a piece of bread.

"Though who knows for how long?"

My bitterness must have shown. He held back whatever he was going to say.

"What?"

"Nothing." He wiped his mouth with a napkin.

"You're not going to start giving me relationship advice, I trust."

I was thinking about what Marina had told me, her uncertainty, her waffling about the wedding. I was angry enough about the whole Susan thing, I might have wanted him to hurt, too. But I shut it down.

"Never." He put the rest of the wine in the refrigerator. "How much do you trust this Isaac's view of things?"

I tabled my personal emotions, gratefully. "He's OK. Why?"

"Because he's the odd detail. I don't think you see how all of this is tied together."

"The two deaths? Carter and Alfonso?"

"I'll admit I didn't want to," he said. "But everything that happened comes out of that one night at the Esposito."

"Greenwood," I corrected. "All I know about it is Rasmussen got stabbed. What else?"

"You know I'm not a 'hunches' guy..."

"But everyone in the story of that night is black, and connected to the music business somehow. And so is Isaac."

Burton hunched his shoulders as if he'd like to agree, but knew how racist it sounded.

"I just can't see where Isaac fits. How did you meet him?"

"Friend of a friend at Berklee introduced us. But I was mentoring him a long time before that night at the Greenwood. Tell me why you think it's all tied together."

"What do you know?" he said.

"Rasmussen got in a fight at the bar and was stabbed. Later on, he died, maybe killed in the hospital."

"Definitely killed in the hospital. Autopsy confirmed it." Burton sat back down on the stool. "I'm still not sure how it all fits together. But in that one bar, on that one night, we got a female singer recruited by a guy with gangster ties and never heard from again, that same guy is trying to rig a dope deal with the man who stabs Carter, and we have an old-lady jazz singer who may or may not be involved. What is the thread that ties all that together?"

"Sweetie didn't do it," I said. "Either kill Rasmussen or Alfonso."

"I'll go with you on Carter. But you don't think she might have been enraged that Alfonso tried to steal from her? Taken it out on him?"

"No. You said she got the money back before he could spend it. And when I talked to her, she seemed bemused by the whole thing, like people getting killed happened in her world all the time."

"Alfonso couldn't have killed Carter because of the timeline—he was already dead when Rasmussen went down. And smothering someone with a pillow? Seems like a woman's way."

"They're sure that's what happened?"

"Medical examiner says it is. And it's a far cry from stabbing the prick again."

I raised an eyebrow. It was unlike Burton to say anything nasty about crime victims.

"Hey," he said. "He's a client. I don't have to like him."

"So. You've eliminated Sweetie as a suspect, then?"

"For both. I got the same vibe off her that you did. She was almost completely uninterested in what happened to Alfonso. Which felt harsh, considering how long they were together."

He started to build a pot of coffee, as if we were going to pull an all-nighter. I did feel energized, part of something important again.

"And she's already moved another stud in to cater to her, uh, 'needs'."

I held in a smile. Sweetie had a lot I'd like to emulate in my old age. Assuming I made it there.

"She is a piece of work."

"But not a killer," Burton said.

"Agreed. Leaving whom?"

Burton adjusted the brown paper filter and spooned in coffee.

"I'd like to talk to this Edward Dare, get a little more detail. Pretty clear he's involved somehow."

"You really have a police contact in New Orleans? Or were you trying to make Isaac feel better?"

"I do. But I'm serious about not running off down there. They're trying to hang this civil suit on me, and I'm still technically suspended. A good murder-clearance rate doesn't buy as much as it used to. I'm getting the feeling there are people up the food chain that would like to see my ass going west."

I shook my head when he held up the carafe.

"I could fly down myself," I said. "Nose around a little."

"I don't think so. This isn't like standing around behind the bar, cogitating on who did what to whom."

That stung.

"I don't think that's a fair description of what I've done." I struggled to sound calm. "Took a few active steps on your behalf, as I recall."

Burton nodded.

"That you did. But these guys are full-on professional thugs. The fact they came up here to operate in Mickey Barksdale's town means they think they're stronger than him. They don't know you or me, they don't live here, and they're a good deal harder than Icky Ricky and Donald Maldonado."

"I get it," I said. "But I don't have to go down there and fistfight anybody. More like reconnoiter."

"Plus Susan won't like that at all."

I thought about the conversation she and I were having when Isaac showed up. I wasn't sure I cared what she thought any more, which told me something.

"Fuck her if she can't take a joke," I said.

33

Burton climbed out of his Jeep in front of the apartment house in Charlestown. Marina had an exam tomorrow and wasn't coming over. A distracted part of his brain acknowledged that things with her were not going well, but if she wasn't going to be with him, he couldn't exactly talk to her about how to fix them, could he?

He locked the vehicle, juggling his phone, an envelope full of interviews he wanted to reread, and a Styrofoam container of Pad Thai. When something hit him between the shoulder blades, the Pad Thai was the first to fly, the container clam-shelling open and spilling noodles all over the late-blooming cosmos. Mrs. Agnolotti wasn't going to be happy about that.

He dropped the phone and the papers and swiveled to meet the threat. It wasn't the first time someone in this neighborhood who didn't know he was a cop thought he was worth a mugging.

"Not a brilliant move, pally," he said, flicking back the tail of his coat to show the gold badge clipped to his belt.

The woman glaring back at him was big and thick, five ten or eleven. The gray leather jacket—was that eel skin?—was tight around her chest, mashing the outline of her breasts. Her makeup was raccoon-eye depth, and her hair high and teased, a throwback to the eighties. She flicked a backhand across his nose in a martial arts move so fast he couldn't dodge it.

"Shit!"

He backed away, reaching for his weapon but knowing he wouldn't get to it fast enough. She moved in close, too close really, and pointed a chrome .38 at his mouth. Blood trickled hot from his lip.

"Don't try," she said. "This doesn't have to get one bit more serious than it is right now."

He held up his hand to show it was empty and reached into his back pocket for a handkerchief. The blood tasted like warm iron.

His mind spun with the possibilities. Nothing major was going on in his professional life right now that would generate this kind of interest, except the investigation into Alfonso Deal-Jones. The Bousquet thing was in the courts, not in the streets. And if she wasn't going to shoot him, what was she here to say?

"It's still not a brilliant move," he said. "Better ways to deliver a message."

She rode up on the balls of her feet, aching to use more of her martial arts moves. Her greatest asset, whether she knew it or not, was that she didn't look that dangerous. She was a little dumpy, a little trashy, over made-up. She'd have been inside his defenses before he knew it, even if she'd come at him head on.

"You're smart," she said. "I don't meet a lot of smart cops where I come from."

"And where might that be?"

He had a good idea, but wanted to keep her talking. Her voice had a familiar lilt, not Southern, but a French tinge layered over the American English.

"I didn't come all this way to shoot the breeze with you, darling." She wiggled the gun. "I've been asked to let you know it would be best if you stayed right here in your own home town." She tilted her head and he saw the whole hair and makeup thing was put on, camouflage. "You haven't been thinking about traveling anywhere, have you?"

"'Anywhere' covers a lot of ground." He eyed the white noodles draped from the tall flowers in front of the building. You didn't have to be a Mensa member to know where this was coming from.

A window, ground floor on the left, slid open with a grinding sound, and Mrs. Agnolotti's phlegmy voice flew out.

"Hey, you! Don't be throwing your garbage around out there!

This is a respectable neighborhood. Daniel Burton, is that you?"

Mrs. Agnolotti distracted the other woman long enough for Burton to step into her and slap the arm holding the gun to one side. He slammed the heel of his hand up under her nose, trying to drive it back into her brain.

She yelped as the cartilage shifted and tried to bring the gun back to bear, but he pressed down hard with his thumb on the nerve in her wrist and heard the weight fall to the ground. He shuffled his feet so he wouldn't trip over it, and kicked it a dozen feet down the sidewalk.

The woman tried a couple of wrestling moves, but he bull-rushed her over the bushes and into the brick wall of the building, crashing the breath out of her. She smelled like cigarettes and cherry cough drops. Her lungs wheezed as she fought for breath, which gave him time to spin her and snap on the handcuffs.

"Daniel?"

"All good, Mrs. A. I'll have her pick up the mess."

The window slid shut. Like most people in his neighborhood, she didn't want to know too much about what went on out in the street at night.

Burton yanked the manacled woman over to the stoop and sat her down hard. His adrenaline was firing, and his breath short and choppy. A muscle in his shoulder twinged. She put her head down between her knees as if she felt faint, and he was happy to see blood dripping off the end of her nose onto the pavement.

She stiffened when he unzipped the gray leather jacket to search her, but he found nothing but the fob for a rental car. He pressed the unlock button and the lights on a green Toyota sedan flashed, down the block.

By the time he located his phone and the envelope full of interviews, he was calm enough to talk to her without wanting to fight. She sat up very straight, staring death and destruction at him, but he'd seen that look a hundred times. Not telling you nothing, cop. They never thought they would. But they usually did.

"I don't even have to ask who sent you here," he said. "I'm so far ahead of your boss it isn't funny."

Her eyes showed a flicker of doubt, then hardened.

"Good for you," she said.

"I can tell you think I'm going to handle this by the book, though. Take you in, find out you have no ID, then we can all muddle around for a while until some sleazebag lawyer comes in and bails you out."

Her lips disappeared as she thought. But she didn't seem worried. Whoever sent her had it all planned out in advance, entrance and exit both.

He took his phone and hit a speed dial, 7.

"But tonight we're not running under legal rules. I'm not officially a cop at the moment, and I take a very dim view of people mugging me."

Someone picked up at the other end, awake and clear, though it was after eleven at night.

"Give me your boss," Burton said. "Tell him it's Burton."

Then: "Got a little problem here, Mickey. Maybe we can do each other some good."

* * *

"It'll go easier if you tell me what you know," Burton said.

He had recuffed the woman's hands behind her, to the slats of an old oak chair he'd rescued from his mother's house after she died, when the sibs were all squabbling over who was going to get her meager possessions. As if they all wanted some tangible proof she was dead.

Heavy feet on the stairs announced Mickey's arrival with what sounded like an entourage. Burton had left his door open.

Mickey took one look at the situation and laid his hand paternally on the shoulder of his traveling companion, a gangly redhead with a sunburn and an incongruous green pompom hat.

"Maybe wait downstairs on this," Mickey said.

The woman stiffened at the implication. The ginger-haired kid looked irked, as if he wanted to ask why he'd gotten out of bed for this if he wasn't needed.

"Mick," Burton said. "Maybe he could clean up the noodles down there?"

Mickey shook his head and waved the kid off. The redhead closed the door behind him quietly enough. Burton guessed if it were anyone other than Mickey, he would have slammed it.

Mickey unbuttoned his short wool coat and walked over to the woman, bent over to look her full in the face.

"Don't I know you?"

"I know you," the woman sneered. "The famous Mickey Barksdale."

Mickey put his hand on her cheek, not a caress but a promise. She flinched.

She was trying for hard-ass, but Mickey's presence shook her. She showed more respect for Burton now, too, the fact he could command that kind of support from the criminal classes.

"That I am, Miss. And judging from your facial expression, you have some idea of my position in the world of this wonderful city."

The mild tone disarmed her. She must have thought Mickey was making conversation.

"New Orleans is a much cooler city."

Mickey nodded.

"Loyalty to the hometown is admirable. And thank you for confirming my suspicion. Frank sent you?"

She licked at the corner of her mouth.

"Can I get a glass of water?"

Mickey turned to ice, the way only he could. His whole body seemed to harden, and Burton considered how much easier his job would be if he could project that kind of menace.

Mickey put his face up close to the woman, who was pale as milk now.

"What is your name, young lady? No." He held up his hand as she started to take a breath to lie to him. "Not your street name. What is the name your mother gave you?"

"Marguerite," she said, after a long silence.

Burton was getting a lesson in interrogation. For obvious reasons, he'd never watched the man at work, but he never expected Mickey's style to be so calm.

"And what does your mother think about this life you've chosen for yourself?"

Marguerite pooched her lower lip out.

"She's not here," she said.

"Not present? Not in your life?" Mickey's voice gentled, a faint false brogue creeping in. "Is she not with us on this earth anymore?"

Marguerite nodded at the latter, as if unwilling to say it out loud.

"Marguerite. Do you mind if I call you Maggie?"

"That's my name." Her voice was stripped of the disdain and bravado. "I don't mind."

"Excellent." Mickey sat in a kitchen chair. "Now say it for me, please, Maggie. Can you be honest with me?"

She nodded, shyly.

"Tell me how you came to our fair city and what you task were charged with."

She started out, halted a couple times, looking for words that might make it sound better. Mickey made a gesture of impatience with his fingertips and she responded.

"Take a stitch or two out of this guy here." She lifted her chin toward Burton. "Something to do with a Dealey-Jones thing."

Burton was miffed—he only rated a stitch or two? He was satisfied, at least, to have the evidence that everything was connected to New Orleans.

"And why was that, dear? You know this man is a policeman?"

She shook her head and then let it hang. She hadn't known.

"Come on, Maggie. Don't make me drag it out of you."

The hint of threat in his voice set her legs twitching. Mickey gave her a come-on gesture. "Why?"

She shrugged. "They paid me?"

"So you work for Frank Vinson, then?"

"I suppose so."

"'Suppose?'"

"Well, the job came through his guy. The one who sets things up for him?"

"Edward Dare," Burton said.

Mickey looked irritated by Burton's interruption. She gave them that frightened nod again, as if the name itself was enough to fear.

"That's all you need?" Mickey turned to him and said.

"Thanks." Burton wouldn't have gotten that much out of her.

"Unlock the cuffs and I'll take her with me," Mickey said. "Rusty's already moved her car."

Burton felt ice in his chest.

"What?" Mickey said. "You don't want a little of your own back?"

As if Burton might want to take some whacks at a woman handcuffed to a chair. He didn't want to give Mickey that idea if he didn't already have it, but he feared for Marguerite's life.

"Mickey."

"Don't sweat it brother. You watch too many of those sleeps-with-the-fishes movies."

"I'm serious."

"Uncuff her." Mickey went cold again. "No one steps on my ground without permission. Not for something like this."

Burton's stomach churned as he took out the universal key and unlocked the cuffs. The skin on Maggie's forearms was cool and clammy. Her fingers curved, as if they were cramped, and she shot him a pleading look.

Mickey stood and turned her gently toward the door.

"Come along then, sweet Maggie. I have a few things to say to you I would like you to convey back to Frank. We both know this Mr. Dare, whomever he might be, wouldn't send you out on a mission without the big boss's approval." He winked at Burton. "At least that's the way we do it here in Boston."

He opened the apartment door and called down the stairs, pitched low so as not to wake anyone up.

"Rusty. The car."

"Mickey," Burton warned, one more time. He felt guilty. He should have known Mickey would have a price. "I do mean it."

As in, you kill this woman, I will have to come after you.

Mickey smiled, all bonhomie and cheer.

"Not to worry, old friend. Marguerite and I will have a little discussion, and I'll put her on a plane home. Intact, more or less."

The "less" part did not comfort Burton.

34

I wasn't being dramatic when I said I felt responsible for Evvie. I'd been the one to introduce her to Baron Loftus, who'd made it possible for Edward Dare to seduce her. So I was thinking about what I could do to help her, if she was in trouble. No one in New Orleans knew who I was. I could act like a tourist, go around to clubs, listen to music, and see what I could see. I wasn't stupid enough to take on gangsters by myself. My success dealing with Icky Ricky and his cousin was equal parts luck and support from Burton's official cop status.

I walked back into the little office I kept in the rear of the apartment to check ticket prices. Even if I was technically rich, I wasn't ever going to be the kind of rich that showed up at the airport and waved my Amex Black to take whatever was available.

As I scrolled through the flights, my landline phone rang. I ignored it. No one I cared about used that number. Even without looking at the caller ID, I was pretty sure it would be the Red Cross looking for my blood or some scammer claiming to be from the IRS, trying to social-engineer me out of my Social Security number.

Only when my cell phone buzzed did I stop and look. *Susan.* I frowned and pressed Answer.

"Elder." Her voice was high, but deadly calm. "Come downstairs. It's Mrs. Rinaldi."

* * *

Mrs. Rinaldi didn't die, which was the most positive thing I could say about the rest of that night. When she told Susan she felt as if a Steinway were sitting on her chest, Susan called 911. Mrs. R. had these spells off and on, and they usually resolved into a case of heartburn and some preventricular contractions, essentially harmless.

She insisted on getting dressed and applying makeup while we waited. Once the EMTs got her onto the gurney, she reached her hand out and squeezed mine. It felt like being swept with a bird's wing.

"As we went, so we go," she said, more of a question than a statement of faith. Her pale blue eyes were watery with pain and worry.

I squeezed back lightly. She'd been my downstairs tenant so long I couldn't remember a time when she hadn't lived in the building. And she'd been a great friend to Henri Voisin, Susan's father, even as he fell into dementia.

"I'm sure you'll be fine," I said. The paramedics maneuvered the gurney toward the door. "We'll check on you tomorrow."

Once they were gone, I closed my eyes and blew out breath. Losing Henri was hard enough—even in the early stages of dementia, he was a genial soul, forever forgetting I didn't drink and offering me sherry, challenging me to backgammon games where he lost track of the play. My life changed a great deal when I sold the Esposito, but that would be nothing compared to losing Mrs. Rinaldi.

I looked around her apartment, the piles of musical scores and opera memorabilia, the small work table covered with tools and glue and balsa wood where she, even with fading eyesight and arthritic fingers, built the miniatures that opera set designers all over the world commissioned as models.

"Thank you for being here," I said.

Susan sat in a stuffed chair by the front window, looking tearful, as if reliving what happened to her father a year ago.

"She was trying so hard not to cry," she said. "Ladies of that age and station are never supposed to complain."

"It's happened before. I'm not too worried. It's been heart palpitations, low enzyme levels, things like that. I know she doesn't eat enough."

Susan stood and stretched her back. "I gather you're off on another adventure, then."

"What do you mean?"

"Burton and the black kid. Something's going on, isn't it? Someone in trouble?"

She was right, but I didn't see why she'd be irked about it.

"True. The black kid's name is Isaac, by the way. One of his friends has gone missing."

"And you're off to the rescue."

This was one of the odder directions our conversations had taken. Why would she care?

"I feel responsible," I said. "I was the one who got her the first gig."

"Which makes you the one who has to solve all the problems."

Anger bubbled under her mild tone.

"I feel like I ought to help, is all."

She paced around Mrs. Rinaldi's tiny living room, stopped to look at me.

"You don't get it, do you? Why this isn't working? You and me?"

"I didn't think it wasn't working."

Though, clearly, it wasn't working smoothly.

"You don't even know why you drink, do you?"

My walls started to go up. Apparently she'd been living on the West Coast long enough to steep herself in some of the crazy pursuits people had out there: gestalt and reiki and touchless massage and whatever else. She wouldn't be the first person I knew who thought a couple of weekend workshops made her an expert in diagnosing psychological problems.

"It's a genetic predisposition, if I understand the science," I said.

She shook her head. "That is too easy. Then you don't have to take any responsibility for it." When she tilted her head to look up at me, I had the random thought her neck must hurt a lot. "You drink because you're bored."

"Bored. I've got work, with Isaac. I've got money, friends. What makes you think I'm bored?"

She pushed a finger into my chest.

"Because you are a helper."

I rolled my eyes.

"No, listen. You like taking care of Mrs. Rinaldi. You looked out for my father. Now you're all ready to run off and solve this problem the boy brings you, whatever it is. You're engaged and you're happier than I've seen you since I got back."

"Even if it's true," I said, "so what? Can't I want to help people?"

She looked sad.

"We can't seem to click. Can we?"

I doubted it was because I was the "helper" type, whatever that meant.

"Modern problems," I said. "You want what you want. I want what I want. We've both been living our own lives as we like them. Of course there are strains."

She sat down again.

"You're so damned good with other people. People who need something. You just don't do intimacy very well."

I shook my head.

"We've been intimate, you and I. Before. *You* were the one who backed away then."

"Fair enough. But I couldn't see fighting that battle with you. The alcohol. And then this."

"Battle."

"Pushing past your walls, then. You're not that interested in being with me."

Her face flushed. It was the first time in a while I'd felt honest emotions between us. I wished they were something other than fear and anger.

I shook my head again.

"What cue am I missing here? I've wanted to be with you since you came back. Since before, even. You're the one holding me off."

"Because I know you're not going to let me get close. That's why. You know how I know that?"

Something valuable was slipping through my fingers. I didn't know how to stop it.

"It's because I don't need fixing. I don't need your help. I stand on my own two feet and you can't find a way to help me. Which you need."

"So?"

"So, go off and rescue someone who needs rescuing, then. Maybe we'll talk when you're done. Maybe not. But I'm not looking for someone to take care of me."

I was confused enough not to know what to say. I took the only way out I could think of. The door.

"We'll talk," I said as I went.

"Sure, Elder. Sure we will."

35

Martines had called to tell Burton they'd unwound his suspension, even though the suit hadn't gone anywhere. Too many questions from the media, he said. Burton was back in the precinct for the first time in days, full of ambivalence about his job and his future.

Antoinette Bordaine had left a voicemail on his desk phone. He'd given her his cell number so she wouldn't call him at the precinct.

"I may have something for you. Call me."

Then she left a number he recognized as a prefix that was not New Orleans. A burner? He wondered why. He left her a message and she called him back half an hour later. He was sitting in his cubicle listening to Martines drone on about how much college was going to cost for his twin daughters. Made Burton glad he and Marina decided not to have children.

He was relieved when his phone chimed.

"Sorry, Lou. CI calling in on a case. I need to take this."

Martines huffed at being cut off.

"Fine. Do your job."

Burton flicked the Answer button.

"Burton."

"Your Creole Belle here, Daniel. How're ya?"

He ran over the small talk.

"You have something?"

"Whoo—no time for foreplay with you Northern boys, is there? Wham, bam, and thank you ma'am."

"Antoinette. I'm on the clock here."

"Ever thus. This young woman you're looking for? Is her name Lily Miller, perhaps? Nineteen years old, AA?"

"AA?"

"African-American, Daniel. Try and keep up."

Burton felt a stab of worry about what he might have to tell Kaylen Miller about her daughter.

"Please tell me she's not a body."

"I haven't met the lady, but I'm sure she has a nice one. She isn't dead, if that's what you mean." Antoinette was almost jolly. He was going to have to hear the story her way.

"Tell me." He used his stop-fucking-around voice.

"I hear you." The playfulness disappeared. "She is fine, relatively speaking. Physically."

"She was with this Frank Vinson character? Your kingpin?"

"Queenpin, more likely. You'd have to meet him to understand the joke. Yes, she was his flavor of the month. Last month."

"And the calendar turned?"

"You got it. 'So long, been good to know you. Here's a hundred bucks to get you home.'"

"But she's OK?"

"Physically, like I said." Bordaine's voice hardened. "What that kind of attention does to a young person? Just once, I'd like to be able to rap Frankie's knuckles."

"Where is she now?"

"St. Agatha's." Bordaine's sentences got shorter, the angrier she got. "The nuns run a drop-in center for people of color who've been abused."

"You said she was fine."

"Come on, Burton. You know there's more than fists and sticks. And if you don't, it's time you learned."

Burton breathed out against his anger at Frank Vinson. He was much better at dead people than live ones.

"I get it. Does she have money to get home? Do we know what her plan is?"

"What's this 'we,' white man?" Bordaine laughed. "Kidding. I've

152

talked to the young lady. She's basically dazed and confused. She doesn't think she can go home—she's playing the whole soiled-dove routine."

Burton made a noise, low in his throat.

"Her mother's pressed me to find her, more than once. I believe she'd want the girl home."

"Thought you might have a special interest. You being homicide and her being alive and all."

"I could ask you one more favor," he said.

"Put her on a plane?"

He was grateful not to have to spell it out.

"Dinner at Antoine's the next time I'm in town?"

She snorted.

"That old dive? I'm talking Herbsaint, the whole nine yards. Bring the Amex Black."

"You get young Lily back to Boston? I'm in."

"I believe we can manage that." Bordaine's voice lapsed into the semi-sweet drawl.

"One thing. I noticed you called me on a burner."

"So?"

"Why is that?"

"First phone I picked up."

"Try again?"

She lit a cigarette, the lighter clanking.

"Let's just say I'm not the flavor of the month in my little world here."

"Wouldn't be surprised to hear Mr. Frank has eyes and ears inside NOPD?"

"Close enough. But also not something we should talk about over the radio."

"Got it."

"I'll text you flight details," she said. "And Burton? Watch yourself. This is one man whose reach exceeds his grasp, for sure."

"Heard and acknowledged. Let's make that dinner soon."

"*Claro*, cher." She made a kissing sound and broke the connection.

He leaned back in his chair and set his boots up on the desktop, relieved that Antoinette had located Lily. He wouldn't completely relax until he knew she was home. There was the distinct possibility that, having been in the bar the night Rasmussen Carter was stabbed, she'd know something that would help with his case.

Assuming Edward Dare, in his role as pimp, had kidnapped Lily to New Orleans, Burton doubted he would have mentioned the fight in the bar that night to Frank. He certainly wouldn't have talked about the deal with Alfonso Deal-Jones. Frank wouldn't see Lily as a danger, but Dare might.

He flipped on his computer. Unlike some of the cops he worked with, the number of vacation days he'd accrued was not at the top of his mind. If Lily didn't return on her own, he might have to fly down to New Orleans. Or if this friend of Elder's who'd disappeared turned out to be Frank Vinson's latest arm candy.

Was Dare ballsy enough to come back to Boston to resuscitate the cocaine deal with someone else? Or to find Frank Vinson's next companion? Much as he hated to lean on Mickey Barksdale for anything, he was going to have to ask him to keep his eyes open. He was starting to like the idea that Dare had killed Alfonso, and it would be considerably easier to arrest the man in Boston than to extradite him, especially from a city where his boss had no political pull.

36

I felt as if I were paddling a canoe in a lake of yogurt, that there was nothing I could do to help find Evvie. I wasn't going to New Orleans—yet. I still needed a fuller version of what happened the night that Rasmussen Carter was killed from someone who had been there.

The morning was bright and brisk, not quite hinting at winter, though you could feel the season sharpening its teeth. I pulled open the heavy wooden door to what had been the Esposito, surprised to find it unlocked, and walked down the noisy steel stairs.

Not until I reached the bottom step did I see anyone. Baron Loftus emerged from the kitchen, a dirty full-length apron over his dressy bartender's costume. Salsa music spilled from the kitchen, reminding me with a quick ache of the days when Marina used to play it loud to drown out the jazz she didn't like. Ornette Coleman, usually. She called him the screecher.

Loftus wiped his hands on an oily rag. I wondered which piece of equipment had given up the ghost.

"Changing a fuse," he said. "Is it too much to hope you've come to buy the place back?"

I felt a sense of fraternity with the man as a bar owner, even if I didn't like him very much.

"It's not an easy business," I said.

"You are not kidding." He swiveled toward the bar back and pulled down a green bottle. "I'm rewarding myself for meritorious service. Can I offer you something?"

I shook my head. I disapproved of bartenders drinking on the job. That would have been the final sabotage of my plans for the Esposito, if I had let myself have a drink whenever I felt like it.

"Couple of questions for you, though."

Loftus poured himself a healthy measure of sickly green fluid into a cordial glass. The bottle was unlabeled, and I did not recognize the whiff of herbs, the tinge of garbage smell. He tossed it off like it was a shot of whiskey.

"Ahh." He made that sound you make when the alcohol burn hits bottom. "Ask away. I'm not likely to see anyone in here until cocktail hour, anyway."

Which interrupted my train of thought. How badly had he screwed up this viable, if not thriving, business? When I sold it, the Esposito hadn't been everything I wanted it to be, but I had a steady clientele—of drinkers, not drunks—and a loyal lunch and dinner business. None of it had been rocket science, but of course, it had all been hard work. Mr. Loftus didn't seem to be up for that part of the business.

Which wasn't why I was here.

"You remember Evangeline? The young woman I introduced to you?"

His bow tie was red with white geese today. He touched it, which looked like a tell. But of what?

"Sure. The singer. Great voice. Though she didn't pack the house the night she was here."

Loftus sounded as if much had been handed to him, and that he didn't particularly value any of it. I wasn't the best judge of people, given my history, but I always thought it was more what you did with what you had than how you got it in the first place.

"She's disappeared."

He wiped the neck of the green bottle, recapped it, tucked it away. He was calculating his response and I wondered why.

When he turned back, his face showed concern.

"You know, I think I did hear that. What does that have to do with me?"

"The last place anyone saw her was here. You must remember

her leaving halfway through the gig? With Edward Dare?"

"Is that the man's name? You were here, though, weren't you? Weren't you pissed he took her away from you?"

There was enough truth in that, my face got hot. Loftus saw it.

"Maybe. I'm just interested in anything you remember."

"Jesus." His irritation was studied. "Are we still hammering on that? Because that is the long and faraway gone."

"A young woman disappeared the night of the fight, too, between Alfonso and Rasmussen Carter. You recall any of that?"

"Everyone else saw more of it than I did," he said. "When I looked up, it was over."

"Did she leave with Edward Dare then?"

"A knife fight between two of my customers, and you want me to remember who left with whom? You've been behind the stick yourself. What do you think?"

I was thinking he was lying to me, that's what. Something about that night, beyond the effect the violence would have on his business, was bothering him.

"How well do you know this Dare?"

His twitchiness hinted at fear. If Edward Dare was some type of bad guy, I needed to know. Burton needed to know.

He sighed and glanced back over his shoulder at the green bottle, as if it held all the answers. I recognized the dragon of addiction sleeping inside him, assuming it hadn't already woken.

"He's a friend of my aunt's." He spoke with deep reluctance, worried, at the very least, about being the target of Sweetie's sharp tongue. "From her New Orleans days. I guess they were tight back then. Maybe lovers."

He tossed the last in casually. I read it as more distraction.

"So he was a regular here?"

"Not really. Only those two times, now that I think of it."

"And he was Sweetie's friend. Not Alfonso's?"

"I saw him sit with Alfonso once. But I couldn't tell you what they talked about."

Burton had mentioned something about a cocaine deal, but Loftus wouldn't admit to knowing about that, even if he did.

"So he was here for Sweetie, mostly." I repeated it to see if he'd embellish, but he didn't.

"Sweetie has a lot of friends," he said.

"And they all hang out here?"

He looked at me with his brows puckered, as if I'd said something stupid.

"Well, it is her bar, isn't it?"

37

Burton got the call from Dispatch about 7:30 the next morning,
not long after he'd pushed the plunger down on the French
press full of Peet's Italian Roast and poured his first cup of coffee.
Marina had been out of touch for several days now, and he worried
whether she was truly getting cold feet—didn't all brides have
doubts? She'd always known about his crazy work hours. It was
late in the game for that to be a problem.

"Burton."

"You know some old broad name of Bogan?"

Burton shook his head at the indifference of the ignorant
dispatcher. Elder was a bigger jazz fan than Burton was, but at
least he respected the music and the musicians, past and present.
The dispatcher couldn't even generate respect for the fact Sweetie
was old.

"Sweetie Bogan."

"That's the one." The dispatcher rattled off an address so fast
he wouldn't have had time to write it down, if he hadn't already
known it.

"What's the complaint?"

Deep sigh.

"Lady asked for you by name. Wouldn't say why. Your call
whether to go or not." The phone went dead.

Burton shook his head. The coffee was the perfect temperature
to drink and he sat and enjoyed it, slipping his way into the day. If
it was an emergency, Sweetie would have called 911.

An hour later, he was dressed and out the door, making a mental note to call Marina during the day and check in. When something bothered her, she withdrew rather than confronted it, and he knew he was going to have to work out what was wrong with her.

The marina and its millions of dollars' worth of boats glinted in the sun like a strange city of its own. He wondered if living close to the water made these people happy, or whether it was like everything else, you got used to what you had, no matter how much you desired it in the first place. That was what fed most white-collar crime: an endless insatiable dissatisfaction with the present and the current.

The security guard, a blonde surfer type this morning, poked at a mole on his arm, looking up with startled blue eyes when Burton walked in. He accompanied him to the elevator and keyed it without comment, apparently recognizing he was a cop.

Burton wouldn't normally have responded to Sweetie without an actual complaint, but things were stuck. He was hoping he wouldn't have to go to New Orleans on his own dime to get some traction.

Sweetie was waiting for him in the doorway, backlit as usual by the sun. He had the odd thought her shadow would make a great target and then wondered why he would think that.

"Detective Burton."

Her hands were trembling as she held them out. As he stepped into her apartment out of the glare, he saw her narrow wrinkled face was tight and angry. Her hair was springy, wired, as if she hadn't had a chance to attend to it today.

"Thank you for coming so promptly. Thank you."

She was the opposite of the cool calm character she'd been the last time he was here. Her energy was spiky, and she tottered as she led him deeper into the apartment, as if she were losing her balance.

"You didn't tell our dispatcher what the problem was," he said.

She didn't offer him a seat or coffee or even an answer, but kept walking past the black and white photos to a door off to the left, one of the spare bedrooms, he assumed.

"It's Enzo," she said. "The security guard for the building found him in the basement. I'd asked him to bring around the car."

She pushed open the door with her knuckles and stepped inside, gesturing Burton to follow.

Enzo was sitting up in the bed, propped by thick pillows. Whoever had gone to work on him had been thorough, if not in a way that threatened his life. Both eyes were swollen to slits, and since he was shirtless, Burton could see all the bruising on his shoulders, arms, and chest. Soft tissue. The black and blue and purple was fresh.

"Enzo, my man," Burton said. "Who did you piss off?"

The man shook his head delicately, as if the sloshing of his brain inside his skull hurt.

"Not me." His voice sounded sandy, as if he might have been choked, too. "This was on account of I work for Mrs. Bogan here."

"Really." Burton raised an eyebrow.

Sweetie looked at Enzo like a puppy who'd crapped on the rug. Burton guessed she didn't do sympathy for anyone but herself.

Burton picked up a water bottle and handed it to the man. The knuckles on both of Enzo's hands were torn. He'd gotten a few licks in.

"And what makes you so sure that's why your ass got kicked?"

Even through the swelling and bruises, Burton caught the disbelieving look.

"Uh, because they told me?"

Burton didn't know if Enzo was making him pull it out of him because he was doped up, or he was just being obstreperous. Sweetie huffed beside him.

"And what was that, Enzo? What did they say?"

"There were three of them." A touch of whine in his voice. "I couldn't do a thing."

That was for Sweetie's benefit. Burton thought Enzo's job prospects were pretty poor at the moment. Sweetie walked out of the room.

"What did they say? What was the message?"

Enzo hiccuped, drank more water.

"On account of the guy who died in the hospital. Rastaman or something."

Burton alerted. "Rasmussen?"

"Yeah. They said they knew Mrs. Bogan had set him up to get killed, and I was the only warning she'd get. She was going to have to own up."

Burton took the water bottle back.

"Really," he said again.

Enzo nodded, winced.

"They said they'd come after her if she didn't confess."

Any logic in that escaped Burton, but he could puzzle it out later.

"Make sure she gets an actual doctor in to see you, all right? You don't want a busted spleen or something."

He stepped out into the hallway. Sweetie awaited him in the living room with a silver coffee service and a plate of muffins—blueberry, if he smelled correctly. His stomach growled and she smiled.

"Come sit down," she said. "Tell me how the Boston Police Department is going to protect me."

He settled himself, took a muffin without being asked, and peeled off the paper. It was still warm: microwave or oven?

"You have no idea who might have beaten up Enzo, or why?"

"I heard the ridiculous story he's telling."

"Why would anyone have the idea you'd killed Rasmussen Carter?"

She poured one cup of coffee, apparently not eating or drinking herself.

She rested her hands in her lap. She'd taken the time to slick back her gray-white hair and put on an emerald-green T-shirt and cardigan combination over black pants. The sweater made her look like the Queen of England, if the queen had been black.

"I'm beginning to wish Alfonso had never taken me to the bar that night." Her fingers twisted, but she was playing the anguish rather than feeling it. "I never would have been involved in any of this."

Burton thought Enzo probably deserved a little more sympathy.

"But the accusation? That you caused Carter's death? No truth to that?"

Sweetie guffawed, showing yellowed, crooked teeth. Whatever she spent her money on, it wasn't dental work.

"Believe me, Detective Burton. I've been around the sun a few times. If I had killed Rasmussen Carter, you wouldn't see my shadow near it."

He thought about that and decided not to drink the coffee.

"That's all I need, then. You're telling me you didn't do it." He killed the sarcasm, which hadn't dented her perfect composure. She sat erect on the couch, legs crossed. "But get some professional medical help in for Enzo. We wouldn't want any more 'accidental' deaths. I'll speak to the precinct about sending someone around to take a statement."

Which he promised himself to do, get this on record. As he rode the elevator down, he knew he didn't believe her completely, whether or not she'd killed anyone. She may not have had an obvious reason for Rasmussen Carter to die—or Alfonso—but she was standing deep in this mess, right up to her spindly shanks.

38

Isaac and I met for breakfast at the South Street Diner, a twenty-four hour joint on Kneeland Street, three or four blocks down from South Station. It used to be one of my favorite places to go after a rough night at the Esposito, when I didn't have a reason to go home and I knew I wouldn't sleep if I did. It was around eight in the morning, and white specks of frozen dew dotted the cracks in the sidewalk.

I was eating oatmeal. Isaac was powering through the full diner breakfast in the way a young man with good cholesterol and a healthy heart could eat: eggs, sausage and bacon, home fries, a short stack of pancakes, and an English muffin, whole wheat.

I put down my spoon.

"Anything from Evvie?"

He shook his head, the question barely slowing him down.

"Not a word. None of her girlfriends knows anything. Her mom hasn't heard from her. The band."

"No father? You know her family pretty well?"

He drank some tomato juice he'd doctored with black pepper and Tabasco.

"Yeah." Then his expression cleared, as if he'd heard me say something else. "Oh, we're not like that. She's like my sister from another mother."

Which made me feel only a little bit better about having slept with her.

"I'm thinking about heading down to New Orleans myself," I said. "Do a little poking around. Unofficially. Burton can't do it, for all kinds of reasons."

Isaac grimaced at the mention of Burton, nodded. He put down his fork and wiped his mouth with a paper napkin.

"I'll go along."

I thought about wandering the night spots of the city, trying discreetly to locate Evvie. A middle-aged white guy with a young-looking black teenager? Wouldn't be a good look.

"I haven't committed to it yet," I said. "It's just an idea."

Isaac frowned. He wasn't fond of the idea of waiting around. He'd been ready to move since he decided Evvie was missing. His phone buzzed and skittered on the table between us.

He turned it over, frowned at the display, and answered.

"Yes."

I stared at the posters on the back wall of the diner, bridges from the various cities of the country: Portland, Oregon; San Francisco; St. Louis.

Isaac's end of the conversation was brief and monosyllabic. He hung up and pulled two twenties out of his wallet, dropped them on the table.

"You're buying me breakfast?" I said, mock-shocked.

He was serious as a priest.

"You can come along or not," he said. "But I think you're going to want to be there."

* * *

We took his car, but halfway to wherever we were going, rocketing down Gallivan Boulevard, I wished I hadn't let him drive. He piloted the souped-up Civic with all the testosterone and unearned confidence of a young male, and no more skill than the proverbial little old lady driving to church on a Sunday.

I winced as he passed a Nissen bread truck on the right and nearly sheared the mirror off a parked Mercedes.

"Be a shame if we didn't survive the ride," I said, as mildly as I could with my heart slamming. I hung on the sissy bar above the window.

"Yeah, yeah."

But he slowed down as we made a couple right-angle turns into a neighborhood. It was a quiet isolated group of homes, on streets that did not connect, stopping in cul-de-sacs or dead ends, in patches of trees and brush.

He turned onto Hopkins Street, parked the Civic at the curb in front of a small ranch-style house painted in Victorian colors, graphite gray for the siding, the trim picked out in raspberry. Wood siding, not cheap aluminum like so many other houses on the street.

"OK," he said. "I know you consider yourself the senior partner. But let me lead this one."

His voice was firm and certain and convinced me. That and the fact I had no idea where we were or why.

"Got it."

I followed Isaac up the concrete path trimmed with flower beds showing the frost-burnt stubs of plants cut back for the winter. A pile of fragrant cedar mulch sat on a blue tarp at the top of the driveway.

The door opened before Isaac could knock. A small very dark woman with her head bound in a red kerchief looked at him with hope.

"You're Regina's boy?"

He nodded.

"She's in here." She pulled the door wide, saw me.

"Hello," she said.

"He's with me," Isaac said.

The furniture in the living room did not match the house's exterior. It was stark and planed, light wood and steel tubes, so the living room felt more spacious. Under a pool of yellow lamplight at the front corner sat a young woman leafing through a coffee table book. She closed it when we walked in and I saw it was a collection of WeeGee photos, an oddly depressing subject for a young woman to peruse.

Girl, really. If she was eighteen, it wasn't by much, though she gave off a sad fatigue that was much older.

"Lily," the woman said. "This is Isaac. Regina Belon's boy? She thought he might be a help to you."

Lily looked at us incuriously. I realized who she was.

"I don't believe anyone can help at this point, Mother. What's done has been done."

Her voice was smooth as warm caramel, and I heard how lovely it would be in song. Her mother's voice was unforgiving.

"We will have some conversation about what you went through," she said. "And some compensation. If I have to run this man down myself and wring his chicken neck."

Isaac sat down on the couch beside Lily and took her hand, an avuncular gesture older than he was. She gripped him so tightly his knuckles whitened.

"I don't know what I can do to help you," he said. "But at least tell us the story."

39

"I don't know the best way to make this work," Antoinette said with an exhalation of smoke. "But Frank wants to talk to you."

"Me." Burton sat in his cubicle at the precinct, a steaming cup and an apricot Danish laid out in front of him. An early breakfast and a little computer searching into Sweetie Bogan's background for gangster connections he didn't know about. Elder had called earlier to let him know Lily Miller had come home, physically OK if not emotionally, and it seemed like an intelligent move to educate himself a little about Vinson's reach and scope. He wasn't sure if Bordaine's call was a result of something he'd tripped over online, or a coincidence.

Because, technically speaking, no crime had taken place with respect to Edward Dare's procurement of young ladies for the gangster's arm. Both Lily and Evangeline—who seemed to be the latest candidate—were over eighteen. What Burton did believe was that Dare was deeply connected to the murders of Alfonso Deal-Jones and Rasmussen Carter.

"How the hell does he even know who I am?" he said.

He took a bite of Danish, not sure he liked what he was hearing. He'd assumed Bordaine was a more or less honest cop, but the reputation of the police force down there, especially since Katrina, wasn't good. He didn't doubt that someone who appeared clean from a distance could be corrupt and he would never know. He hoped he was wrong about Antoinette, not least because he liked her.

Her voice gave him nothing.

"He has feelers out all over the place. He's like a big calamari. You know as well as I do, cher. Information is everything these days."

He could have pushed it harder, but he didn't think he wanted to know right now where she stood in relation to Frank Vinson.

"Well, he must know I'm not going to fly down there to talk to a gangster. What's the pitch?"

"What he'll tell you?" she said. "Or what I think?"

She was asking him to trust her. Half an hour ago, he wouldn't have had a qualm.

"Start with him. What do you think he'll say?"

She inhaled, coughed.

"Frank is the king shit around here, you understand. Has been for years. He is, shall we say, connected in political ways as well as running his own businesses."

"Not too new an idea," Burton said. It was what Mickey was after, eventually. "But I've got no political pull to speak of. Not here, and definitely not down there."

"Not what he'd be after. You have a little bit of a reputation down here, you know."

That surprised him.

"Not from the Kathleen Crawford business."

She chuckled.

"You weren't here that long, but you made an impression. Good and bad."

"So, what? Frankie's going to help out a street cop who's already in the shitter with his own department? Does he think he can turn me?"

"Politics." Bordaine almost spit the word. "He's doing what every intelligent gangster over the age of seventeen is doing, trying to make himself legitimate. He sees the legal thievery that the banks and real estate developers get away with and thinks it's safer."

Burton nodded.

"And he thinks I could foul him up somehow?" Which, truth be known, he'd do for any number of these assholes. "I'm that big a risk in his mind? Tell me your take."

He sipped his coffee but it was too cold to drink. He'd lost his appetite anyway.

"Oh, I believe he's sincere enough about wanting to be legal, not get pulled into anything that's going to dirty his shirt. But specifically, I think he's trying to save Edward Dare's ass."

"Dare's that important?"

"To him. Edward is really the brains, and Frank is smart enough to know it. Frankie has all this power because of who his daddy was. And his granddaddy. Dare is the guy who's pulling the whole operation into the twenty-first century."

"The brains? He's done some stupid things."

"But without him? Frankie's just another old-school gangster. Part of the city's history, not its future."

"You've thought about this a lot." He heard an acceptance of the status quo in her voice that troubled him.

"These assholes quit stealing and pimping and dealing drugs," she said. "It's better for everyone. Better for the city."

He didn't like the implications.

"You're a mouthpiece for Frank, then? Or is it Dare? You have an offer for me I can't refuse?"

"Don't be an asshole. I'm working for a better city here. Task force, in fact."

The two scariest words in law enforcement, as far as he was concerned.

"Pitch it," he said. There wasn't going to be any big dinner in New Orleans, if he ever went again.

"Seriously, Burton. We're trying to keep a lid on things. Especially now."

"Pitch it."

She sighed her disappointment. He didn't care. He'd use Mickey for information, but he'd never let Mickey use him.

"Edward Dare was, and is, Frank's gofer, on the surface. The ambassador to the world, where everyone works out, no one smokes cigars, and public perception is as important as profit. You feel me?"

"So…"

"We would like to preserve Dare's position in this—he's the only one pushing Vinson's organization out of the darkness. The politicos think he's someone they can deal with."

Burton frowned. Sounded like there was also a coup brewing, to take Vinson down.

"You're a little higher up the food chain than you represented to me, then."

"No. Just doing the job they asked me to do."

"I think Dare killed Alfonso Deal-Jones. I'm not letting that go."

"No one's asking you to. We just need a month or two to stabilize things."

"Months? That does me no good."

"What about the girls?" she said. "Frankie taking them in, feeding them dope probably, maybe abusing them? Couldn't you concentrate there first?"

"Maybe." There was no way he was letting Dare slide for a murder for even a week. Antoinette had squandered his confidence. He wasn't going to tell her his plans. "What are you asking for?"

"Open a case on Frank. Kidnapping, reckless endangerment, whatever you slick Boston cops use. Give us time to settle the situation before you take on Dare."

"I'm going to need to talk to him eventually. And not months from now."

"Not a problem. I'll make it happen. Just give me a little time."

"Sure," Burton said. "Let me take this up the line."

But his gut told him she was lying to him. As long as he was in New Orleans, Edward Dare was safe as houses.

40

I watched through the street door as Susan double-parked to let Mrs. Rinaldi out, then drove up half a block to an open spot. I stepped down off the stoop to meet the old woman, navigating her new walker shakily along the sidewalk. She seemed weightless as I helped her up the stairs, lighter than the folded walker, which I carried in my other hand.

"I am awfully glad to be home," she said. "The noise in that place! I can't imagine how they expect anyone to sleep."

She was gray and tired, and I wondered if doctors and nurses ever saw a patient like Mrs. Rinaldi as more than a dicky heart.

I got her into her apartment and settled into her favorite chair in the living room, a straight-backed rocker with a leather seat. In the kitchen, I put on water for tea.

Susan walked in, her cheeks flushed with the cold morning, and unwound a long filmy blue scarf from her neck, stuffed it in the pocket of her coat.

"She looks very tired," she said.

"Hospitals. Do we know what it was?"

Susan and I were still dancing around each other after the semi-argument the other night. But she had at least called me and asked for help resettling Mrs. Rinaldi.

"You were pretty much right," she said. "Dehydration. A touch of malnutrition. Not so much that she wasn't eating enough calories, but not a very good diet."

I couldn't remember seeing the woman eat a meal, now that I thought of it. She would nibble. But I was her landlord, not her caregiver, and this episode made me wonder whether she had relatives, maybe children. I didn't know, which made me feel like a very bad friend.

"Elder, dear." Mrs. Rinaldi's frail voice floated in from the living room. "There's a box of Lorna Doones in the cupboard above the sink. Don't you think they'd be a treat with a cup of tea?"

Susan and I smiled at each other, the warmest moment we'd shared in days.

"Sure thing, Mrs. R," I said.

"Can you handle things with her for a bit?" Susan said. "I'm waiting for a call from the people I work with in Oregon. They want to know when I'm coming back."

She dropped that like a small bomb, but I didn't react. When, not if.

"We're fine here." I poured boiling water over the tea bags and put the timer on. "I'll wait to pour yours until you come back downstairs."

Carrying her coat, she walked out, stopping to say something to Mrs. Rinaldi that made her laugh, a sound like a small bell that made me feel better. The apartment door closed behind her.

When the timer dinged a couple minutes later, I squeezed out the tea bags, put a sugar bowl and creamer on the tray with the tea and cookies, and carried the whole thing out.

"I brought the cookies, Mrs. R. But I hear you haven't been too much for the vegetables lately. Does a carrot for a cookie seem like a fair trade?"

But in the few minutes between the time Susan left and I carried in the tea, Mrs. Rinaldi had left the earth. I set the tray down on a side table.

Her head was lolled back against the headrest of the rocker, her mouth slack enough to show her dentures, the gums an unnatural pink. I put my ear down to her mouth and felt nothing and heard nothing. No breath, no sound.

"No," I said softly, as if I might disturb her.

I wiped my hands down over my face, feeling a loss that outweighed the woman's presence in my life. One more piece of my past, my history, gone. It was a selfish thought, but in a moment like this, your nature shows.

Susan rushed back in the door as if someone were chasing her, fear paling her face. She stopped short when she saw my expression, Mrs. Rinaldi's slackening body in the chair. Her sneakers squeaked on the hardwood floor.

"No." She stepped over Mrs. R's outstretched legs and touched two fingers to the side of the woman's thin neck. "Just like that?"

I nodded, cramped by grief.

Susan stepped over to the old black phone on the side table.

"There's been a death," she said, when someone finally answered. "There isn't any hurry."

* * *

It took a surprisingly short time for the EMTs to show up, pronounce what Susan and I already knew about Mrs. Rinaldi's state, and take her body away. They were polite and respectful.

It was late morning before we were done. Susan and I looked, but found no next-of-kin notification, and I knew I was going to have to take care of burying Mrs. R.

I locked the door of the apartment behind me, thinking about how to set up a memorial. Susan had stayed with me the whole time, for which my shaky self was grateful.

"When you came running in," I said, "before you knew she was dead. Did something happen? Bad news from Oregon?"

I selfishly hoped they'd told her not to come back, that there was no job for her. I wanted her to stay even more now, with me. Mrs. Rinaldi's death underlined how empty my life was of friends, even those at a second or third remove. Without the grounding effect of a real relationship, I might slip back into places and practices I thought I'd left behind.

We climbed the stairs and stopped outside the door to what would forever be Henri's apartment to me. Hers now, for the moment. She pushed the door, unlatched, open wide.

"I was madder than hell," she said. "Until I realized you weren't the kind of creepy landlord who played tricks like that. Misusing master keys?"

She was trying to make light of something, and not succeeding.

"What happened? And no, I'm not weird enough to break in. Unless I thought..." I gestured down the stairs. "Something like that happened."

She nodded. I hoped she believed me.

"Then you have to see this."

She led me back to the bedroom, which still held the masculine flavor of her father's occupancy. On top of the bedspread, arranged as if on a body, were a filmy bright blue bra and panties set, as if Susan had been deciding what to wear. Nothing too unusual about that, except that the underpants were pinned to the bed with a long thin knife, right through the lacy fabric of the crotch.

41

"It's not just nerves, is it?" Burton was doing his best to control his irritation. This was a side of Marina he thought she'd conquered: the worrying, the indecision, the self-flagellation. The not telling him what the real problem was. "We've got plenty of time to resolve things."

The wedding was scheduled for late March, during Marina's vacation from the culinary institute, also when Burton could take some time off without crippling the division. Homicides usually fell off during Boston's frozen winters.

"It doesn't feel right," she said. "Nothing does. For a while, I felt good, and now I don't."

"Something I did? Or said?"

She shook her head firmly.

"It's me, Daniel. Not you. It's Carmen, it's Rasmussen being killed. It's all the chaos."

"Carter," he said thoughtfully. "So there was more there than you let on."

She wiped her eyes. He saw no tears.

"I don't know. I didn't realize. Maybe if he hadn't died, it wouldn't bother me so much."

"Good enough." He rose from the banquette, leaving his lunch untouched. "You'll let me know what you decide, yes?"

Outside the restaurant, he stopped and leaned against the brick front of the building, opened and shut his smarting eyes. He'd sensed something was wrong, but hoped it was temporary. He understood one aspect of it, because of his work. When you lost someone you cared about by violence, your relationship with them came to a screaming halt in a moment. All the unshared stories, the actions not taken, were consigned to an emotional trash bin, never to be seen again. The cut-off was final and terrible, and nothing healed it completely, even time. It didn't mean he had to like it.

His phone buzzed. He cursed it, cursed his job, cursed his own state that wouldn't let him do what he knew he should, walk back into the restaurant and tell the woman he loved they would do whatever they needed to do, together, to get past where she was.

He shook his head, took out the phone, and thumbed the Answer button.

"Burton."

"Martines. Where are you?"

"Scheduled day off, boss." He felt like working now, as long as no one new had died.

"I've got something that looks a little wrong. I need you there. You remember Mrs. Miller?"

Kaylen Miller, the slim, regal woman so worried about her daughter's fate in New Orleans.

"Yes."

Martines gave him an address in Mattapan.

"The patrolman, god bless him, decided he was a detective, and pronounced it as suicide. But you need to go."

He felt a pinch where his liver was and wished he'd eaten his lunch.

"OK. I'm on the way."

42

"It'll be a lot safer if you move in with me for a bit," I said. "Your doors were locked, right?"

She nodded, yanked the knife out of the mattress, and handed it to me, wadded up the ruined underwear and threw it in a wastebasket. She was never someone with a lot of fear, but this had shaken her. She was pale and seemed to have shrunk.

"I don't understand," she said. "Who'd want to intimidate me?"

I felt guilty for not saying it to her, but this had to be the result of my poking around Rasmussen Carter's death.

"It could be directed at me," I said. "But I doubt it."

"That's bullshit." She walked away, sneakers rubbing the wooden floor.

I turned over the knife in my hand, folded the blade back in until it clicked shut, then pressed the button that opened it again. This was not a cheap article. The steel of the blade was chased with depictions of a fox and bunches of grapes, the handle a yellowed bone with silver rivets. It was a weapon, not a junky toy, and I wondered who'd wanted to frighten Susan and me so much he'd left it behind.

She stood in the center of the living room, her arms folded across her chest.

"You know goddamned well what this is about, Elder." Her face was livid. "Someone's using the connection between you and me to back you off of whatever you're doing."

I felt like shit. The fact I hadn't intended any of this meant nothing. As had happened more than once before, my actions dragged someone innocent into my troubles. Only in this case, it was a woman I loved.

"I didn't mean for it to happen," I said. "But you're probably right."

Contempt curled her upper lip.

"That doesn't matter, does it? If this is the outcome?"

She had me cold there.

"My apartment is secure. I don't feel safe with you staying in yours."

I'd put in double locks and an alarm system last year, during the Olympics thing.

The smoldering look was anger-fire, nothing pleasant.

"If this is some trick of yours to get me to move in…"

The fact that she didn't believe me put me over the edge.

"Your choice," I said. "Pack a bag for one night. I'll get a locksmith in the morning and double up the locks on your apartment and the ground floor door."

She stared at me, as if deciding whether to believe me or go to a hotel. She opened a hall closet and pulled out a leather duffle, already packed.

"I may be staying overnight, but I'm goddamned if I'm going to sleep with you."

My anger spilled over. I started for the door.

"I'll give you a set of keys. Come and go as you like."

She deadpanned me, not making a sound except to sniff as I locked the door to her apartment behind us: horse, barn door. I got it. And she sulked behind me all the way up the stairs, only bumping into my back when I stopped dead on the landing. The door to my apartment was ajar.

43

I pushed Susan to the far side of the foyer, away from the door. My heart kicked like a tom-tom and blood roared in my ears. I was still angry at the blatant threat to her, and so I didn't do what would have been smarter, which was call the police. I'd been in fights before, and while I didn't love them, I'd learned not to freeze.

I was assuming whoever was inside was the person who'd cut up Susan's underwear. They'd had to break in to get into my place. My unvarying habit was to lock the door, even if I were only walking downstairs to get the newspaper.

Sounds of breaking glass from the living room. I tipped the door farther open with my knuckles and hoped whoever it was—burglar, vandal—hadn't found the .38 pistol I kept in my bedside table.

I still held the switchblade, pushed the button to open it. I could wave it, at least, maybe scare whoever it was. The snick of the mechanism echoed in the silent moment. I felt the intruder stop and listen.

"Police are on their way," I barked. "You've got about two minutes to get your ass out of here. And leave your booty behind."

Booty? I winced.

"Thievery is the least of your problems, Mr. Darrow." The voice from the darkness was deep, cultured. Familiar.

I stood in the doorway, shielded by the door.

"I've come to remind you that nothing that happened at the Greenwood is any of your business. I killed Mr. Carter because he would not let go."

I was absorbing what he said and forming an answer when a dark bulk rushed at me out of the shadows. I braced myself, got my hands up, and felt the shock in my arm when the assailant ran right onto the knife in my hand. I felt a slow meaty impact as the blade plunged into soft tissue, then a gritty scrape—against bone, maybe. My wrist wrenched badly, sending an electric pain up my arm.

Warm fluid coated my hand. I released the knife and stepped aside, letting the body fall to the carpet on the landing. All I could see from my angle was long, well-groomed gray hair, and the back of a green wool jacket. I had a very good idea who I had stabbed. Edward Dare made a low coughing sound. One heel slammed into the floor, twice, and his breath rattled in his throat.

44

"You know damn well this was murder," Kaylen Miller said to Burton as he sat in the bare rectilinear parlor of the neat house in Mattapan.

He was sitting on what might have been the least comfortable couch he'd ever known. The paramedics were long gone, carrying Lily Miller's body out with them, and her mother was holding herself upright with obvious effort.

Burton thought he'd seen all the possible reactions to suicide and murder, but Mrs. Miller had a unique ability to balance her tears and her anger with a rigid control of what she was saying. And, yes, he was angry, too, but not sure at whom.

"How do you mean?"

Lily, Kaylen Miller's only daughter, had composed herself on the bed after taking the pills, wearing a black T-shirt with a gold fleur-de-lis on the front and a pair of white linen pants. Rolled up in her hands was the sheet music for a jazz tune, "Misty," as if making a comment on her decision.

"Detective Burton." Kaylen's facial skin looked loose, as if her bones were eroding from within. He had the fanciful idea only the power of grief kept her upright, that if she let go of that, she might collapse.

"My girl was about as innocent as a child of nineteen could be. She was a star in her studies, she sang in the church choir—did you know she'd been accepted into a Berklee program?"

He did not, and that made him feel worse. That was Elder's world more than his, but he understood what it meant. He was starting to hate the fact that he only learned about the lives of victims after they died. How many times had he thought he might like to get to know someone whose lifeless body lay before him?

"I did not."

Though there was nothing he could do for this woman in an official way, he would sit and listen to her for as long as she needed. He owed her that much.

"Why did this happen, Daniel? Can I call you that? Why would she do that?"

Her voice rose toward breaking at the end of her question, but it did not shatter.

Burton did not know Lily's answer to that. Frank Vinson, Edward Dare, maybe even Antoinette Bordaine, owned some of this guilt. But he shook his head. He was the only ear here today.

"It was abuse, you know." She was matter of fact about it now. "Lily was not beaten or hurt, no. But her spirit, her loveliness, they were stolen from her, along with her dream." The tears broke through. "Whoever did this to her. He needs to be punished."

Something they could agree on, then. He wondered how much Kaylen knew about Frank Vinson, how Lily had come to be in New Orleans. How much had Lily confided in her mother before she decided on her choice?

He sat with his hands tucked between his knees. When he was sure she wanted him to speak, that it was his turn, he did so reluctantly.

"If I've learned anything in my work, it's that balance never returns after something like this. We like to think the world works in mysterious ways, that for a loss, there's a gain." He shook his head. "Things change, but they almost never return to what they were."

He believed the world was indifferent to human problems, but he didn't want to say that to her baldly. All someone could do in a situation like this was endure, hold themselves together long enough for the pain to fade a little, and to let life back in.

"I know." She pushed a tear from the corner of her eye. "And I hope you know, when I put pressure on you to solve this murder, today, tomorrow, a year from now, if that's what it takes? It's love speaking, understand? For my daughter's sake. Not hate, but love."

His bosses wouldn't allow him slack in investigating a suicide, but her words were as much of a reason as he needed.

"I believe Lily's situation has something to do with another case I'm working on," he said. "I will tell you that I don't leave people behind."

She lifted an eyebrow as if skeptical of his pronouncement. He saw the energy powering her anger desert her, her shoulders slump, her maintained calmness crumble.

"I think it's time for you to go now," she said. "Thank you for your concern. Consider it motivation. We will talk again."

That promise lodged in his mind as he walked down the flagstone path to his vehicle, as if he needed more motive to untangle this mess and afflict the perpetrators responsible.

45

"No, I'm not giving you this case." Martines was as firm as Burton had ever seen, as if the bureaucrat had grown a skeleton. "I know the two of you are friends."

Burton had rushed in to the precinct when he heard.

"Not my point, Lou. I'm positive this is connected to the Deal-Jones case."

Martines made a sour face every time Burton said Alfonso's surname, probably at the complication of the hyphen.

"I don't care." Martines fingered the chest pocket of his white shirt. He was in a nicotine deprival period, which always made him pissy. "If I'm a surgeon, I don't operate on my own heart. Am I right?"

That was assuming he had one. Burton gave ground, for now.

"But it looks like self-defense, right? Nobody's thinking about arresting him?"

"You know that's not up to me," Martines snapped. "I doubt it, though. His witness backs the story. And the guy had already trashed his apartment. Almost like he was looking for something."

Martines looked at him suspiciously.

"I have to be sure Dim-Sum doesn't short-arm this. Because if it is who I think it is, it's connected to my case."

Jon Demeter, the detective nominally assigned, had a tendency to let his assumptions dictate what evidence was important, not the other way around.

"I'm not going to dignify that with an answer. Come into my office."

Which was as good as an answer, as far as Burton was concerned. He'd have to bird-dog the man.

He followed Martines inside and closed the door, expecting to get chewed out. Instead, Martines handed him a slim folder.

"Victim's name is Edward Dare. Ring a bell?"

"Shit." While he was concerned for Elder's state of mind, this was a solid link to Alfonso's murder. And maybe Rasmussen's. "It is connected, then. This is the guy who pimps for the New Orleans gangster I was telling you about. The one who lured Lily Miller? I like him for the Deal-Jones murder."

Martines flicked him a dark look, as if feeling manipulated.

"Dim-Sum... Demeter's not going to like it," he said.

Burton made a farting sound with his lips.

"He'll be overjoyed. He's keeping his effort level low until next March."

Martines frowned. Was he really that clueless about the men he managed?

"When he retires," Burton said.

Martines took back the folder.

"You can explain it to him then. That it's connected to a case already on the board."

Chickenshit.

"Sure. Where's Darrow?"

Blank look. Jesus.

"The citizen who was defending himself?"

"Conference Room B."

The nice interrogation space, the one they used for interviews with children, rape victims, anyone who didn't need leaning on. Burton turned to go, noticing the broken cigarettes in Martines's ashtray.

"You ought to get some air freshener in here, Lou. It must be like a diabetic standing out in front of a bakery, inhaling the exhaust."

"Burton." Martines whip-cracked his voice. "No favors, right? Straight and narrow."

He nodded.

"No other way, Lou."

186

* * *

Burton looked at his old friend through the one-way glass for a moment. Elder looked hollowed-out, shrunken, old as a grandfather. His sparse blond hair stuck up in all directions, and his shirt was misbuttoned. He stared directly into the mirror, his eyes mapped with red capillaries, the terrible route of his emotional state against the whites. He lifted his chin, as if he knew someone was watching, and nodded.

"Where's Susan?" was his first question when Burton stepped into the room. "Is she all right?"

An open toy box in the corner spilled colored foam blocks. A poster on the wall extolled the need to limit screen time to an hour a day. The room felt more like a doctor's office than an interrogation suite.

Burton kicked himself. He should have checked.

"I'll check on her. She wasn't injured?"

"Neither one of us was. Only that poor bastard I killed."

Burton raised his hand to stop the flow of words.

"Someone read you your rights?"

Elder nodded miserably.

"Very first thing. The whole thing should be cut and dried, though. Self-defense, right?"

He winced at the unintended pun. Burton told himself to treat this as if he didn't know the man.

"Tell me exactly what happened."

Elder took a deep breath and laid his hands on the table. Dried blood stained the folds of his knuckles, wedged under the cuticles of his fingernails. Burton pushed a plastic box of disinfectant wipes at him.

"Someone broke into Susan's apartment while we were… downstairs. To leave her a message, apparently." He described the bizarre scene with her underwear. "He must have thought we were out of the building."

"Taking care of Mrs. Rinaldi."

Elder raised his eyebrows.

"I get the EMT reports when something happens at your address. So you were already angry when you headed up the stairs?"

Elder shook his head.

"Scared shitless when I saw my door open."

Burton rolled his wrist. Tell it.

"He confessed to killing Rasmussen Carter." Elder's voice strained. "Then he rushed me."

"And you stabbed him."

His friend's face torqued.

"I didn't even realize the knife was in my hand. I put up my hands to stop him, and he ran right into it."

His voice shook and the tears threatened to spill over. The pain Elder felt now was nothing compared to what he'd have to live with later. Killing someone, even in self-defense, would be with him forever.

"Easy, my friend," Burton said. "I doubt like hell anyone's going to give you legal grief over this."

But it was not the law's effect on Elder he worried about, so much as his taking on the weight of killing someone. Nothing ever lifted the stain of that guilt completely. Not even time.

46

"I'd had a drink," I said to Susan. "Even if it was only the one. Maybe if I hadn't?"

Her reply was quick and severe.

"I was there, Elder. You did not murder that man. He practically threw himself onto the knife."

What she could not know was the moment of sheer berserker rage I'd felt when Dare rushed me, how I'd shoved the blade forward into his body when we collided. Self-defense, sure, but in the moment, I was happy to kill him.

We'd taken a room in the Marriott downtown, not too far from the library and Copley Square. The police would not let me back into my apartment until the forensic people were finished, which could be days, even if Burton pushed. And neither of us wanted to camp out in Susan's apartment. It wouldn't be any quieter or any more anonymous.

I sat in the room's desk chair with Susan behind me, her strong fingers digging into the locked-down muscles of my trapezius and neck.

"I know this sounds a little hypocritical, considering. But maybe you should have a drink. One. If it would calm you down."

I held down my nausea, which surfaced every time I realized I'd killed Edward Dare. Violence had brushed up against me often enough when I hung around with Burton, but I'd never had such a direct relationship with it. If I'd been prone to clichés, I would have said it would change me forever.

"Strictly medicinal, right?" I tried to smile, but suddenly I was awash in tears, my cheeks hot and wet.

Susan came around in front of me and knelt. I didn't deserve her sympathy, but she held me until the storm passed.

"I'm going to have to do something about this." I walked out of the bathroom, blotting my face with a hand towel. "I don't know what, but I have to make up for it somehow."

Susan shook her head. She'd changed into a long emerald-green T-shirt and lay on the bed, propped by pillows.

"I don't think it works that way, and neither do you. Eye-for-an-eye in reverse somehow? Let us not forget the man was a pimp and a gangster. And a would-be drug dealer."

What was useful in my conversation with Burton was that we agreed the two deaths—Carter and Deal-Jones—were connected. We didn't know the motive for Carter's, other than what Dare had shouted at me, but that would come.

"Besides, bringing back the balance to the world is Burton's job." She patted the bed beside her. "I know you don't think you can sleep, but tomorrow, as we optimists like to put it, is another day. Come sit with me."

I climbed onto the too-soft mattress and arranged myself beside her. She wrapped her arms around my shoulder and gently forced me down, so my head lay in her lap. I knew I wouldn't sleep, but I concentrated on lengthening my breath, clearing my mind. My rational sense would deal with my responsibility for what had happened, but it would take my emotions a while to catch up.

47

"You are not fucking going to New Orleans," Martines snarled. "There's no need. And no budget. The entire case took place right here in Boston."

Burton knew it was a long shot, but he had to play it. For Elder's sanity and for his own sense of completion.

"We don't have a motive."

Martines loomed in Burton's cubicle entrance like an angry bear.

"Dare confessed to Darrow that he killed Rasmussen Carter," Burton said. "But he had no reason to. Carter didn't try and keep him from luring Lily Miller away. And it was Deal-Jones who stabbed Carter that night, remember."

"Burton. You know as well as I do, we don't do motive here— least important leg of the stool. Facts: Dare confessed to killing Carter. Dare is dead. Carter is dead. Case is closed. By facts."

"That doesn't say who did Deal-Jones, though." Burton reined in his growing irritation.

"Carter. Obviously. You know what your trouble is, Dan?" Martines leaned into the cube. "You indulge yourself too much."

Burton stared at his superior. He supposed he had to listen to whatever the Lieutenant wanted to get off his chest. Unless he wanted to quit right now.

"No, really. It isn't enough to do your job—which you do very well, by the way. No one's arguing that. But everything has to be a fucking crusade with you. Why can't you accept what's happened and move on?"

"You have to ask that? Lieutenant?" He leaned hard on the title.

All this time, he'd been hoping he was wrong about Martines, that he was more than the political animal he appeared, the manipulator of budgets and schedules, without much feel for the human side of the work. His patience with that notion was worn out.

"Because if we don't know the whole story." Burton was as patient as if explaining to a rookie. "If we close a case without knowing it all? How many times might a murderer skate?"

Martines shook his head.

"You know, they warned me about you when I was assigned here." He reached for his empty shirt pocket and frowned.

"The fuck does that mean?"

Martines puffed up his chest, as if it might make him look stronger. "That you've always considered yourself a force of one. Your own little homicide department."

Even in anger, Burton could smile at that. Whether he got it or not, Martines had articulated a homicide detective's prime directive: you don't dilute your concern for a victim with worry about how much it cost or where it took you.

"Only in the sense that someone's got to talk for the dead, Lou. Seriously. All that other bullshit? That's your job."

Martines flared at having his professional life called bullshit. He shook his head.

"What you don't see," he said, "is how that leaves you out on a limb. Unprotected."

"Never needed protection," Burton said. Certainly not from a bean counter. "If I do my job."

Martines nodded.

"Don't be surprised if a change is coming, Daniel. For you, I mean."

48

I could not get myself to sleep, while Susan snored softly beside me. In a perverse way, I was proud I couldn't, that my brain and body both realized I'd done something elemental, that my existence on the earth from here on in was altered. I would never be the person I'd been before I killed Edward Dare.

I climbed down off the bed and paced the room. I would have made myself a cup of coffee, but the in-room machine was one of those cheap plastic makers with the pre-made coffee sachets, undrinkable. I slipped into my pants and shirt and sat down at the desk to pull my socks on.

"What?" Susan spoke from the darkness, wakened either by a dream or my moving around.

"Nothing." I grabbed my car keys, a room card, and a jacket. "Going for a walk."

"Mmaazzz." She agreed and was quiet again.

In the lobby, I checked the clock, thinking it must be early morning by now, but it was only ten forty-five. Because I used to drink in bars in this neighborhood, I knew where to park my car so I didn't have to pay. The alley around the corner and behind the garage across the street was lit with a single feeble yellow bulb, but my car was still there. Unticketed.

I turned on the engine and shivered until the heat started blowing. I had no idea where to go, except that I wanted to be moving, escaping from my thoughts. I dropped the Volvo into gear and backed out of the alley onto Exeter Street.

Boston was never the all-day, all-night town New York was,

which was one of its charms. Even tonight, a weekend, the streets were relatively empty, except for the bars and clubs the students frequented.

Driving around my city calmed me down, and as I drifted over toward the South End, I saw how much more gentrified the neighborhood was becoming, a long way from where it had been when I acquired the Esposito. I doubted I could afford to live there now, even if I sold the building I owned on Comm. Ave. I wasn't going to spend my father's money on real estate.

The fancy new door of the Greenwood appeared to the right, and a parking space ten feet down the curb made me feel as if I ought to take it, if only to acknowledge my luck. I hadn't planned to head here, but most of what had happened seemed to center on the place. And as Susan suggested, maybe a drink would calm me down.

For a Saturday night, the bar was not doing the kind of business it should. The lights were up higher than I would have run them and only a half dozen tables were occupied. What would have worried me if it was still my bar was that I didn't recognize any of the customers. None of them were the neighborhood folks who'd patronized the Esposito. They looked like semi-dressed up suburbanites, in from the hinterlands for a night on the town. The equivalent in New York of bridge crossers from New Jersey. A little Neil Diamond, a cocktail or two, and home to relieve the sitter by eleven, congratulating themselves for living the night life. I almost headed back up the stairs.

The reason I didn't was that Baron Loftus saw me and raised a hand. He was slouched behind the bar, a sour expression pulling at his face. He wore a blue-striped shirt, for fuck's sake, and the bow tie tonight was printed with tiny replicas of SpongeBob SquarePants. Too much for me—he probably had a fedora on the rack out back.

Which was dark, the kitchen lights turned off, except the red Emergency Exit sign at the far end of the hallway by the fire exit.

"No chance of a burger?" I nodded toward the kitchen.

"Cook quit." He rolled a toothpick across his lips as if he'd seen it in a movie. "We weren't doing that much food business anyway."

I felt a pang at everything he'd done to ruin what I'd worked so hard to build. I tried not to wince at the bubblegum pop coming out of the speakers as I looked around.

"Doesn't look like you're doing much bar business, either."

His skinny shoulders rose and fell.

"You're here, aren't you?"

I shucked my jacket and hung it on a hook under the bar. He stared expectantly.

"Macallan 18," I said. "Water back."

He free-poured the Scotch with an accuracy that would have impressed me if I hadn't seen the line edged into the shot glass. He pushed it forward.

"On the house. A little lagniappe for the former owner."

I eyed the amber liquid warily. It was Sunday morning by now and I had been allowing myself that single drink a day. But I'd been doing it alone, trying to make it ceremonial, without anything to make it feel like a social act.

Loftus registered my hesitation, but didn't know what to make of it. I left the shot glass where it was, sipped some water.

"How's your aunt?"

His face showed a phony concern.

"Sweetie? Not well," he said. "She's been ill for quite some time, but she seems to have taken a turn."

I recalled my conversation with the feisty old woman, how she represented a big part of jazz history to me. I wished some bright young thing from Berklee would visit her, try and collect those stories.

"Sorry to hear that." I turned the whiskey glass in my fingers. "It was a pleasure spending time with her."

Loftus tugged at the ends of his bow tie, as if to be sure they were aligned.

"Just try being family," he said. "Her money put me in this place. And don't think she doesn't let me hear about it every day."

Nothing for me to say to that. I picked up the shot glass and sniffed the whiskey. Loftus looked as if he wondered if I were going to drink it at all.

"Are you still booking acts for that Isaac guy?" He wiped the bar on either side of me unnecessarily.

I hadn't talked to Isaac since yesterday, when we'd been at Lily Miller's house. I hoped the young woman was doing better.

"Off and on. Why?" I took a sip of the whiskey and welcomed it back.

Loftus reached under the bar and pulled out an envelope, stamped and postmarked, addressed to Isaac Belon, c/o The Greenwood, Mercy Street, Boston.

"This came here for him. I don't know why he'd be using me as an address. If you see him?"

"Sure. I'll give it to him." I tucked the envelope into my jacket.

Loftus leaned against the back bar, as if he had all night to chat. No one was pressing him for drinks, so maybe he did. Neil Diamond slipped into "Cracklin' Rosie" and the couple at the far table by the stairs started swaying back and forth. The whole bar seemed to be running in slow motion.

"You're some kind of detective," he said.

I took another small bite of the Macallan, felt the heat and the light, put the glass down. I was very pleased with my self-control.

"Not really. I've gotten involved in a couple of situations, is all."

"But you're friends with that cop."

I cocked my head. We were getting closer to whatever he was asking.

"Friends is a little strong. We get thrown together."

Silence built between us, an uncomfortable one. I took another minuscule sip.

"This really isn't my thing, you know," Loftus said. "The bar, the music. I was trained in art history."

It was evident he didn't take running the Greenwood seriously.

"It's not for everybody."

"Sweetie thinks I'm waiting for her to die."

Whoa—did I all of a sudden look like Dr. Phil?

"You know she's rich as a bastard, don't you? Married into it thirty, forty years ago."

"Uh, Baron…"

"And lucky me, I'm her only living relative."

He sounded so bitter, I finally figured it out.

"So she's got you whipped into running the place for her? Until what? She dies? Sells it?"

He nodded. I sank the rest of the shot and stood up to go.

"Sorry to hear that. It's a tough enough business, without feeling like you're doing something you don't want to do."

"She'd let you run the place, if you wanted to come back."

"Baron. I used to own the joint. Even if I needed a job, I have no interest in being a manager."

He snatched the empty shot glass and the water glass, as if shutting off a drunk.

"Make sure your pal gets that envelope, all right?"

He slotted the glasses into a dishwasher tray at the far end of the bar, then stood there with his arms crossed, staring out into the unpopulated darkness in the corners of his bar.

* * *

I drove back to the hotel, trying to parse the strange conversation. The drink did distract me from my guilt, momentarily. I thought it was possible that I could accept my own responsibility at some point, that what I had done would not poison my life. I'd done what I could for Marina, and at some cost to myself. It didn't feel as if I were done.

Back in the hotel room, I hadn't been missed. Susan still curled under the covers, and when I crawled in naked beside her, she pushed her warm bottom back at me as we spooned. Eventually, my mind exhausted itself enough to sleep, though my dreams were fitful cartoons of blackness and blood, the killing of Edward Dare perched on my shoulder like a dark bird that had adopted me.

49

Burton frowned at the lack of security as he strode in through the lobby of the Marriott. The hotel had repurposed one of the old mansions in this part of the city, and the check-in desk was tucked in back, out of sight of both the street doors and the elevators. He wondered if a city building inspector had ever been inside.

Carrying the shopping bag from Au Bon Pain, he exited the elevator on the fourth floor and checked the numbers. He rapped on the door for four twenty-five with the back of his knuckles, heard the cover of the peep hole slide open, and grinned.

"Wakey, wakey," he said as Elder opened the door.

His friend looked irked, which Burton didn't understand until he heard the shower running in the bathroom. Elder wore a pair of silky green undershorts with black badgers on them and a plaid flannel shirt.

"That's a good look on you," Burton said.

Elder took the bag, looking as if he wanted to push Burton back out the door.

"If there's no coffee in here, you're a bigger asshole than I think."

Burton walked through the room to an armchair by the window, not before catching a flash of pink flesh through the open bathroom door. Elder reached and closed it with his foot.

"Nice night?" Burton looked at him innocently.

"None of your fucking…"

"Lovely night." Susan emerged from the steamy bathroom wrapped from neck to ankles in one of the hotel's terry bathrobes, a towel turbaned around her head. "And room service breakfast delivered, to boot."

Burton had never been one of her fans. He'd seen how her leaving the first time crushed Elder, as well as all the back-and-forth across the country, where neither of them seemed able to make up their mind what to do. It made his current troubles with Marina look minor.

"You're welcome," he said.

She dipped a curtsy.

Burton sat down, crossed one leg over the other. He'd had enough coffee already this morning.

"Your apartment is cleared," he said. "I leaned on the crime scene people to finish up fast."

Elder saluted him with a chocolate croissant.

"And the cleaners will be in this afternoon."

Susan shook her head.

"I am never going back into that building." She shuddered and the tie on the robe loosened. She yanked it tight.

Elder nodded.

"Except, Mrs. Rinaldi," he said. "We need to find out her next of kin. Clean out her place."

"Shit. You're right."

Burton knew Elder's tenant had died, but that didn't have anything to do with this.

"That's all I got." He grabbed a pastry from the bag. "Just wanted to bring you up. Elder, where will you be later?"

He would have covered this now, if Susan weren't here.

Elder read that, nodded.

"Mr. Giaccobi's? Eleven o'clock?"

"Then."

And Burton slipped out the hotel room door into the sound-dead hallway, having accomplished what he needed. Elder was not, at least at the moment, immobilized by his guilt.

50

I dropped Susan off in front my building. She got out reluctantly. "Stay in Mrs. Rinaldi's apartment for a while. You don't have to go upstairs. See if you can find any family information. I'll pick you up for lunch."

She shot me a tight-lipped smile and slammed the door of the car, headed for the stairs without a word. I shook my head, but I waited until she was inside before I put the Volvo in gear and drove off. I had a chore to do before I met Burton.

Isaac was renting an apartment on the edge of Roxbury, one of four in a converted Victorian. The block was still sketchy. A couple of the buildings had eyeless plywood windows, one ranch house with a '57 Chevy sitting up on blocks in the side yard. The overall effect was chain link fence, grilled doors and windows, and security lights up in the eaves. I expected to hear pit bulls barking.

Isaac's building, on the other hand, was painted a tasteful dark-green with plum-colored trim, a color scheme that reminded me of the Painted Ladies on Alamo Square in San Francisco. The lawn was clipped close, the flowerbeds neat and mulched, and the Adirondack chairs on the porch were hardwood, barely weathered.

I pressed the button next to a single name: Isaac. I supposed if you didn't know which Isaac you were looking for, he wasn't going to help you out.

A scratchy voice rained down from above the door. I looked up at an all-weather speaker.

"It's Elder, Isaac. Need to talk."

"Uh… Sure."

The door lock buzzed and clicked and the door kicked itself open. I stepped inside and started up a long central staircase. The hallway was aggressively empty: no bicycles, tricycles, recycling bins, or trash. The air smelled like lemon polish and tea. Someone was keeping up standards for the block. Either that, or this was the first instance of gentrification for the neighborhood.

"Elder. My man."

Isaac stood in the carpeted hallway outside his apartment, a mug in hand. He was barefoot, in a pair of black cotton slacks and an unbuttoned white linen shirt with thin blue stripes.

"Did we have something going on I forgot about?"

I shook my head and handed over the envelope Baron Loftus had given me the night before.

"Special delivery."

He scrunched up his eyebrows and took the thick square envelope of cream-colored paper, looked at his name on the outside. He was clearly wondering why I was delivering it when I could have addressed it and stuck on a stamp. But I had an intuition that I needed to know what was inside.

Also, as I was driving around the city, I realized I needed to keep busy, stay in motion for a while, occupy my brain and body with something other than the visceral sense-memory of the knife in my hand sliding into Edward Dare's belly, the darkness and chaos that had created in my brain.

"I didn't know if it was important," I said. "Someone handed it to me last night."

"Who's it from?"

"I don't know. But I got it at the Greenwood. From Loftus?"

He looked more confused.

"Come in. I've got coffee on and I know you won't turn that down."

I understood why he wasn't too happy for company when a statuesque black woman, ten years his senior and naked except for a towel around her waist, walked into the living room.

"Who was it, Isaac?" Then she saw me. "Whoops!" And she

turned around, not in a terrible hurry, and walked back into what I assumed was the bedroom.

Watching the muscles in her back flex and loosen, I felt jolted by something sad, less lust than regret. I believe that was the moment I realized I'd lost Susan all over again.

Isaac was distracted, ignoring the woman, and I wanted to advise him that most women I'd known would tolerate many things, but being ignored was not one of them. It was none of my business, though. Maybe it was a one-night stand.

He picked up a letter opener from a small walnut secretary I happened to know was 18th Century Chippendale—there'd been one like it in my house growing up. It was worth as much as the whole building. I looked at Isaac differently then. Like a jerk, I'd assumed he was a ghetto kid on the make for something better. It was a lovely example of an object changing your perspective of a human being.

Inside the envelope was a small stiff card, the same color as the envelope, the size of a wedding invitation. I saw black cursive. Isaac frowned as he read it. He tossed the card down on the coffee table and stepped to a laptop sitting on the glass top.

He keyed in some characters. When I moved to see what he was doing, I could see the card.

Evangeline is at home at 2321 Coliseum Street. PLEASE.

The last word, all in capitals, was underlined twice.

Isaac brought up Google Maps and found the address. He pinched his fingers wider on the screen until the street name was visible. The Garden District.

"She's in New Orleans," he said.

We knew that. Or rather, I knew that. Isaac didn't know all the things Burton had told me about Edward Dare and his boss, Frank Vinson.

"What's the address look like?" I said.

He shifted to street view and fiddled with the display to line up the photos around the address. The building was three stories high, a low set of garden apartments with a cast-iron fence around a central courtyard. It looked benign, a lovely place to live, out of place among the mansions around it.

The "PLEASE" had hit me in the chest.

"You think it means she's being held?" Isaac said. Despite how worried he'd been about her yesterday, he didn't sound relieved to know where she was. "In there?"

"I don't think so."

I thought she was more likely a prisoner of her own wishes and desires. Burton had told me the Edward Dare story, how part of his job was supplying suitable out-of-town arm candy for Frank Vinson. Probably, the local women in New Orleans had caught on to his ways.

"But they will likely make it harder for her to leave. Before they want her to, anyway."

"And who's 'they'?" Isaac was too bright not to see I knew more about who might be holding Evvie than he did.

The woman, dressed now in a short burgundy leather skirt and a dark gray top, came out and sat on the couch beside him. I smelled a faint sophisticated perfume, dry and herbal.

"Whachu got there, hon?"

I had the impression she was leaning on the accent, trying to convince me she was something she wasn't. Isaac ignored her, staring at the screen.

"Y'all going to New Awlins?" She wheedled for his attention.

I assumed now she was not a hooker, the way she almost begged for his attention.

She huffed and pushed herself up off the couch when he didn't answer, flashing the tops of her thighs.

He turned to me.

"I don't know. We going to New Orleans, Elder?"

51

"No," Burton said. "No one's going to New Orleans. Not you, not your freaky little friend. This whole thing is too tangled up for it to be safe."

He'd dumped everything he knew about the connection on Elder, including the fact that the organized crime cops in the city were leery of confronting Frank Vinson.

"It's their job, not yours. And if you think stabbing someone in self-defense was a traumatic experience, wait until a couple of thugs do a second-line dance on your head."

What worried Burton most was that Elder wasn't seeing the risk clearly, as if he were some kind of avenging angel on behalf of the young woman. Before, when Elder wound up in the middle of one of these cases, it was, if not accidental, a function of proximity to a victim or a witness. Now, though, he acted like he wanted to sacrifice himself, in the name of helping a young woman he barely knew.

"I get it," Elder said. "I've thought about it."

"Then why take it on yourself?"

Old man Giaccobi's coffee shop was busy for this time of day, just before lunch. It must have been the run of cold, gray weather, people needing a mid-morning caffeine hit. But it was also that Giaccobi had created a neighborhood oasis, not unlike what Elder had had in the Esposito. Maybe once his string with Homicide ran out, this would be the kind of business he might do.

"But if I don't do it, who will?" Elder said. "Your bosses won't let you go. And I'm worried Isaac will go off half-cocked and take it on by himself. You think I'm naive, what do you think he is?"

Burton understood. The kid was barely out of his teens, full of the piss and vinegar a young male had. And yet... he was black. Which meant he might fit in better in places down there than Elder. Assuming he knew how to act.

He erased that thought.

"Look. You remember I know a cop down there?"

Elder turned the tiny white cup over on top of his saucer. A diva shrieked an aria out of a speaker above the restroom door.

"And I remember you told me you weren't sure you trusted her."

"I trust her to do the right thing." He hoped he was right. "This is not a law enforcement issue, unless the girl's being held against her will. My contact could ease in and make sure this Evvie's all right. Would that be good enough for now? Because these are not your Icky Ricky class of gangsters, Elder. These are serious thugs."

He watched Elder cool off, see the sense. He understood Elder thought of the kid as a nephew or something, and that was why he'd been ready to jet off and solve all the kid's problems.

The old man slipped a fresh espresso in front of Elder—Burton smelled the lemon peel—and raised an eyebrow at Burton, who shook his head.

Elder turned his head from side to side, slow and heavy.

"I don't think we have a lot of time. The 'PLEASE.' Remember? And you were the one who told me what happened to that other girl who went down there. Lily? She came back in rough shape."

Burton insisted.

"Don't do anything until I talk to my friend. I'm sure she can organize a wellness check without triggering a gun battle. We'll find out what the situation is before we jump in."

He felt Elder bending toward agreement. Burton hoped he'd overruled the do-gooder gene for now. No cop in his right mind would walk into a situation the way Elder intended without a SWAT team at his back. Was he suicidal all of a sudden?

"What?" Elder said.

"Regardless what Bordaine finds out," the time for sweet reason was past, "you get on a plane heading south and I'll have you picked up at Louis Armstrong the minute you touch down."

Elder looked shocked. Good. Burton worried that throwing up such a hard "No" might make his friend resist automatically. The man could be mulish.

"You say so, Dan."

He detected mock-meek in Elder's tone, but he wasn't going to push it.

"I will talk to Antoinette and have her look into the girl's situation."

"Soon," Elder said.

"Today. I will call her today."

Elder settled into a disgruntled slouch, staring over Burton's shoulder.

"If she—your cop friend—can't get Evvie out of this? I am going. I have a plan. Isaac says he knows some people."

Jesus. Now it was the both of them. Burton rolled his eyes.

"'Some people.' Right. Let's let the professionals do their work. All right?"

Elder leaned over the table and picked up the cup.

"All right," he repeated. "For now. Not that the professionals have been doing such a great job already."

"You think that's what this is all about? What I do? Saving lives and punishing the wicked?" His laugh was rough. "I'm not an angel, pally. My job is facts. Evidence. Building cases. White knighting things is a hell of a lot easier than that."

The silence hardened like concrete. Elder checked the clock over the door and stood up, rattling the crockery.

"Tomorrow, OK? I'll call you. And you'll tell me where we stand."

The coffee shop door banged shut behind him, tinkling the bell. Mr. Giaccobi looked at Burton, who shrugged. And he wondered what that meant, in another way, what Elder had said: where they stood.

52

Burton thought I was out of my zone of competence, thinking about going to New Orleans, but Isaac and I together would present an innocent enough front not to trigger the antennae of the local gangsters. They'd see a blobby middle-aged white guy with thinning hair and a young black kid as civilians, or if not, as an interpretation that had more to do with sex and race than any threat to them. I believed, with the element of surprise, we could slip into the apartment house where she was, talk to Evvie, and get her out, if that's what she wanted.

I stood outside under the awning of Mr. Giaccobi's and regarded the rain sheeting down, wishing my jacket were waterproof. The chime on my phone went off and I welcomed not having to step out into the downpour right away.

"Meet at Gwood? Sweetie wants to talk. BL."

Loftus. I frowned—how had he gotten my number? And what could Sweetie want to talk to me about now? I was all done with what happened to Rasmussen Carter and I hadn't left any open questions. Which is not to say I wasn't interested in what she had to say.

I flagged a cruising cab and ducked into the back seat, gave him the address of the Greenwood.

* * *

A laser-printed paper sign taped over the stained glass window reported that the Greenwood was closed until 6 PM. More evidence Baron Loftus had no idea how to run a tavern. You built customer loyalty in a lot of ways, but the most obvious was never being closed when your customers expected you to be open.

I shook my head. I was doing that a lot lately.

The door was unlocked, which didn't make a lot of sense, either. I walked down the stairs, my soles ringing against the steel risers. The lights were turned very low, except for one bright spotlight on the tiny triangular stage in the corner.

Instrumental jazz flowed from the sound system, a cut above Loftus's usual choices, but still not hard core. As I stepped off the bottom stair, a diminutive figure dressed in a long white evening gown stepped out of the shadows, the white light glinting off the diamonds at her ears and around her neck. The short white hair was slicked back under a sleek cap of feathers, like something Edith Piaf might have worn in the Forties.

The stereo cut out and without a word or a gesture, Sweetie took the standing microphone between her hands and began to sing.

"*Look at me...*"

Her voice cracked, making me think of the Leonard Cohen line about where the light comes in. Listening to her sing "Misty," however creakily, was for me the equivalent of sitting on a stool next to Leonardo Da Vinci while he painted the Mona Lisa, or watching Michelangelo chip out the Pietà. It was virtuoso in idea, even if the imperfections of execution were all too obvious.

She finished the song with the flourish it deserved. I couldn't do anything but applaud, even as I suspected the applause was the whole point.

She blinked in the light, then tottered around to the steps leading down from the stage, not shuffling, but unsteady on her feet. I turned up the house lights and met her at the bottom of the staircase, my arm ready to brace her, if she wanted it.

"Lovely," I said. "I don't believe I've heard the song sung better. Grace and feeling."

She used my forearm to step down, looking pleased.

"Age," she said. "I wouldn't have believed it when I was young.

But it brings you as much as it takes away. And it's always taking something away."

The house lights were crueler to her appearance than the stage spotlight. The evening dress drooped where age had diminished her body at the chest and hips, and the white fabric, satin or silk, bore shadowy stains down near the hem. Her collarbones were delicate as twigs, and the skin of her bare shoulders and chest had the dry crepey look no amount of lotion could ease.

She started for the small table at the end of the bar near the kitchen, her posture straightening as her joints moved and the muscles warmed. I wondered how long she'd waited in the wings to make her appearance, and, too, I wondered what all this drama was in aid of. If we had anything else to say to each other, I couldn't imagine what it would be.

"Come sit with me," she said.

The table bore a fat bottle of Pinch, a blended whiskey I used to drink before I discovered the single malts. I wouldn't have trouble refusing that. Two crystal glasses were crosshatched with cuts so they glittered like ice. She pulled the cork from the bottle.

"Drink with me," she commanded.

I sat down across the table.

"Rather not," I said. "It's nothing personal."

The whole setup felt dangerous, but I was more interested in the fact that the song of the whiskey was not reaching my ears. Was I that much of a snob about Scotch?

"Please."

She poured for both of us. I pulled one of the glasses over to my side of the table, and left it there.

"Thank you. Baron said you wanted to talk to me."

Sweetie shot back the Scotch like a housepainter on a coffee break and poured herself another.

"I used to come in here once in a while," she said. "When you owned it."

That surprised me. I'd have thought I would have recognized her.

"Really? I wish you would have told me."

She shook her head and played with the glass. I smelled the whiskey now, but it smelled wrong, industrial or off in some other way I couldn't define. I started to feel anxious.

"I liked very much what you did with the place, back then." She looked around the room with some disdain. Now I guessed where she was going.

"It was satisfying," I said. "But it was time to move on. Do something different."

"Well, you and your police chum have certainly done that. Can I infer that you're not interested in owning your own establishment again? I could make you a very attractive offer."

"Baron isn't working out, I guess."

She shook her head.

"He doesn't have the heart for it. And I don't like what the place has become."

We agreed on that much at least. And I wondered if the small surge of excitement that the idea gave me was reliable. She was talking about selling the bar back to me, not having me manage it, as Loftus had suggested at first. I had to admit, the freedom of not having the business, being shut of the daily anchor of work, wasn't everything I'd hoped for. I hadn't run back to Planet Drunk again, but I could sense how the formlessness of days might roll over on me.

Yet, I didn't need the money, as I had when I first bought the bar. And I did enjoy getting up in the morning and knowing there was nothing I had to do.

"No, I don't believe he does." I hoped she didn't sense that I liked the idea. "I think I've had my day in this place, though. Your nephew will be fine—he's just learning how hard it is to run a business like this, day to day."

"I wish you would consider it more thoroughly." She drank her whiskey down, all at once. "I do understand that Baron is not up to this particular challenge."

Her voice was harsh, implying many more unhappy days for Loftus, beyond his failure at the bar business. There were days when I was glad not to have any living family.

"But if the idea doesn't grasp you…" she said. "I learned a long time ago not to force myself to work at something I didn't love. Not for long, at least." She poured herself more Pinch. "I was hoping the bar would take for him, but apparently not."

We sat in silence for another minute.

"Well, thank you for the offer. But I think it's time for me to go."

She brought her full attention to bear on me, back up from what felt like a deep reverie. Her aged face showed regret.

"My cigarettes," she said. "They're in the back, in my coat pocket. Would you mind?"

I stood up.

"Back of the door?"

"Yes."

I didn't need to turn on the lights to find my way out back. I walked straight to the coat rack on the back of the door to the supply closet and touched the leather jacket hanging there. The silk lining breathed out a sweet perfume as I plunged my hands into the pockets for the cigarettes.

Which meant both my hands were trapped when someone slammed me hard across the shoulders with a closet rod or a thick broomstick. It cracked on the impact. I went to the floor, feeling the jacket's lining tear as I dragged it down.

The hitter kept swinging. I curled up and rolled away from the blows, my arms tangled in the jacket, fetched up against the cold stainless steel wall of the refrigerator, unable to protect my head.

The impacts moved around—the hitter was methodical about striking wherever I wasn't covering up: slamming, moving, slamming me again in another place. I heard a gasping out breath every time the stick hit. He was putting serious effort into it.

The stick made direct contact with the bone at the point of my shoulder. A shock like lightning went up my arm, which went limp, dead as hanging meat. I tucked it underneath me, out of the way, but that only exposed my back, a larger target. My kidneys took a hit apiece, left then right, and I groaned, deep in my chest, kicked out my legs, made contact, and heard a whispered curse.

That only increased the frenzy. My torso felt like a side of beef being tenderized, but the hitter finally ran out of steam. I realized I was going to survive this.

He—or she?—panted. I struggled out of Sweetie's torn jacket and tried to stand up.

"The fuck?" was all I could manage to say.

The voice bore an accent I couldn't place, elements of the Canadian French I remembered from childhood trips to Nova Scotia, mixed with something southern.

"Best you stick to bartending, cher."

Stunned, bleeding from my nose and mouth, the pain started to come. I didn't have the brainpower to puzzle out who thought I was a threat. All I knew was that whoever it was had not come to kill me, and a craven part of me was grateful enough to want to hug his legs and weep.

"Yes," I said.

"Remember that."

A whoosh of air and a blow landed on the crown of my head that drove me back down onto the floor. In that micro-second before the world went black as death, I believed that was exactly where I was going. The land of the dead.

53

"What do you mean you just found him there?"

Burton felt himself redlining, over-revving, ready to slam this effete little motherfucker up against a wall and bang some answers out of him. He had been attending a memorial for Lily Miller when Marina texted him the news that Elder was in the hospital. He wondered how she'd found out. And he wondered if he was supposed to take it as a message that this was the only communication he'd had with her since last week.

He hadn't looked at the message until after the service, standing on the sidewalk in front of the community center in Mattapan, so he was also feeling guilty about not responding right away, too. The hospital would not let him in to see Elder until later, even when he flashed his badge.

And Loftus was acting too cool for someone in the police eye. He claimed he'd walked into the Esposito—pardon, the Greenwood—to start his day and found Elder unconscious on the floor. He'd done the right things, started first aid for the bleeding, called 911, but Burton sensed he knew much more than he was saying.

"I told you, Detective. I was late today." He arched his eyebrows. "Personal business. When I got here, he was lying in a heap on the kitchen floor."

"The main door was locked? How did he get in?"

Loftus looked impatient.

"He used to own the building, didn't he? It wouldn't surprise me if he had keys."

Burton shook his head. When Elder gave up the Esposito, he gave it up altogether. There was never any talk about going back, getting behind that bar again.

"Then why? What was he doing here, getting the crap kicked out of him?"

Loftus's confusion seemed genuine, though he did tend to whine.

"I told you I don't know. Maybe he got drunk and had an attack of nostalgia."

Burton stiffened. Loftus saw it, backed away, and put the bar between them.

"You can't think I wanted something like this to happen?" The whine spun higher. "I'm on thin enough ice with this place as it is. It's not going to help my reputation if people get mugged here."

Burton had no official standing with respect to this case. The district detectives who'd caught it gave him all kinds of side-eye when he talked to them, not relaxing even after he told them he was the victim's friend. But he and Loftus were alone here, and the bow-tied youngster not only knew why Elder had been beaten, but there was also something he wasn't telling about the murder of Alfonso Deal-Jones.

Loftus's forehead gleamed with a light coat of sweat.

"I do not know how, Loftus, but I am convinced you're responsible for more of this than I know. You need to understand it's not just cops who look out for each other. That man is a friend of mine."

Loftus was one of those inflatable clowns who bounced back after every blow. Burton wasn't making an impression.

"I get it, Detective. I just can't help you. I don't know Mr. Darrow except as the former owner of the bar. And the music thing. Why would someone want to get me in trouble?"

Which did bother Burton. If Loftus hadn't lured Elder down to set him up, who would benefit from implicating him? He wasn't stupid enough to bring Elder here for a beat-down.

And then, what had Elder done to precipitate it? The only reason he was sitting in Mass General was that he'd learned something or done something that threatened someone.

"There are a lot of keys to this place around," Loftus said, out of the blue.

The sudden admission said Loftus was about to dump someone in the shit.

"Yes?"

"Well. The workmen I had in. Plumbers, electricians, painters. And the owner, of course."

"You don't own the place?" Burton had been guilty of an assumption.

"No. No, I'm only the manager."

"Then who owns it?"

"She never comes in here, though. Not when we're closed." Loftus was playing hard to get.

"Who is it?"

"Sweetie," Loftus said. "My aunt. Sweetie Bogan."

54

Burton sat in his Jeep in the hospital parking garage, in no hurry at all to go inside and visit Elder. When he called, the nurse said he was in and out of consciousness. She couldn't guarantee they'd let him in to see him, even if he flashed his badge again. He was procrastinating—he'd never liked hospitals, as a visitor *or* a patient. Then, as he opened the driver's door to get out, his phone rang.

"Burton."

Static, short blips of voice, then he realized the parking structure was interfering with reception. The caller ID read a 504 area code—New Orleans—and he thought it might be news about Evvie, the woman Elder and Isaac were so worried about. He shut the call off, jogged inside to the elevator down to the ground floor, and stepped outside again to redial the number.

"This is Bordaine. That you, Daniel? What happened? You drop your phone in the toilet?"

Burton felt a charge. He was hoping for some good news to bring to Elder.

"I was in a parking garage. What do you have?"

"You owe me," she said. "Bigly, as one of our politicians loves to say. There is nothing more fun than messing up a nice New Orleans fall morning by ruining Frank Vinson's day."

"What? You find the girl?" This could be one of the pieces to the puzzle.

Bordaine sniffed loudly.

"We call them women these days, Burton. And yes, I had one of my people go over to talk to her."

He didn't want to read too much into her tone, but she made it sound as if the whole thing had been easy.

"I still owe you dinner," he said. "Regardless."

"Damn right, *cher*. Look, the girl is fine. And before you back-check me, yes, we did it the usual way, separated her from everyone else, assured her she was safe to talk, even had our psych guy ride along."

A little more than a *pro forma* welfare check, then.

"All good, then." He was relieved.

The Zippo clicked, smoke rushing past the phone at her end.

"Well, from your perspective, anyway. The woman is healthy, no apparent signs she's using anything more complicated than too much facial scrub. More to the point, she seems pretty practical about the deal she made. Frank's gotten her gigs at some of the lesser clubs in town, but legitimate ones."

"Was he there at the time? This Frank guy?"

Bordaine made an exasperated noise.

"Burton. They're both adults. There was nothing I could point to and say, this is illegal. Or even harmful. *I* wouldn't want to spend my nights underneath that fat of a man, but that's mostly a matter of taste."

"No bullshit." He thought about Lily Miller, how the experience had broken her. "You think it's on the level?"

"As level as it's going to be with that boy," she said. "The young woman in question—pretty name, by the way—told me in confidence she thinks she's gotten everything out of the relationship she's going to get." Bordaine gave a husky laugh. "I got the impression she was a little tired of our music scene. It gets nasty."

OK. Here was something tangible he could bring to Elder and his pal, even if Elder wasn't in any shape to head off to the Big Easy at the moment. And if the two of them would get off his back about Evangeline, maybe he could fit the rest of this together and solve the murder of Alfonso Deal-Jones.

"Good enough, I guess." He never celebrated a dead end, but in this case, he was grateful for her help. "I do owe you."

"Burton, look." Bordaine lowered her voice, as if someone might overhear. "I burned some of my cred on this, all right? Best if we don't be in contact for a while."

He played back their previous conversation, his own questions about how straight she was.

"That's fair. Thanks again, though."

And he cut the connection.

Walking into the hospital through the revolving glass doors, he tucked the phone in his pocket and wondered how much he could trust Bordaine's report. She didn't have any reason to lie to him, though, and assuming Evangeline returned to Boston, that would verify her tale.

* * *

Elder was sitting up, or half-lying down, depending on how optimistic your viewpoint was, sucking a straw stuck into something that looked like a coffee milk shake. He seemed awake. The dark blue and purple bruise puffed up the entire left side of his face. It looked like a Phantom of the Opera mask.

Burton felt guilty. As a homicide detective, he rarely encountered physical violence directed at him. It seemed like every time Elder got tangled up in something, he took the brunt. There had been the time Burton was almost stabbed to death on a ballfield.

"Elder."

His friend's eyes were bloody inside, as if the beating had broken a bunch of his capillaries. He set the sippy cup on the tray table and winced.

"I'm fine," he said. "They won't let me out, though."

Burton smirked.

"Yeah. Hospitals suck. I know."

"Wake you up to take a sleeping pill. Crap in a metal pan." He shifted his weight, grimaced. "Did you talk to Sweetie? About who might have done it?"

"Sweetie? Why?"

Elder scoffed.

"You didn't talk to the other detectives? She was there in the Greenwood, trying to sell it back to me. She asked me to meet her. I went out back to get her cigarettes for her and *bam*! This happened."

Burton fumed. He'd asked the district guys to keep him in the loop. They obviously hadn't bothered.

"I'll look into it. What's the prognosis here? You ready to leave?"

Elder shook his head.

"They're watching my liver enzymes or some fucking thing. Make sure I'm not bleeding internally. I could have told them my liver wasn't first-rate. Should be out tomorrow."

Burton guessed he was being optimistic.

"Take this in and think on it, then. Your friend Evangeline? Alive and well in New Orleans. My cop friend down there verified everything's kosher. She'll be back in a week or two."

Elder brightened.

"Good. You tell Isaac?"

"How hard did you get hit? I don't know the kid's last name *or* where he lives. I'll leave that to you."

Elder started to nod, then stopped short as if it hurt.

"He was in this morning."

Burton was feeling the hospital heebie-jeebies. He buttoned up his coat.

"Anything you need?"

Elder grinned weakly.

"Pants and a shirt. And a decent cup of coffee. And tell Susan where I am."

"That much I can do. The latter, I mean. And I'll come by in the morning, see if you need a ride."

Elder nodded, reached carefully for the milk shake.

"Espresso," he said. "Quad shot."

55

Sweetie Bogan, Burton thought as he rode the elevator to the ground floor and left the hospital. The street in front of the doors was jammed with vans and cars picking up and dropping off patients, an ambulance with its lights turning trying to squeeze through, people in pajamas and robes and track suits limping on crutches and walkers, families in formation. A single security guard in a green hi-vis vest stood in the middle of the mess, tweeting his whistle and trying to direct the melee.

Burton nodded as he eeled his way through the crush.

"Hang in there, buddy."

"Bunch of fucking lunatics," the guard said. "They should be glad I'm not armed."

Sweetie Bogan. Burton climbed the stairs in the parking garage and unlocked the Jeep. He'd dismissed the old woman as a suspect, partly because of her age, but more importantly, because of her long relationship with Deal-Jones and the fact that she'd gotten her money back. Had that been a mistake? She wouldn't have been strong enough to beat up Elder.

He pulled out his phone to check messages. Predictably enough, Martines had already texted him three times, each one snarkier than the last, looking for an update before he went into some Very Important Meeting. Burton smiled as he deleted them all. The last message...

He touched the number and the phone dialed it automatically for him.

"Willos." Burton's PBA lawyer.

"It's Burton. Got the text. What's up?"

Willos's voice was low and tight, as if he were in a group.

"Not on the phone. Plough and Stars. One hour."

Burton pursed his lips. These old-line Irish cops were always trying to remind you of their roots.

"Give me a hint."

"There's only one thing you and I have in common, isn't there?"

The phone cut off before Burton could say another word.

* * *

It didn't take that long to drive from Mass General to the Plough and Stars, but he ate up almost fifteen minutes finding a legal place to park. Cambridge had always been tight, in more ways than one, but there was so much money in the city now, the crowding was worse than he'd ever seen.

He found a semi-legitimate spot in a loading zone near a defunct produce market, an eyeless brick building behind a high chain-link fence. A sign stuck in the ground announced more condos coming.

He locked up and started up the street for the bar on the corner. A folding chalkboard sat outside, touting a shepherd's pie lunch special and Trivia Night at 7:30. He stepped inside under the green and yellow sign and located Willos in the dimness by his shock of white hair. It wasn't fair how many of these Irish guys kept their thick hair into their sixties—Burton had been balding since college.

Whatever Willos had to tell him, it wasn't going to be pleasant. The lawyer had already bought him a drink, which he hadn't ever done since the beginning of all this. He mounted the backless stool like a saddle and nodded at the glass.

"Bridge. How is it? That for me?"

"You're going to want it."

Burton was tired of all the drama.

"Someone else die, did they?"

"Near as, as far as you're concerned."

"Jesus, man. Spill it." Burton picked up the shot glass and sniffed. Irish whiskey, of course.

Willos looked past the taps and into the mirror, straight ahead, as if he were forming the best words to use.

"The Bousquet thing?" Burton said.

The lawyer, resplendent in his charcoal suit, hard-starched white shirt, and red tie, nodded and lipped the foam off the top of his dark beer. Guinness, no doubt.

"They want to settle it."

Burton felt a surge of hope.

"That's a good thing, isn't it?"

Willos sank a quarter of the pint.

"For the city? Sure it is. For you, not so much."

Burton drank the whiskey, medicine for the blow that was obviously coming.

What he knew about the lawsuit was that it was the brain child of a couple of obscure bent cousins of Antoine Bousquet, the Belgian clothes designer Burton arrested for murder last year. Burton had sucker-punched the man while arresting him, and though the department had cleared him, Bousquet later died at the hands of one of his business partners. The ownership of Bousquet's three buildings in Chinatown was left in limbo, and the city had taken them in a RICO finding. The cousins sued the city and threw Burton into the mix, claiming his history with Bousquet made the man more vulnerable to his killer.

"The city doesn't want the fucking buildings, now that they have them," Willos said. "They're firetraps. And the mayor's saying something about the city not being in the real estate business."

He wiped condensation from the bar with a paper napkin.

"But they want you gone."

"They—the Bousqueteers?"

Willos nodded.

"They offered to drop all the suits if the department severs ties with you."

Burton felt like he'd been slammed in the gut with a sledge hammer.

"And they'd do it, too, the fuckers, wouldn't they? The brass?"

Willos gave him a minuscule lawyer's nod.

"They'll let you resign, Daniel." To his credit, Willos looked as if he were swallowing something nasty. This was not the kind of precedent the PBA wanted to see. "Full pension, bumped up as if you'd been a captain."

Burton whistled.

"They really want me gone, don't they?" He signaled the bartender, a hipster with arm garters and a thick ginger beard, for another round. "I won't quit until this case is all done. *Solved*."

Willos nodded. He'd been a street cop once. He understood.

"An expression of agreement is all it would take at the moment."

More fucking lawyer-talk, words without meaning.

"Can you get me some time to think about it?"

Willos's frown was the answer.

"They're already pushing me pretty hard. Day or two at the outside."

"Good enough," Burton said. "You push them back and tell them I'm thinking about it. I'll get them an answer. Maybe it will shake them up a little if I don't roll right over."

56

The dreams from the painkillers were spectacular: colors I'd never seen, in nature or in my imagination, winged flashing shadows and shafts of excruciating bright light, tiers of granite and brown sandstone blocks ranging up the sides of high hills. A sunrise on the wrong side of the sky.

I came out of it—I couldn't call it waking up—to find a nurse with her back to me fiddling with the IV port, the saline bag hanging down from its stainless steel skeleton. My brain was still half-in, half-out of hallucination, so the white-coated figure with the syringe seemed normal to me. I felt warmed, that someone from the medical team was taking care of me. I watched the thumb press down on the plunger of the syringe, and realized it was all wrong.

"You," I said.

The face left tracers of light as the body turned away and left the room. The afterimage raised a great wave of irrational fear in me.

I reached for the call button taped to the frame of the bed, but weakness coursed through my muscles and my hand would not obey the impulse from my brain. Physically, I was limp, but the clay of my flesh seemed to harden into concrete, my breathing pushed hard against the flaccid muscles of my chest. I could not force sound out through my mouth. The cry for help screamed itself dead in my throat, and I knew a deep wave of sadness, regrets for things I'd done and things I'd been afraid to do.

Which was the moment I realized I was dying, that the person who killed Rasmussen Carter was not the dead Edward Dare at all. But it made no sense.

My mind raced, as if the fact of my body being immobilized by whatever was in the IV now gave my mental processes more fuel. Why me? Why now? I had most of the answers to my questions and Burton's, but the knowledge was going to leave with me. And I could not even close my eyes so I could die in the darkness.

57

"I can't do this right now," Burton said.

Marina showed up at the precinct half an hour after he got the news from Willos. His cubicle was usually quiet late in the afternoon, and he'd been sitting there, staring at the fabric walls, and contemplating his future. It didn't feel as if he had a choice, but he didn't want to jump too soon if he could figure a way to keep his job. Not only did he need to do the work he did, he hated to give the brass and the rest of the politicians in the department what they wanted.

Marina was sitting on one of the visitors' benches in the lobby. When she stood up and walked to meet him, the cop on the desk started to say something, then subsided when he saw Burton nod.

The third floor was deserted, Martines's office dark. He walked her into one of the actual conference rooms. His cubicle would have been cramped, and too public.

"Tea?" he said.

She nodded and he stepped out to the machine, got himself a coffee, too.

They sat on opposite sides of the scarred table. She wore her chef's whites. A stain the color of raspberries kept drawing his attention. It looked like blood.

"I'm sorry to come here," she said. "But we have to talk. We never seem to be in the same place at the same time any more. It's like you're running away from me."

His temper stirred. He closed eyes.

"You know what my job's like, Marina. You've never known me when I wasn't doing this. All of a sudden, it's a problem?"

She tugged the label on the tea bag, squeezed it out with her fingers. He winced. Culinary school had toughened her hands. He saw scrapes and tiny knife cuts all over, in various stages of healing.

"I'm not so sure that's what the problem is," she said. "That's only the reason we can't find the time to talk. It's more about what we don't talk about."

More than one of his married colleagues had warned him about brides and the emotional whiplash leading up to the actual day. He'd wanted to think Marina was too mature for any of that, but apparently not. The idea of yet another relationship talk made him want to roll his eyes. What else was there to work through?

"Is this the whole Rasmussen Carter thing again? I thought we talked about that."

"It's the fact you take me for granted."

His head snapped up. Of all the complaints he could have anticipated, that wasn't even on the list.

"What do you mean? We talk. I pay attention to you."

She touched him on the back of the hand with one finger.

"You don't feel how comfortable you got once the whole thing was settled? We were going to get married, now you had that part of your life figured out, you didn't have to worry any more."

"Not fair," he said. "I never even expected to have this, to have you. You know I can't always be where you want me to be: it's the nature of the work. And it's not like you're sitting home waiting for me. With school and all."

"Is that what you want? Someone to sit home and wait for you?"

"Of course not." He shook his head. "This is still about Carter, isn't it? You never got over it."

She shook her head half-heartedly.

"At least be honest about it," he said.

Burton felt a terrible urge to cut and run, walk down the stairs and out the doors of the police station, out of Marina's life, out of this work, and not come back. If no one wanted him around, what was the point of staying?

She tilted her head to the side and inspected him. Did he love her? Was he willing to bend himself to this latest upheaval? She didn't seem to want to meet him anywhere near the middle.

He pushed the coffee mug away, shook his head.

"No. Never mind." He held her gaze. "We've been through enough crap together to know how this works. And that it works. If you don't? If you don't want this? Say so. Right here."

She twisted away, as if he'd hit her.

"I'm confused, Daniel. I don't know what I want any more."

He took a deep breath, and with it, what felt like the risk of a lifetime.

"I'm not letting you go, Marina. Not until you say to me that's what you want to do, to be done with me."

She closed her eyes, but he knew the pain was not something she was going to think away. He'd worked through all his worries and reluctance already. It surprised him that it had taken this long for her doubts to surface.

"Can we hold off on the wedding for a little while?"

"Of course." He felt relief. How this resolved was more important to him than the flowers or the church. "As long as you need."

"And you'll talk to me? Every day?"

"If that's what you need." He hoped he wasn't promising something he couldn't deliver. "I'll make it happen on my end. How about you? Will you talk to me?"

58

Burton wanted Sweetie to come down to the precinct, but as soon as she heard he wanted to interview her, she called her lawyer. Burton informed the lawyer he would bring Sweetie in on a material witness warrant if she didn't comply. The lawyer proposed a compromise by offering his conference room. Burton was inclined to push, but Sweetie must have called someone else, because Martines came by to tell him to go to the lawyer's office. Burton looked the lieutenant in the eyes and wondered whether he knew about the plan for Burton to "retire."

The lawyer's offices were in a low glass and stone building on Dudley Street. The attorney introduced himself as Donald Millington. He was a lean black man, so average looking you wouldn't see him in a crowd: six feet, a hundred and eighty, wearing a dark suit that wasn't disgracefully cheap but hadn't cost him a couple thousand dollars, either. His voice was unremarkable, too, a medium tenor.

"My client isn't feeling too well today, Mr. Burton. I hope you'll understand if I don't let this run very long."

Typical lawyer, trying to establish that he was in charge. Burton fingered the small white card, embossed in gold type, that Millington handed him: name, number, a small gold fleur-de-lis in the upper right corner.

"I'm not familiar with your firm," Burton said. "Are you admitted to the bar in the Commonwealth?"

Millington pulled a small, amused smile.

"I'm not sure that's what's at issue today." He laid a hand on

Sweetie's shoulder. "Perhaps we should get on with it?"

Sweetie looked old and tired, as if something was wearing on her. She was dressed all in black today, wool trousers and a cashmere sweater with pearl buttons ranged along the V-neck. The skin of her chest looked dry and gray.

"Ms. Bogan. I'm following up on a crime that took place in your bar, the Greenwood."

She rolled her eyes.

"My nephew's bar. Baron Loftus. My bow-tied cross to bear."

He noticed she didn't ask what crime.

"A Mr. Elder Darrow was severely beaten there in the bar. You've met him, I believe?"

She gazed out the street-level window at the sign for the MBTA station. She acted vague and drifty, and Burton thought she was already setting herself up to seem unreliable.

"I… Well. Perhaps. I don't know."

"This would have been last Sunday, at the bar. You had a conversation with him. About…"

"Oh yes," she said. "A nice young fellow. And a jazz fan, or so he said." She stared at Burton. "Some people say that just to get close, you understand. There aren't that many true fans out there anymore. The music is dying."

He resisted her attempt to drag him down another path.

"Well, right after you spoke to him, he was beaten. In the kitchen of the bar. Would you know…"

Millington held up a blunt-fingered hand. He'd been writing notes on a yellow pad with a fountain pen.

"I think we can stop right here for a moment. Mrs. Bogan isn't quite…"

"How terrible!" she cried. "He didn't seem like a thug."

She wide-eyed Burton and he had the definite sense she was fucking with him. As did Millington, apparently, whose mouth twitched.

"Were you still there?" he said. "The man was quite badly beaten. You must have heard something."

He was having a hard time contrasting this wavery old woman

with the sharp on-point one he'd first met. She fluttered a hand, bony and spotted.

"I might. I think." The lawyer watched her like she was the pot of gold at the end of the rainbow, which Burton guessed she might be for him. "He's not a young fellow, is he? Balding? A little soft around the middle?"

Elder would love that description.

"Maybe if you could recall what you two talked about?"

She made a disappointed face.

"Probably my nephew. This friend of yours, did he used to be a bar manager?"

Close enough.

"Yes."

"Baron—my nephew?—has been running that bar I own. Maybe you've heard of it."

"The Greenwood," Burton said.

Sweetie made a face as if a bad smell had floated into the room. The lawyer relaxed in his chair, unworried now about where the conversation was going. Burton wondered what he'd missed.

"It's a stupid name." There was a flash of the woman he'd first met. "These children and their irony. Do you know who Chester Greenwood's supposed to be?"

Burton shook his head.

"He invented goddamn earmuffs." She sniffed. "Though it was his wife's idea, originally. Have you ever heard anything so absurd?"

"So you were discussing the bar? Maybe you were asking him for business advice?"

He winced as soon as he said it. He'd led her right to a plausible answer. The way she was shining him on was making him impatient.

"Yes! Exactly." She rearranged the pad and pen on the table in front of her, as if too embarrassed to meet his look. "I gave Baron the job to keep him busy. But to learn to work, too. He's terribly spoiled, you know. Flunked out of Tulane, which is not as easy as it sounds."

She cut the lawyer a look, as if it might be his fault. Another New Orleans connection.

"So you were discussing your nephew's management of the bar with Mr. Darrow. That was it?"

Her energy was returning, as if she found it too hard to play vague for long.

"That was it. I went to the rest room, and when I came out, he was gone. I assumed he'd left, so I did, too."

"You didn't ask him to get you your cigarettes?"

She looked appalled.

"I'm a singer, Detective Burton. I've never smoked in my life."

He hadn't expected complete candor, but her story varied from Elder's significantly. Maybe she didn't know he'd survived the beating. The only new information was the New Orleans connection to Baron Loftus.

"Do you know where I can find your nephew?" he said.

"He better be behind the stick at my tavern." Her voice was sharp as a blade. "He knows I won't fire him, but I can always make his life more miserable than it already is."

Burton didn't doubt a word of that. He needed to get to the Greenwood before she could call.

"You're Homicide," Millington said. "This Mr. Darrow died?"

"No. But the attack is connected to another case I'm working on. Which, of course, I can't talk about."

"Of course," Millington said.

Sweetie had checked out, staring at a Picasso print on the wall.

"Thank you both," Burton said, as he stood to go. "You've been a great help."

Millington smiled as if he knew Burton was lying.

59

"I thought for sure you were dead, man."

Isaac knotted his hands, uncharacteristically subdued. The floor of my hospital room was littered with paper wrappers, a torn nitrile glove, some bits of vomit-soaked gauze, a minor chaos.

I did, however, feel better than I had in months, all my previous aches and pains smothered under whatever drugs they were feeding me now.

And I was deeply confused, not to mention still petrified by the feeling, before I'd passed out, of being trapped inside a body that could not move. Isaac had shown up a few seconds after I stopped breathing and knew immediately something was wrong, had the presence of mind to mash on the call button. Whatever antidote they'd given me to whatever poison it had been, my return to life felt like a whole-body case of shaking off pins and needles.

"Good thing." My throat was dry as sand, my tongue too thick to articulate whole sentences. "K'you."

Isaac started kicking the debris on the floor off to one side, as if embarrassed.

"Good thing I came to talk to you." He came back to the bedside, hands in his pockets. "I heard from Evvie. That's what I came to tell you. She's booked a flight back."

I sensed his relief, how much he thought of Evangeline. My mind wasn't completely connected up yet. I had little to say.

"She texted me the time." He held up his phone.

My head cleared slower than a cloud on a winter day. The fog lifting also meant my pain could reassert itself. I tried to think of

233

it as a signal that I was getting better. It didn't help.

"Great."

The nurses had told Isaac he was a hero. He looked uncomfortable.

"I guess I should go."

"No." Fear tore through me. I didn't want to be alone again. Not yet. "Stay a few minutes."

He shrugged, sat down in a chair and crossed his legs, his discomfort obvious. I remembered how, as a younger man, I'd been uncomfortable around the old, the sick, the infirm, as if I could pretend I wouldn't be in one of those states eventually.

"Wha' happened?" I said.

A tall woman in a long white coat swept in like a gust of wind. She was slim and dark-haired, her exposed forearms ropy with muscle. A triathlete maybe, or a dancer, with all that barely suppressed energy. Her faint perfume ticked a memory I couldn't pin down.

"What happened was that someone tried to shuffle you off this planet." She was angry, and for a second, I thought it was directed at me.

"How's that?"

She looked unsure how much to tell me. I beckoned with my fingers.

"I'm supposed to wait for the lawyers," she said. "But I'm so mad, I'm ready to spit. Who are you that someone would come into my hospital and try to kill you?"

She was talking too fast for me to process, bouncing on the balls of her feet like she couldn't stand still. She looked over her shoulder and saw Isaac in the chair. Then she stuck her head out the door and yelled into the hallway.

"Hey! Can we get someone in here to clean this crap up?"

Isaac hunched.

"Hello," I said. "My name is Elder Darrow."

She stopped moving around, then stepped up to the bedside when an orderly came in with a broom and a big steel dustpan.

"Shit," she said. "I'm sorry. Jane. Jane Newkirk. Doctor. This has thrown the entire hospital for a loop."

"Imagine that." My head was clearing, but she missed the sarcasm.

Now the aches and pains started chorusing, an atonal bellow. I supposed they took me off the painkillers until they could figure out what my killer might have injected into the IV. I tried to hike myself into a sitting position and winced.

"Oh, God."

Dr. Jane jumped to the other side of the bed and grabbed the call button. "Do you need help? I have a lot of sick people to look after."

She didn't see the humor in that, but it made me crack my first smile of the day. Isaac lifted his head.

"I don't believe so." I tried to stay calm, wondering why I was supposed to keep her from freaking out. "Can you tell me what happened?"

She glared at me as if I were stupid, which given my pharmaceutical levels, was probably a reasonable diagnosis.

"Someone tried to kill you," she said again.

"I get that." My throat cleared. All my pain was back in force, my tongue was looser, but at least the words weren't reverberating inside my skull as they had, bouncing around, unable to escape. "But how?"

She looked worried, glanced at Isaac.

"I don't think we better get into that right now."

"Someone injected succinylcholine into your IV." Burton stormed into the room, making it crowded. "Call it sux, because it does. Right, doc?"

"Oh. Right." Newkirk, turning her face away from him, scurried out the door as if she were a mouse and Burton a thirty-pound coon cat.

He and I shared a look.

"She's a doctor?"

I shrugged.

"We need to get you out of here, to some place safer. Do you remember anything?"

The drugs had crushed out my memories, except for what the

nurses told me, after they brought me back, that I'd been unable to move or breathe. I shook my head, then started.

"Wait. The perfume."

"On the woman who just split?"

"Yes. I smelled that, as I was going under."

Burton grabbed his phone.

"I've got a car outside. Maybe they can grab her. Anything else?"

"Other than that? *Nada*. Someone in a white coat messing with the IV."

"You triggered someone," Burton said. "Or something."

"Sweetie?" I didn't have any trouble remembering the crap being kicked out of me.

"Alfonso's like her forgotten man. She's definitely key."

"You talking about Alfonso Deal-Jones?" Isaac said. "That dude is a mean motherfucker."

Burton whirled on him.

"Wait, what? You know him? How?"

60

"Elder goddamn Darrow."

Susan made a grand entrance that afternoon, carrying a tote bag with some clean clothes, a handful of CDs, and a small boom box. Isaac slipped out the door too quickly for me to thank him. Burton looked surprised to see her here.

"What the hell happened?" she asked him.

I'd forgotten that I'd put Susan on my medical paperwork as an emergency contact last year. She was as angry as she was worried, and Burton looked as if he wanted no part of whatever came next.

"I'm out of here," he said. "But I'm putting someone on the door until you're released. That woman was no doctor—she may have come back for another bite of the apple."

"What woman?" Susan said.

"I'll let Elder explain." Burton pointed a finger at me and left the room.

Susan stepped in close and inspected my face. Bumps and bruises always look worse as they're healing. I didn't get a lot of physical punishment, but I knew it would be a week at least before I could stand to look at myself in the mirror.

"Well," I said. "I got mugged the other day. Sunday, I think."

"So seriously you end up in the hospital? They weren't after your wallet, then."

I didn't want to drag her into this, but minimizing it might put her in danger, too.

"Then last night, someone apparently tried to kill me."

"Kill you?" She was tough, but that wasn't something you shook off. "For what?"

"I suppose it's got something to do with Rasmussen Carter and the jazz singers."

I wished a real doctor or nurse would come back in and re-hook me up to the painkillers. My back and ribs felt like they'd been pounded flat, and my head throbbed, as if all the unnatural substances in my body were leaving through my skull.

"So you're proving the point I made the other day. Remember what we were talking about?"

I closed my eyes, no energy for a fight.

"Do we really have to go back over that now? I can't help what happens."

She dragged Isaac's chair over to the side of the bed.

"That's a matter for discussion," she said. "But I'm not the type of woman who kicks a man when he's in a hospital bed. Tell me. The whole bloody thing."

* * *

I hated being alone in the hospital, so I stretched the story out as much as I could, beginning with Alfonso Deal-Jones's stabbing of Rasmussen Carter.

"Carter died in the hospital?" she said. "This very hospital?"

"But not of his stab wounds. Someone helped him along with a pillow."

"And he and Alfonso were fighting over a woman?"

"Carter was grooming this young woman as a singer. A man named Edward Dare convinced her to move to New Orleans as a career move. Deal-Jones stabbed him because he thought Carter was attacking Sweetie Bogan."

Susan shook her head.

"And someone beat Alfonso to death?"

I nodded.

"He and Dare were putting together a cocaine deal, which Dare's boss wouldn't have approved of."

"So where does the old woman and her nephew fit in? And the bar?"

"Sweetie Bogan and Baron Loftus, who now runs what used to be the Esposito."

"Sounds like an overly complicated episode of *Murder, She Wrote*."

She plugged in the boom box and cued up a compilation of instrumental tunes, mostly trios, at low volume. We wouldn't disturb anyone.

"I know. If I wasn't in the middle of it, I probably wouldn't believe it myself."

She focused her wide eyes on me, her look charged with worry, a little sorrow.

"There's no way you'll let this go, is there?"

"Oh, no. I am done with all this." I waved my hand around the room. "I never had to deal with this kind of thing when I was involved before, and I'm not doing it again."

She gave me a level look.

"You're full of it. You know why you're so deep in this?" She didn't wait for me to answer. "You're flat out bored. Once the bar got sold, you didn't have enough to do. So you made something up."

Here we went again. I thought about the way I got into this, doing a favor for Marina.

"I was trying to help out a friend. You can't beat me up for that."

"Where it started, looking into what happened to the sleazy guy, Rasputin whatever?"

"Rasmussen Carter."

"Elder. The man was murdered. Normal people don't agree to help out their friends by investigating murders. Not civilians, anyway." Her cheeks showed high red color. "And, if I have to remind you, it almost got you murdered, too. For helping a friend."

My head was clearing, which made me think I could convince her. The nurse popped in to hand me a couple of pills and a little plastic cup of bitter liquid to wash them down. I sniffed around her before I took them: no perfume.

"I know you think I go looking for trouble. But I don't. Really. I was just trying to help out."

"Then maybe you ought to stop being an amateur at it," she said crossly.

"What do you mean?"

"There are people who do this kind of thing for a living. With training and certifications and licenses, that kind of thing."

I snorted and a muscle in my neck tweaked.

"You want me to be, what? Some kind of private eye? Like that would be safer?"

Her stare was cold as aluminum.

"You don't want to be safe, Elder. You don't ever take the easy way. It's something I like about you, if you didn't keep getting into situations like this."

Being on my back in a hospital bed seemed like a terrible time to have a relationship talk.

"I guess that's true. It's probably one of the reasons we're attracted to each other. You're not exactly easy to be with, either. No certainty."

I thought she might get offended at that, but instead she laughed out loud. She stood on her tiptoes and leaned over the rail to kiss me, while George Shearing noodled his way through "Misty."

"Keep being yourself, Elder. And get well. Maybe we can find a way to make things a little more certain. I'll see you."

61

I knew I'd have to wean myself off the painkillers at some point, but man, did I feel good. Considering the beating I'd taken, my body hadn't sustained permanent damage: just bruises and muscle pulls, all soft tissue injuries. And despite the fact I was paying for the most expensive health insurance on earth, the hospital wanted to get rid of me as fast as they could. They pushed me out the door on Thursday, right before noon. Someone must have notified Susan, who picked me up and brought me home.

"The last thing you want to do is sit in one place," she said, helping me up the stairs into the apartment. "Movement's what keeps the blood flowing. The healing."

Climbing left me weak in the knees. It was clear my brain wasn't giving me the best advice. I flopped into my leather armchair and put my feet up on the ottoman.

"That must be why they pitched me out on my ear?"

"Stop grumbling. If you feel sorry for yourself, it's going to take that much longer to feel better."

"You try getting the shit kicked out of you," I said.

"What?"

"Nothing."

She brought her face down close to mine.

"Healing is mental, Elder. You start pissing and moaning, you're just going to drag yourself down."

"They teach you that out in woo-woo land?"

I winced. The dose of painkillers they'd given me this morning was wearing off.

"What time is it?"

She kissed me on the forehead.

"Two hours until the next one. You'll have to tough it out. Don't start cheating on them."

"Jesus, you sound like we're married."

That word hit the floor like a brick. She was shaking her head, almost before I disavowed the statement, the notion, the very idea.

"It's the drugs," I said. "I didn't mean anything by it."

She set the pill bottle and a glass of water on the side table next the chair.

"I think I'll go down and put my apartment back in order."

At least she was calling it her apartment now, and not Henri's.

"I will be here." I picked up the pill bottle and started to work the childproof top. "Come back upstairs when you're done. We can have lunch."

62

Burton was heading in-town on Cambridge Street when his phone rang, the caller ID showing Fortin's Produce, which he recognized as one of Mickey Barksdale's fronts. Mickey came on with none of the usual pleasantries.

"You're going to want to see this, Burton."

"Mickey. I'm in the middle of something. Actually, working."

Burton always tried to be in the middle of something when Mickey called or dropped by. Ever since he'd saved Burton's life on that ball field in Charlestown, Mickey acted like he owned a piece of him. He was too sly to be overt about it, but the fact that he felt comfortable calling Burton out of the blue made Burton uneasy.

"Dan'l. I am not fucking around here. You show up, you're going to save at least one life. Maybe two."

"Seriously, Mick. We have to do this right now?"

Mickey also loved his drama—Burton couldn't make it easy on him. But Mickey didn't lie, either.

"Daniel. I have here in my office, through a set of curious events too extraordinary to describe, the very person who tried to send your bartender pal off the planet. Do I perhaps have your attention now? I assume you know he almost passed on us."

Burton's chest bumped, close to panic. How could Mickey know so much about something that happened only hours ago?

"You have someone following me, Mick?"

Mickey laughed wetly.

"If I do, boyo, I probably had a good reason, don't you think?"

Burton shook his head. Mickey was his weak spot, that much he understood. But sometimes he was the lever who moved the rock up the hill, and this felt like it might be one of those times. Not that he needed any encouragement to find out who'd tried to kill Elder.

"At the market?"

"Correct. And do me a favor? Swing by Dunkin' and grab me a coffee? Light, two sugars?"

"Fuck you, Mick."

"How long's it going to take? You're at the hospital?"

They were going to have a discussion about Mickey surveilling him.

"Half an hour."

He was goddamned if he'd hurry.

* * *

Fortin's Produce operated out of a storage bay off Hanover Street, behind where the Haymarket operated on Fridays and Saturdays. The place was a relic of the time when the entire area hosted a wholesale and retail produce market.

Burton located a parking space around the corner on a fenced-in lot he knew belonged to the apparently homeless man sitting on an upturned drywall bucket at the entrance. He slipped him a twenty.

"Tito."

The bum tipped his greasy Red Sox hat, the one with the 100th anniversary logo, and adjusted whatever was weighing down the pouch of his sweatshirt. Burton guessed a .38. Very few people knew that Tito drove home to an eight-bedroom house in Dover on the weekends and had put three sons through Boston College on the proceeds of a string of parking lots across the city. This was only one of them.

Fortin's entrance was hung with vertical plastic strips, the interior warmer than the day outside. Racks full of boxes displayed oranges, grapefruits, lemons, limes, apples, pears, and other more exotic fruits on the left side of a narrow aisle. All the vegetables—

the usual lettuce, tomatoes, cucumbers, onions, as well as some Burton didn't recognize—sat in crates along the right.

He picked up a knobby purple ball he didn't recognize, then put it down and picked up an apricot. Almost tasteless when he bit into it. He spit the pit out on the floor. He was stalling.

The produce stall appeared unmanned, but Burton knew better than to think anyone but an idiot would steal from one of Mickey Barksdale's establishments. Even if produce wasn't his primary source of income.

Deeper into the skinny, dim aisle, the temperature got colder. Normally, he could trust Mickey not to fuck him over, but this case made him more nervous than usual. He didn't grasp its underlying logic yet, why Alfonso Deal-Jones had been murdered, and he couldn't be sure Mickey wasn't the driver behind the whole thing.

"Dan'l."

Burton stepped to his right, in through a doorway into a rough drywalled room, and immediately felt warmer. Mickey sat behind a sleek Scandinavian desk, both of the extra chairs to his left occupied.

"Nice office, Mick."

Hidden in behind the rough market stall, Mickey's space was carpeted, wallpapered, heated, and furnished to a respectable level. He'd always been more concerned about his own comfort than Burton was, despite the fact they'd both grown up poor.

"Close the door, will you? It's fucking raw out there."

"November in New England, Mick. You want heat, go to Florida. What's going on?"

He saw immediately what was going on: the two chairs Mickey did not sit in were occupied by women. One of them was Sweetie Bogan, who sat with her camel's hair coat wrapped tightly around her, hands in her lap, as composed as if they were all drinking tea. In the other chair, her arms tied behind her and her ankles duct-taped to the chair legs, was the woman pretending to be Elder's doctor not an hour before. And, wonder of wonders, Burton recognized the face now. This was the woman who'd tried to assault him outside his apartment, but her hair and makeup were entirely different.

"Well," Burton said. "I've met Mrs. Bogan." He nodded politely. "And I'm not sure I know this other person's name. I certainly recognize her though. Not Newkirk, I presume?"

She stared.

"Here." Mickey pointed his cigarette at two syringes lying on top of his desk. "I thought you might appreciate it if I disarmed everyone while we talked."

Mickey was playing the grandee again, as he liked to do. Burton understood what drove him, growing up poor in a shitty family situation. And Burton hadn't ever seen Mickey exercise his criminal tendencies on anyone who couldn't fight back. He'd been a terrible bully until puberty hit.

"Very thoughtful, Mick. She get away from you the night she tried to cancel my ticket?"

Mickey glared. "You were the one who asked for mercy."

Burton's sudden rage toward the woman who'd tried to kill Elder surprised him. He wanted to smash her face in.

"Let's talk, then."

"Where shall we start?" Mickey said. "How about you, Ms. Newkirk? Or is it Doctor? Is that your real name?"

The woman duct-taped to the chair tried to shrug, but it was awkward.

"Jane. Job of work, Mr. Barksdale. You know how that goes."

An honest to god contract killer. Burton understood the causes of most of the homicides he worked, having been in the business this long. Most of them were anything but puzzles, usually a loss of control by someone without a lot of impulse control in the first place, exacerbated by alcohol, drugs, passion, or greed. What he'd never been able to understand, except intellectually, was the professional, the person who, for no other reason than money, would terminate your chosen victim. The few he'd met looked cold from the outside, but his experience said they were broken in more serious ways than your average drunken killer. But he did not want to know Jane Newkirk's story.

"That your real name?" he said.

"Wouldn't mean anything to you."

"Millicent," Sweetie said. "Millicent Vinson."

Burton flashed on the surname. Millicent shot Sweetie a murderous look. He was glad she was secured. The hate didn't seem to faze the old woman.

He assembled the pieces.

"You're from New Orleans, then. So what brings you to my city to knock people off? Or to try to, I guess. Since you haven't succeeded."

"You haven't figured that out, I can't help you. I don't teach the Murder for Dummies course any more."

Mickey reached across and slapped her on the back of the head, not lightly.

"Millicent," he said. "My Ma used to go to the Bingo on Friday nights with a neighbor name of Millicent. Nice old woman."

Millicent's eyes burned cold.

"You think you'd like to be an old woman some day?" Mickey said.

"Not if it means giving you anything."

"Children." Burton looked at Mickey. "Mick. Why am I here?"

"Other than the fact she tried to kill your best friend?"

Mickey sounded hurt, as if he'd thought he was Burton's best friend. Or at least a friend. Burton shook his head. Unbelievable. He wasn't going to kill her.

Mickey looked disappointed, as if he'd read Burton's thoughts. Burton turned to Millicent.

"Why Darrow? You people don't usually pick on civilians."

She shook her head.

"He's no civilian. The guy took down Edward Dare. Who is—was—a very valuable member of my employer's organization. Insults like that don't go unpunished."

Sweetie spoke up, in a low honeyed voice that distracted him. He could listen to her read the phone book.

"Your father's organization, you mean."

Millicent tried the hard look on Sweetie again, but it bounced off.

"So what?"

"If I told him once, I told him a hundred times," Sweetie said. "Keep your goddamned family out of your business."

Burton tried to fold that new knowledge in.

"You know Frank Vinson?"

Her gaze reminded him not to underestimate her, just because she was old. Or a woman.

"I spent the best fourteen years of my life in New Orleans," she said. "If I'd been a country singer, I would have gone to Nashville."

"So you do know him."

Sweetie glanced at Millicent.

"In every way," she said. "Including the Biblical."

"No, Sweetie." Millicent snapped. "I know that's what you wanted. But you're not my fucking mother."

"Whoa, whoa." Mickey slapped his hand on top of the wooden table. "This family shit is all very touching. It's also not why we're here."

What were they doing here? Burton thought. Nothing he got out of Millicent was going to be admissible.

"Since you know how to navigate the hospital. That must mean you also killed Rasmussen Carter?"

"Who d'at?"

"The other guy you killed in his hospital bed."

"Oh, yeah." Millicent's voice dulled, as if she saw she had no way out. "Weird name, huh? I didn't get the sux until later."

"Why did Dare claim he did it?"

Her smile twitched.

"He did? Probably trying to save his own ass. Dad—Frank—was very unhappy with him."

Sweetie bore in.

"That damned cocaine deal."

Millicent lifted her chin.

"Edward was way off the reservation on that one," she said. "Frank didn't like his people freelancing. Doesn't."

Something wasn't passing the logic test for Burton, but it didn't matter at this point.

"So you killed Deal-Jones, then."

Millicent shook her head.

"Nope. I knew who he was." She gave Sweetie a hooded look. "Not in the Biblical sense. But he wasn't on the list."

"List?" Burton said.

"Manner of speaking."

He nodded at Mickey. "Can we talk?"

Mickey got out of his chair and walked around the end of the desk farthest from the two women, led Burton out the door.

Burton leaned on the frame, blocking the doorway with his back.

"I'll take her with me," he said. "Let me call a patrol car. You can get Sweetie home?"

Mickey shook his head.

"It's not going to work that way this time, sport. These assholes stepped over my personal line. Killing people in my city? There has to be a response."

Burton thought about Mickey saying "my city," the same way he had. Both of them felt the responsibility, if in different ways. He wondered if he were ready for a head-to-head with Mickey Barksdale.

"What is Sweetie doing here, anyway?"

Mickey laughed.

"She brought me the bitch. She knew what these freaks from New Orleans were up to, and she saw a chance to help me out."

"You've known her for a while?"

Mickey tapped the side of his nose.

"I'm not going to kill Millicent, you understand. So you don't have to worry about that. We have that level of respect for each other, am I right?"

Burton considered whether he was crossing a line. If he was, he didn't feel terrible about it, especially on Elder's behalf.

"You deliver her to the airport tomorrow morning. Alive and unharmed. I'll put her on a plane."

Mickey's smile was icy.

"Whatever you say, Dan. I'm just sending a message to her

daddy. About who runs the game here."

Burton still hesitated.

"I'm serious. Alive and unmarked."

"And I said not to worry. By the way." He tapped Burton on the chest. "You owe me a dollar. For that apricot you ate."

Burton opened his wallet, took out a five, and stuffed it in Mickey's top pocket.

"Keep the change."

63

Sweetie was a pretty fast walker for a woman on the far side of eighty. If she'd known where he parked the Jeep, she would have beaten him there. He deliberately slowed his pace as they walked back up Hanover Street, to see if he could make her impatient enough to give something away.

"He is a formidable man, Mr. Barksdale," she said. "Though you would think gangsters would have more sense than to fight with each other all the time. It has to affect the bottom line."

He unlocked the car door with his key. He understood Mickey's sense of territoriality, his ownership of some part of the city. He looked at it mainly as what the city could do for him. Mickey was sentimental about Boston, which Burton could agree with.

"I've known him since we were kids. We grew up on the same street."

"Will he kill her? Despite what he said?"

He was helping her climb into the high seat of the Jeep and almost let go when he heard the question.

"Mickey keeps his word. But I still would not want to be Millicent today."

He decided he didn't feel guilty at all about leaving the assassin to Mickey's ministrations.

Sweetie fastened her shoulder belt. He climbed in and started the engine, pulled away from the curb, and headed up Merrimac Street.

"But at least your mystery is solved," Sweetie said.

"Really. How's that?"

"Well, if Millicent really did kill your friend Rasmussen in the hospital…"

"Not my friend, but OK…"

She frowned at the interruption. Burton sensed she was constructing a story on the fly, not saying what she really thought happened.

"If Millicent killed him in the hospital, and then tried to kill the other man. The one who was your friend."

"Elder Darrow. The first man she killed was Rasmussen Carter."

He liked to speak and remember the true names of the people whose deaths he dealt with. It was tempting to forget they'd been humans, had lived and eaten and drank and loved.

"What I'm trying to say is this: if Millicent did those two deeds, she must have killed Alfonso. Don't you think?"

He did not, actually. In his experience, people who killed more than once favored the same method. Millicent, the professional, had tried to confuse things by using different modes, but on the whole, shooters tended to shoot and stranglers tended to strangle.

"Mmm." He wasn't going to agree, but he encouraged her talkative mood. "Am I dropping you at home?"

"Please." She was impatient with him, as if she could tell he wasn't convinced of her theory. "Listen. I'll tell you what I think happened."

They turned off Chelsea Street onto 13th. He nodded.

"Edward Dare's job was finding girls for Frank Vinson, somewhere other than New Orleans, where Frank was too well known. That, and covering Frank's ass, was as much as he had to do with anything."

He believed Dare was doing something more important than that, even if she seemed to understand the New Orleans mob pretty well. It could be a power play against Mickey, for example, if Frank found out Mickey was trying to legitimize his business.

"Did you work for Frank, too?"

"I told you I lived there for fourteen years. And I was beautiful. And I was a headliner. Singer." Not bragging now, matter of fact. "Don't you think he would have wanted me?"

Not a yes or no answer, but the only one he was going to get.

"So. Dare was his pimp, more or less."

She frowned at the word.

"Frank really isn't interested in sex that way," she said. "Anyway. Dare and Alfonso were trying to put a cocaine deal together. With *my* money." She was hurrying to get the story out before he dropped her off. "But Frank has always been death on drugs. So when he found out, he had Alfonso hit for dealing with Dare."

"And Dare would've gotten away with it?"

"He would have been punished. But he was important to Frank."

"And Carter?"

"Millicent took him out for trying to keep Dare from bringing that girl singer to Frank."

"That's a nice neat story," Burton said.

A little too neat for him, and he wondered why she was selling it so hard. He didn't believe Sweetie had killed anyone, but she could be protecting someone though.

The doorman at the apartments, seeing it was Sweetie, hustled out of the atrium to help her down from the Jeep.

"You'll see it eventually," she said, as she leaned on the uniformed man. "You'll come around."

64

I swallowed a painkiller dry as soon as Susan was out the door, as much to defy her as because I needed it. She acted like she was only staying around to save me from myself, and I didn't need someone playing nurse or hanging around because she pitied me. I'd moved in her direction quite a bit since she returned from Oregon, trying to make something between us work, and she kept changing her mind about what was wrong. First, it was my drinking, which I agreed was something to be concerned about. When we met, I was not in control of it, as I was now.

Now, though, she'd convinced herself I was looking for ways to put myself in danger, to risk getting the crap kicked out of me. Did she think I had a death wish? Or was she just looking for another excuse to leave?

The pill took effect and I sat up straighter, realizing I hadn't had my ceremonial drink in a couple of days. Was it a good thing or a bad thing that I didn't crave it? The half-empty bottle of the good Macallan was in the cupboard over the sink. If I could reach it.

I started to hitch myself up out of the chair. A zing of pain shot up my spine, disregarding whatever comfort the painkillers were supposed to provide. I sat back. It would be stupid for any kind of addict to mix the pills with booze. I could wait.

That thought set me perseverating about whether the pills—I assumed they were the same opioids the whole world feared being addicted to—could turn me into a different kind of addict. If you had the gene, I was sure, you could get addicted to almost anything.

My heavy thinking was relieved when a knock sounded on the

apartment door, Susan coming back from checking her apartment. I should listen to her—stewing in my own unhappiness was no prescription in favor of mental health.

"It's open."

"I heard they let you out of the hospital," Marina said, walking in.

She wore a pair of black skinny jeans, a hunter orange hoodie with a zipper down the front. For some reason, I was irked that she wasn't Susan. Either that or I was just in a mood to fight with someone.

"I'd say that's fairly obvious. No kitchen school today?"

She frowned at me.

"Teacher's day off. I guess they need to take time and talk about how bad we all are. How are you feeling?"

"Like someone dropped me into a big metal garbage can and pounded on it with a baseball bat."

"Ooh. No fun there. Do you need anything?"

"A little peace and quiet, maybe." I was acting like a prick, but I couldn't seem to control the momentum of my nastiness. "I wouldn't waste a day off trying to make me feel better. Isn't Burton around?"

"There is news on that front."

The painkiller didn't seem to be full strength. My torso rippled with aches, a bolt when I moved the wrong way. I wondered if the hospital had given me placebos, either by accident or on purpose.

"Yeah?"

"You can put off your appointment with the tailor. We decided to postpone the wedding."

My first thought, uncharitable as hell, was that Burton must be relieved. Then I was angry on his behalf. Seemed like the women in both of our lives liked to complicate things.

"You get cold feet?" I said.

She slumped into the love seat across from my chair, her face drawn, plum-colored bags under her eyes telling me she hadn't been sleeping, I wondered why I couldn't muster any sympathy for her.

"As good as. It's both of us, though. But more me than him, I guess."

"Because I know Burton wouldn't fuck you over like that."

She shivered as if a cold wind had passed over her and scooted forward on the cushions. Her dark eyes sparked with anger.

"Why are you being such an asshole? I thought I could at least talk to you about it."

"Complain, you mean. And who's the asshole? I'm not the one who dumped my fiancé."

"I didn't dump him. We're taking a breather. To make sure this is what we really want to do."

"Whatever." I closed my eyes as the second pill finally kicked in all the way and a fuzzy wash moved through me. "You know how much I believe in being loyal to people. And that isn't it."

She stood up, shaking.

"I don't need a lecture from you on relationships, Elder. I thought..."

"You thought I'd give you absolution? For fucking over my best friend. I don't think so."

I wiped saliva from my lips with a tissue, aware I was acting all out of proportion to the situation, but unable to control myself.

She looked ready to cry, but angry tears, not hurt ones.

"So this means we're not friends any more?" she said. "Burton gets all the claim on your loyalty?"

It wasn't her words so much as the devastated look, the sagging shoulders, the tears, that finally pierced my half-drugged self-absorption.

"Aw, shit," I said. "I didn't mean..."

"On, no." She raved. "Don't you pull that give-with-one-hand, take-with-the-other stuff with me. If you want to know what happened? If you want to be a real friend? To him and me? Climb out of your pit of self-pity. Talk to your very best pal Dan Burton. It's not like you're limited to one friend at a time, you know."

And then she stalked out of the apartment like an Amazon on the hunt.

As the door slammed, I raised my head up above the pain for

long enough to realize I'd been a complete asshole. If I'd known why, maybe I wouldn't have felt so stupid. I picked up the pill bottle in my hand and rattled it—supposed to be a week's supply. I wondered if I took them all at once—would that ease the pain?

65

Burton couldn't ignore the nagging fact of the Bousquet cousins wanting him to quit in exchange for dropping all the lawsuits. The idea of retiring hovered in the back of his mind like a lesion, burning all the time. He wondered if Willos had any more leverage than he appeared to—maybe he was a creature of the brass, too, committed to making things run smoothly.

As much as he hated the idea someone could force him to do something he didn't want to do, buried in that possibility was the tiniest spot of bright light. He'd never worked seriously at anything other than being a cop. Maybe there was something else out there that would interest him as much, feed his need to serve, to put things right. And maybe it would be something that would make it easier for him to keep things steady with Marina.

After meeting with Mickey, Sweetie, and Millicent, his never-fail bullshit meter was clanging like the bells at a railroad crossing. On the ride back to her apartment, Sweetie strained to convince him that everything that happened was because the people from New Orleans poked their noses into Boston. It didn't surprise him she tried to point fingers everywhere but at the people who'd been here all along. The tinge of desperation in her insistence gave him a good idea who she was trying to protect. And what.

He backed the Jeep into a space in front of the Greenwood and looked at the fancy stained glass window in the door, thinking about how much—not fun, exactly, but community, companionship—the old Esposito had. He didn't worry so much as he used to about Elder falling into a nasty drunk. The bar had suited him, though, given him a structure to his days that he didn't have now.

Because Sweetie pushed so hard on the notion that Edward Dare and Frank Vinson were the source of all the problems, Burton guessed she was trying to divert his attention. Other than the pay-as-you-go protection she hired to take care of her after Alfonso died, there was only one possible person in the world she would cover for.

He wasn't surprised to find the door to the bar unlocked, but it did worry him when he pulled it open and started down the stairs into complete darkness. One of the things he'd loved about the old Esposito was the fact natural light never entered. But the bar should be open. No good reason to be closed on a Thursday night. He stepped lightly on his heels, so the stairs would not make noise.

At the bottom, he stepped off toward the kitchen door, where a bar of light spilled from the back room, shadowing the legs of tables and the upturned chairs. He stepped behind the bar into the kitchen doorway, feeling cold air that said the back door was open. Someone whistled a snatch of classical music—Beethoven?—over and over, seriously out of tune.

Burton unholstered his weapon.

"OK. Let's everybody stand still here for one minute."

The whistling cut off mid-note. Burton stepped into full light to see a man holding a red plastic case full of liquor bottles. They clanked as he set them down on the tailgate of a U-Haul truck.

The man looked like a small barrel stuck on top of long skinny legs. Despite the chill, he was wearing tight Levis and a T-shirt from the Strand bookstore in New York. His shoulders and biceps strained the fabric, and his bald head shone white under the light. He sighed as he reached into his back pocket and produced a hard pack of Marlboros.

Fishing one out, he extended the pack to Burton, who shook his head. He seemed unconcerned by Burton's firearm. Burton wasn't pointing it at him. Yet.

"Bubba," the man said. "You a mate of Loftus?"

"No. And you are?"

The man gestured at a paper in the pocket of his T-shirt, asking permission. Burton nodded. The back of the truck was stacked with cases of beer, wine, liquor, and glassware. An enormous Yeti cooler stood open to one side, probably for the perishables.

"Yard sale?" Burton said.

"Man hired me to clean the place out." He passed the paper to Burton. "Cash in his hands."

Burton glanced at the paper, a generic permission slip for one Jonny Buono to remove items from the Greenwood Tavern, signed by Baron Loftus.

"Why?" Burton said, holstered his weapon.

Buono shrugged, his doughy face a drinking man's.

"It's legit," he said. "I checked the guy out online. He's the owner of record."

"No," Burton said. "Why's he clearing the place out?"

Buono lit the cigarette without asking, a little more comfortable than Burton liked. The cold night air blew the sulfur smell of the match back in his face.

"Didn't tell me. The rumor mill says he was running the place into the ground." He looked around. "Too bad—it's a nice location. Used to do a pretty good business, I understand."

"Rumor."

"I own a bar up on the Hill."

Burton assumed he meant Savin Hill or Winter Hill, not Beacon. Everyone in Boston thought their hill was the only one.

"So, this is like Christmas for you."

He wasn't ready to believe an anonymous piece of paper that Buono could have printed out himself as proof the guy wasn't thieving. Buono's back went up.

"Helping the guy out," he said. "He told me working the bar was killing him and his aunt needed some kind of medical care. No health insurance, obviously."

"He wear anything unusual?"

Easy way to tell if the guy had ever actually met Baron Loftus.

"Yeah. Bow ties. Light-skinned black guy. Twitchy."

Now Burton was convinced that Sweetie had been trying to distract him from Loftus, her nephew. He was going on the run, as much evidence of his guilt as Burton needed. He showed the man his credentials.

"You have some way to contact him?"

Buono reached into his pocket and held up a ring of keys.

"He gave me an envelope to return them in when I got done."

"Let me see."

Buono walked around to the front of the van and reached in the window, pulled out a small brown padded envelope, already addressed and stamped. To Sweetie's condo.

Burton's mind leafed through the possibilities. Was Loftus there now? Would Sweetie's protection extend to hiding her nephew, if he'd been the one who killed Alfonso? Or was he gone already, with the cash Buono paid him? Down to New Orleans. Or Mexico.

Burton handed back the envelope.

"I'm going to assume what's going on here is what you say it is. But don't take anything from the office: paperwork, licenses, any of the files."

Buono's disappointment told Burton he'd been contemplating that very thing. The liquor license itself would be worth something, even if the ownership was clouded.

"The man said 'all' contents." His protest was half-hearted.

"You think I can't find you in a bar on Savin Hill?" Burton said.

He'd guessed which hill correctly. Buono's shoulders fell. Burton knew he'd have to follow up, make sure the man wasn't taking things he shouldn't have.

"Anything you say, detective." Buono stubbed out his smoke on the linoleum and Burton was tempted to feed it to him. "Anything you say."

66

"I didn't find any emergency contacts for Mrs. Rinaldi," Susan said, an hour later when she came back upstairs.

I was still feeling bad about the way I'd treated Marina, but at least my pain was finally under control. I knew I'd miss Mrs. R., but at least she'd had the chance to die at home.

The double dose of painkiller was in full force. I had no intention of moving out of my chair. My thinking was about as spry as it ever was, but my body felt as if it were wrapped in one of those weighted comfort blankets, holding down my legs and torso.

Susan inspected me.

"I kept hearing a noise in her gas stove."

I teared up. "Which I checked for her four times." My tongue was taking up a lot of space in my mouth. "She was always a little nervous about mechanical things."

"Are you feeling OK?"

"It's nice." My head was drifting, not trending toward sleep so much as a very soft landing on some faraway planet where my aching body had nothing to do with my mind. "She was always a good tenant."

Susan arranged herself in the armchair across from my recliner, pushed the sleeves of her maroon cotton sweater up her forearms.

"I feel like I ran away from something I shouldn't have," she said. "A few minutes ago, I mean."

My unintended crack about marriage. It wasn't any more than a slip of the tongue, but she'd shied away as if I'd actually asked her to get married. I loved her, I but I knew better than to think we were ready for that.

"It's fine," I said. "The drugs are messing with my filters. Don't take it too seriously."

She tucked her legs up under her and studied me.

"You took another pill, didn't you?"

I closed my eyes.

"I do not need another mother. The pharmacist said I could take a second one if the pain persisted."

"It's going to persist until you heal, dumbass. What you're doing is how people accidentally overdose."

I shrugged, wished I hadn't. Maybe the drugs weren't as good as I thought.

"Let me tell you a story," she said.

I reclined the chair as far back as it would go and crossed my hands over my chest as if I were lying in a coffin.

"Very funny. I never told you this, but I was married once before."

That penetrated my fuzziness. I wondered why she'd never mentioned it.

"So why am I telling you this now, you ask?" She looked down at her hands.

"Because you need to. I'm listening."

She nodded, as if I'd promised something I hadn't offered before.

"My size," she said. "People have underestimated me my whole life. You've seen that."

I had. It was a hot button for her, and I couldn't blame her. People, especially but not only men, talked down to her, patted her on the head (sometimes literally), and told her how cute she was.

"Derek." The name made her falter, as if it brought a bad taste into her mouth. "He seemed to be better than that. He always treated me as if I were a full-sized person. Never talked down to me, minimized what I could do, who I was. I thought he loved me for *me*."

She colored.

"I was eighteen. No one had ever taken me seriously. So I started taking myself seriously. Which caused the problem."

Damned if I was going to interrupt, even if I couldn't guess where the story was headed. Nor why she thought she had to tell it to me.

"The problem..." I said.

"The problem? My father was the banker in town, only bank, locally owned. The small town version. Bricks and mortar, know your neighbors, boost the town."

"Henri wasn't your father?"

She shook her head.

"My father's brother. But more of a father to me than my own, really. Especially afterward."

Which I assumed meant she'd lost her biological father. To death?

"I'm sorry."

"Let me tell it and I'll be done with it. And you'll understand. Derek was older. He developed shopping centers. Or so everyone believed, since all his properties were out of the state."

I had a feeling what was coming.

"Daddy was so pleased I'd married a businessman, not the poet who'd caught my eye in college." Her voice hardened as she went on—she'd already wrung all the pain and grief from it. "He convinced the bank to underwrite Derek, for more money than the rules allowed." Her voice hitched. "He put his reputation out there to help because Derek was my husband."

I needed to say something to bleed off the tension.

"Derek defaulted?"

She shook her head.

"Derek absconded. Took the money my father's bank loaned him to build a mega-mall outside Seattle and disappeared."

"And your dad?"

"About what you'd expect. He lost his position. But worse, he lost his confidence. In people, in himself, in his professional abilities."

"He's all right?" I was afraid she was going to tell me he'd killed himself.

"They moved to Arizona to get away from all of it. It took everything they had, after he repaid the bank. Which is only to tell you why the 'M' word makes me gun-shy."

"You've had people tell you this before, I'm sure. But you know other people's crimes, their mistakes, don't belong to you."

"I needed so much to be taken seriously," she said. "I can read people like that clearly now. But I had no defenses then. If Derek stole everything I owned or beat me up, that would have been between him and me. But he fucked over my entire family, just by marrying me."

It made a twisted kind of sense, but only because I cared for her. I understood how a story from your past could freeze you.

"These pills are pretty strong," I said. "It wouldn't hurt that much if you came over and sat with me."

I shifted to one side in the recliner. She wouldn't take up much room.

"I don't think so, Elder. Not today. You're a little too fragile."

Which I understood to mean she was feeling too fragile herself right now.

67

Burton pulled up to his building and was stunned to find a parking space in front of the street door, two cars long. No backing and filling, he swung in the Jeep nose first. Marina's green Mini Cooper was parked halfway down the block, and he almost pulled out again and left. He thought they'd come to a decision. But it would be better to face up to her than to run.

He didn't believe Millicent Vinson's avowal she hadn't killed Deal-Jones. He could, however, imagine Frank Vinson waving his hands and wanting everything in Boston connected to him—Edward Dare, the bar fight, the aborted cocaine deal, even his seduction of the female singers he brought to New Orleans—wiped clean. What made Burton most curious was why Frank picked on Boston. Was it the closest city where he found the women attractive? Or was there something else going on, something to do with gangsters trying to extend their territories?

But if Millicent confessed to killing Rasmussen Carter and trying to kill Elder, what did she gain from lying about Alfonso? Unless it was because she'd been in the same room with Sweetie and worried the old woman might wreak revenge on someone who'd killed her lover? Nah. Too convoluted.

He also wondered if Sweetie knew Baron Loftus had bailed on the bar business. He checked his watch as he walked up the path. Sweetie would be at home—she didn't go out that much any more, or so she said. But he needed food and sleep. Tomorrow would be soon enough to go talk to her again, see if she knew where Loftus had gone.

His weapon was chafing his back. He'd spent too much time sitting today. He removed the holster and tucked it into a duffle bag with a set of gym clothes that needed washing, carried it inside.

The hallway was dark, and when he waved his hands, the motion detectors didn't turn the lights on. He pulled the flashlight off his belt and used the narrow beam to light his way up the stairs. Someone was cooking chili.

He had the door to his apartment open before he realized it was unlocked, then remembered Marina had a key. As he stepped inside, the overhead lights burst on, blinding him.

"Drop the bag."

He blinked away the shards of light dancing in his vision and saw Marina sitting on the couch, her ankles strapped together with duct tape, her hands in her lap. Surgical tape, white as cotton, covered her mouth. Her hair was disheveled and the jacket of her chef's whites was streaked maroon, dark drying blood. From a nosebleed—her upper lip, underneath her nose, was also crusted. His rage spun up.

"The bag."

He bent his knees and laid the duffle with his weapon on the floor. You never tossed a gun down, even if it was in a bag. The reason Sweetie tried so hard to convince him the New Orleans people were responsible for Alfonso's death was right here in front of him.

"Mr. Loftus."

Baron stood behind the couch, within easy reach of Marina. The long wicked blade in his right hand glinted in the light.

"You couldn't leave this alone."

"It's not my job to leave a murder alone."

"Lift your jacket and turn around."

The young man was madly disordered, his white shirt untucked, speckled with blood that was probably Marina's, his green bow tie so far off plumb it looked like a stuck propeller. His face was gray with strain.

Burton complied, knowing Loftus would assume a cop carried all his weapons on his belt. The bag with the pistol was in reach, but he wasn't stupid enough to think he had a chance to bend over, unzip the zipper, and pull out the weapon before Loftus would be on him with the knife.

"Let's just keep this whole thing civilized, Baron, can't we?"

He let the tails of his jacket fall. A knife was actually a more frightening weapon in the hands of someone driven by emotion. Loftus was desperate enough for anything.

Burton walked across the carpet to the club chair farthest from the end of the couch where Marina sat. Tactical decision, separate the two of them as much as possible, make it hard for Loftus to cover them both at once.

"I thought you'd be out of town by now, Baron. Why stop back here and cause yourself more trouble?"

Loftus's eyes stretched wide. He breathed like a tired runner. Burton hoped he wasn't dosed up with pharmaceutical courage.

"Because of you, you son of a bitch. Because you fucked me up with Sweetie. You're the one who gave her the idea it was me."

"It was you what, Baron? That you hated the bar business?"

Marina was moving her eyebrows, but Burton didn't understand the message she was trying to send him.

Loftus sneered.

"That old bitch knows nothing about bars. It was a pretty sweet setup, since she didn't care whether it made money."

Burton connected a couple of dots.

"As a place to sell drugs, you mean?"

"Wholesale. There's deliveries in and out of there every day, all kinds of people. No one would notice one or two more."

"Isn't cocaine passé by now? A little old-school?"

Loftus showed him teeth.

"Old white people, man. They're the only ones with money these days. Discretionary income." He chuckled. "Poor man can't afford to get high any more."

"Boo-hoo." Burton doubted his premise, but Loftus was more interested in justifying himself right now than threatening Marina. It was as if they were the audience he'd needed all along, people to tell him how smart he was. "So, you were connected with Alfonso and Edward Dare? What did the three of you fight about? Who got what?"

"Small ambitions. Both of them thought this was a one-time thing. Alfonso only wanted some money he could call his own. Dare was scared shitless his boss would roll up on him."

He waggled the knife at Burton.

"You know how much traffic goes through this city? Everyone focuses on New York, but if you own Boston, you own the Northeast. Upstate New York. Even Canada. There's no wholesale hub up here."

Loftus had big eyes, but the reason there was no wholesale drug trade in Boston was Mickey Barksdale. Mickey was greedy enough, but he understood that trying to bring his operations into legitimacy was inconsistent with drug running. Especially on a scale that would attract not only local but federal law enforcement. Ever since the Olympic debacle, Mickey had been ruthless about pushing obvious gangster activity underground.

"You ever meet a man named Barksdale?"

Loftus lifted his lip again.

"Washed-up old school gangster guy? Gotta move with the times."

Burton did not think wholesaling the fad drug of the eighties was moving with the times, but you couldn't argue with a fanatic. He needed a plan for moving this along, but at the moment, all he could think was to keep Loftus talking.

"So you and Alfonso fought over keeping the party going?"

Loftus looked confused, shook his head impatiently. He held the knife down by his side as if he'd forgotten he was carrying it. Burton stood up, calculating whether he was close enough to jump the fool and try and disarm him. He could put up with a cut or two, as long as they weren't near anything vital. Then, before he cuffed him, he might slap him a few dozen times for causing so much trouble.

"Sit down over there." Loftus pointed the knife at a wooden chair Burton had bought at a yard sale, one of those heavy cherry-armed chairs with the Harvard seal. "I'm serious."

He raised the knife toward Marina as Burton hesitated.

"All right, all right."

He lowered himself into the chair.

"So, what, then? You and Alfonso get into it over the deal going bad? And you killed him?"

Loftus shook his head, tossing a brief gleaming glare as he checked Marina's bonds.

"Alfonso was a leech." He knelt in front of Marina and started to cut away the duct tape. Burton wondered what he was doing, whether he had a plan or if he was just spitballing.

"Dare only instigated the deal in the first place because of Sweetie's connections. She was tight with Frank Vinson, Dare's boss."

"Sweetie." Of course. He'd thought all along she was somewhere near the center of this, even without evidence. "So, she was in on the cocaine deal, then?"

Loftus straightened up and stared at Burton as if he'd proclaimed his belief in a flat earth.

"For fuck's sake. She isn't that smart."

Marina peeled the rest of the tape off her pant legs. Burton couldn't figure out why Loftus had freed her.

"Yeah, it was her money. But that was it. Alfonso should have known you don't take anything from Sweetie Bogan without consequences."

"You're saying she killed him."

"Fuck, you're thick. No, she didn't kill him. 'Fonso stole the money to finance the deal from her, which I told him was a bad idea. He had to back out when she caught him. Dare was more pissed off than she was. He was taking a risk to get free of the guy he worked for in New Orleans. I guess Vinson's death on drugs."

Literally, Burton thought. "So Dare killed him."

He understood what was going on—Loftus needed to confess. It was part brag and part unburdening. But it would be too straightforward of him to just come out and say he'd done it.

"And that's a big no, too."

Loftus was relaxing, as if some internal pressure was bleeding away. Burton wondered if he could persuade him to put the knife away and sit down, pretend they were all good friends assembled to listen to his problems.

"Dare wasn't any better than a pimp, really, for Vinson. It wasn't any more complicated than that."

"Doesn't leave too many more possibilities, Baron."

Loftus emitted a long sigh.

"Do you have any bottled water? All this talking is making me dry."

Burton recognized the point of balance they'd reached, where the guilty party comes to terms with responsibility for the act, but cannot bring himself to say the words out loud. Burton tried prompting him.

"So it was you? Who killed Alfonso? But why? Because he was stealing from your aunt? I get that you were protecting her. He was loyal to her for all those years and then he was screwing her over."

Marina, deep in the butt-sprung sofa, gathered her legs under her as if she were about to jump, but he shook his head. Burton didn't want Loftus to remember she was there. He was pretty sure the danger was over, that Loftus had talked himself down. Now they needed to find a way for him to surrender without hurting anyone. Or himself.

Loftus moved so he stood between Burton and Marina, as if he sensed they were sending messages back and forth.

"Protect Sweetie Bogan?" Loftus laughed shrilly. "That woman needs protection like I need bow ties." He ripped the one he was wearing off and threw it. "She made me wear them. I did it for myself. By myself. That was my money Alfonso was trying to steal, too."

Burton nodded, getting it finally.

"Sweetie was going to take care of you when she died."

Loftus's mouth worked.

"Do you know what she's worth? I was only running the bar because she asked me to. She was the one who told me about Alfonso stealing the money. Her money. My money."

Burton felt that sense of completion, when the gears of a case meshed and the solution moved forward. As motives went, it was one of the standards.

"So, she pointed you at him."

"And she didn't tell me he'd given it back."

Burton shook his head. He believed he'd seen a sliver of evil in the woman, but he hadn't wanted to believe it. Revenge had been as important to her as recompense.

"Or that he was my father." Loftus groaned. "She made me kill my own father."

Tears glistened on Loftus's brown cheeks. Burton had thought the surprises were done.

"Sweetie is your mother."

Loftus nodded, waving the knife. Burton focused on making sure no one got hurt. Even the murderer.

"What's the end game here, Baron?"

Loftus looked up at the ceiling, as if befuddled by his emotions and Burton's question both.

Then Marina lifted a leg and planted her boot in the back of Baron's knee, collapsing the joint and causing him to lose his balance. His arm swung wildly behind him and as Marina came up off the couch, the blade sliced her along the outside of the upper leg, turning her chef's whites garnet in a second.

Burton caught Loftus as he pitched forward, took his wrist in both hands, and cracked it over his knee with a sound like a tree branch breaking. Then he swung the man, light as a bundle of sticks, and shoved him down into the chair, handcuffed his unbroken arm to the struts of the chair. Loftus groaned.

"You all right?" He went to Marina.

She pressed down on the slit in her leg, which oozed blood rather than pumping. A good sign. No arteries cut.

"Fine," she said. "Were you going to let him talk at us all day?"

68

My first official act was to change out that frou-frou stained glass window in the door, in fact, replace the entire door with a steel-clad one. I was astonished that in the months Sweetie had owned the place and Baron Loftus had been managing, no one vandalized that window. Shades of gentrification, I guess.

I'd made some other changes, too, even if I didn't give in to my first impulse to try and recreate the Esposito. I didn't do nostalgia. I did, however, reinstate the old name.

Sweetie squeezed a fair price for it out of me, if not the astronomical sum she demanded at first. She needed it for bail. Burton had dropped me hints that her hands were not very clean in the matter, especially in Loftus's murder of Alfonso Deal-Jones. He might even have brought some pressure to bear. She was subdued, almost polite, the day we passed papers in the lawyer's office.

But I was back behind the bar again, at least until I could train Isaac as manager. I really didn't need the day to day, and he needed a job for a year, since Stanford had revoked his scholarship when he postponed.

The music from the speakers was a favorite of mine, Keith Jarrett's Köln Concert, but no one, Isaac included, was too impressed with it. I cared not—I was in charge again.

The black and white pictures of Diz and Miles were back up on the walls, the ferns donated to a nearby nursing home. The lights were turned low against the cold night outside. November is as cruel a month as April, as everybody in New England knows. The only fly in my eye was that the kitchen was dark.

I didn't know if I'd fractured my relationship with Marina irrevocably, but I also held her responsible for Burton's depression. The wedding was adjourned *sine die*, and I believed it was her insecurities, not his, that made that so. Needless to say, he and I weren't talking about that.

"Something about this feels pretty good." Burton drank several ounces of the whiskey sour I'd mixed up in a pint glass for him. I don't think he knew Marina and I were on the outs.

"You're such a philosopher," I said.

"No food tonight?"

"Still have to find a cook."

He flicked an eyebrow.

"You ask Marina to come back?"

"School's got her all tied up. And I believe she has higher aspirations than working in a dive bar."

Burton thought about that. Maybe she wasn't talking to him very much lately, either.

"Where is she, anyway?" I said. "I thought she might come down with you."

I invited a few people in for what I was calling a soft reopen. I still had a fair amount of cleaning, painting, and redecorating to take care of, but I wanted the word to get out that the Esposito was back. Lily Miller's mother sipped sherry at a table by herself. Susan was here. Pedey Thomas, from the newspaper, was haranguing her about something at the far end of the bar. A scattering of the old regulars occupied four or five tables.

He shook his head.

"She went to the memorial service. For Carter."

I winced. Burton had dropped enough breadcrumbs about their relationship troubles that I understood Rasmussen Carter was a bigger obstacle to their happiness in death than he had been in life. If he hadn't been murdered, Marina's memory of their time probably would have faded. But someone dying unexpectedly leaves them full in your life, in your memory. You're denied a chance to say all the words you need to say to settle the relationship. You get stuck, in other words, and I feared Marina was in that kind of state.

He shrugged, acknowledging what I was thinking.

"She'll work it out," he said, not hopefully. "Or she won't."

"Things all squared up with New Orleans?" I knew how angry he'd been that he couldn't go after Frank Vinson, for what happened with Lily.

"My contact down there is in trouble. Got a little too chummy with some of the darker elements." He sounded rueful.

"Too bad for her."

"Saved me from buying her dinner."

I left him looking down into his glass and walked down the bar. Pedey headed for the men's room as I arrived.

"Hey," I said to Susan.

She smiled, easier than I'd seen her since before I was in the hospital. I was still not quite sure where we were, but she'd made a point of telling me she cashed in her return ticket to the West Coast. I'd always had hope for us, but now maybe she had some, too.

"How's Burton?" she said.

"Rough and ready. I guess they're still negotiating how and whether he retires. I get the sense it's a done deal in his mind, though."

"That's going to be hard."

"I think he's accepted it. The force never treated him that well: the maverick thing. All that kept him out of trouble was that he built great cases."

"Not this one, though." She shook her head.

"No. Loftus will probably deal his way out of most of it. He started throwing the racial card around."

"Huh. This city. I'm surprised it took him that long. You need to watch out for Burton, Elder. You know he's not the kind of man who'll let you know how he's feeling."

"Yes."

She looked around the bar.

"Happy to have the place back to yourself?"

"Moderately. It means I'll have to start going to work every day. For a while."

Which I knew she'd like.

"Do you good."

Pedey returned then, picked up his glass, and toasted me.

"Wouldn't have guessed I'd be so glad to see this shithole back in business." He shook his head. "Jesus. Neil Diamond?"

I laughed and looked down the bar at Isaac, dressed for success in a white tuxedo shirt, black onyx studs, arm garters, and tight black pants. I didn't want to tell him he looked like the old elevator operator at Filene's, but if he was going to manage the place for me, he'd have to learn about the dry cleaning bills the hard way.

The music shifted to my guitar hero, Wes Montgomery, picking out the opening notes of "California Dreamin'." Isaac called down to me.

"Boss-man. The fuck is this, Rod Roy?"

"Rob Roy, junior."

I grinned and moved down the bar to help him. He'd be fine, even joked that most of the clientele probably wouldn't know he wasn't Baron Loftus, if he put on a bow tie.

I plucked out my worn copy of Old Mr. Boston's bartender's guide and passed it down to him, pulled down the sweet vermouth so he didn't grab the wrong bottle. As I did, the phone on the bar chimed. Isaac's. True child of the digital age, he ignored me to check his message.

I laid the book on the bar next to the phone. He tapped the screen and a video came up. His eyes went wide as he watched it. He turned the phone in my direction and restarted it.

Evangeline, in a long, sleek, brilliantly red sheath dress, sang from a small stage in a dim nightclub, the air around her smoky and low.

"*Look at me...*"

The smoke seemed to bother her, making her blink.

"You see what I see?" Isaac said.

She blinked three short, three long, three short. I wasn't sure what she was trying to say until the sequence repeated, as the camera zoomed in on her face, full-frame. Her eyes showed distress.

"Oh, fuck," I said. "It looks like we're going to New Orleans."

About the Author

Richard J. Cass is the author of the Boston-based Elder Darrow Mystery series. The first book released in the series, *Solo Act* (Five Star Publishing, 2015), was nominated for a Maine Literary Award in 2017. The second book released, *In Solo Time* (Encircle Publications, 2017), is the origin story for Elder and his friend, Boston homicide detective Dan Burton. *In Solo Time* won the Maine Literary Award for Crime Fiction in 2018. *Burton's Solo* and *Last Call at the Esposito* continue the story of Elder and Burton and the Esposito Bar & Grill.

Cass's short fiction has been published widely and won prizes from *Redbook, Writers' Digest*, and *Playboy*. His first collection of stories was called *Gleam of Bone*. He blogs with the Maine Crime Writers at https://mainecrimewriters.com and serves on the board of Mystery Writers of America's New England chapter.

He lives in Cape Elizabeth, Maine, with his wife Anne, and a semi-feral Maine Coon cat named Tinker, where he writes full time. You can reach him on Facebook at: Richard Cass – Writer or on Twitter at: @DickCass.

9 781645 991144